BEST

BONDAGE EROTICA

OF THE YEAR

VOLUME TWO

BEST
BONDAGE EROTICA
OF THE YEAR
VOLUME TWO

Edited by

RACHEL KRAMER BUSSEL

Published in the United States by Cleis Press, an imprint of Start Midnight, LLC, 221 River Street, 9th Floor, Hoboken, New Jersey 07030.

Printed in the United States.
Cover design: Jennifer Do
Cover photograph: Shutterstock
Text design: Frank Wiedemann

First Edition.
10 9 8 7 6 5 4 3 2 1

Trade paper ISBN: 978-1-62778-302-6
E-book ISBN: 978-1-62778-515-0

CONTENTS

INTRODUCTION:
ALL KINDS OF KINKY

One of the things I love best about bondage as a practice and as a subject for erotica is how versatile it is. You can restrain someone with kinky items like handcuffs or bondage rope, elaborate bondage furniture, or household items. There are so many avenues to explore and the nineteen stories you're about to read in *Best Bondage Erotica of the Year, Volume 2* get kinky in all kinds of ways, with all kinds of pairings.

Bondage travels beyond the home in a few of these stories. In "Headspace" by Evan Mora, a workplace gets a kinky makeover of a kind when two lovers put a very adult spin on a certain holiday. A piano player discovers how submitting to the will of her teacher can unlock beautiful notes, and so much more. Whether these bondage scenes take place in bedrooms or more non-traditional venues, what they all have in common is how the players revel in losing one element of movement in favor of all the breathless pleasures that await them.

You'll find everything here, from long-term D/s couples to a chef and sous chef engaging in an extremely spicy encounter. You'll meet a leather library sex fantasy come true and a woman who gets to watch a bondage scene starring the man she's fantasized about take place before her eyes. You'll read about a stocking fetish and a sadistic but effective personal trainer. Bondage is also a way for lovers to connect and reconnect, to learn new things about each other as they play. Alexa J. Day serves up some "Restorative Justice" as an apology takes on a very heated meaning for Michael, and he loves every minute of it, telling the reader, "Bound, I feel stronger than ever, my muscles flexed hard in my shirtsleeves." Discover how bondage and power are intimately intertwined in this racy story of a couple working out their issues and their kinks in mutually satisfying ways.

You may be used to hearing about bondage as an act for two people, but there are lots of trios here who explore the art of restraint in fun and creative ways. In "Table for Two" by T.R. Verten, John is forced to observe his lovers, straining for them as they flaunt their desire right before him. In "Unicorn" by Jacqueline Brocker, a man who's restrained outside has a woman try to come to his rescue—only to discover that the last thing he wants is to be released from the control of the woman who's watching him. And in "Trade Show" by D. Fostalove and "A Constructed Threesome" by Dr. J., the triple plays come with a few unexpected twists.

From the opening story about a very wild escape room with a woman and the two Dominants she answers to through the closing story, about an art model and the artist she lusts after, and with all the naughty tales in between, you'll discover all sorts of erotic explorations. In "Escape," Veronique Veritas writes, "He lingers on the rope encircling my waist and I know what's coming next now, just not quite when." This delicious tension of being made to wait, of wanting more while also wanting the person (or people) who hold the power over you to decide what happens next, is played out in all of the stories here. It's part of the thrill of bondage, of submitting, of putting yourself in the hands of another person. I hope you enjoy the many thrills this book serves up as much as I did.

Rachel Kramer Bussel
Atlantic City, New Jersey

ESCAPE

Veronique Veritas

Although I'm lying down, I see a partial image of my two favorite players standing in the room. They're appreciatively taking in the scarlet walls, blackout curtains, and my naked body bound skillfully to the table by them just moments earlier. It's just us tonight, as I've closed my escape room parlor for a "staff training event." As trendy as the rooms are, I've been making enough money to indulge in closing for a night of personal gain.

I catch the dim light shifting into different patterns on the woman's tight black latex shirt and miniskirt. She sets the timer on the wall and numbers start to flash.

"I think we can beat the last record easily," she says. Her partner immediately sets to puzzling out the first coded message on the other side of the room. It shouldn't take them too long to put the pieces together, at least I hope. I've purposely made things easy for them ever since we talked in the beginning.

In the meantime, she walks over to me and traces her fingers across my shoulders. The room temperature is just below comfortable; my nipples already stand firm as she drifts her fingers lower to pinch them.

"I have a feeling you're the key to getting out of here, aren't you?" she whispers. *She's on the right track*, I think, as I clench and feel the tiny round plastic ball with the key to the room deep inside me.

"One step at a time," I say, teasing. She looks back at me again with that pouty look I love before turning to her partner. He holds a paper with the first puzzle on it.

"The first clue is 'warm,'" I hear him announce.

"My turn!" she says, and takes up the next puzzle as he joins me.

As he stands above me in his black mesh shirt, I notice his gaze turn toward something on the other table next to me. Within seconds, he lifts a leather strap and traces it along the paths of the black bondage rope: beneath my breasts, crisscrossing my stomach, circling my hips. I bite my lip, ready to drift away into the sensations.

He snaps the leather in the air and brings me back to attention.

"Maybe we can make you talk," he growls, reminding me of the characters we'd discussed.

"I'll never give up my country's secrets," I spit back. "Not even if you use that thing on me all night."

I try not to let the anticipation sparkle in my eyes as he brushes it purposefully across my legs, then snaps it higher up to just barely smack my pussy. It stings my skin and I moan, squeezing my hands into fists beneath my bound wrists. He places a smooth hand on my breasts as they rise and fall with my ragged breath.

"Our country won't be forgiving if they find out you held us in a room like this. If you give us the location of the key, they'll go easy on you. And maybe we will, too . . . "

I try to strain myself away even though I can barely move. His mouth moves to my exposed neck and he licks me in one long, deliberate stroke, ending with a kiss on the edge of my chin. I shiver as I hear the woman's high heels click across the floor again.

"She's obviously not going to talk yet," the woman declares. Her voice sounds like it might be lower, toward my legs. "The other clue is 'wet,' by the way. So what do you think that means?"

Warm and wet and right in front of you . . . I think, wanting so badly for them to get it. For *me* to get it . . .

"If you don't talk, I'll have to use your mouth for something else," the man says, and from upside down, I see him strip his black pants and walk toward me again, his erection already stiff and uncompromising. The table I'm on is a sort of modified massage table, so he's able to carefully lean down the top part where my head rests. He moves over my mouth and eases in the head of his cock; he knows to pulse more gently when he hears me gag at deeper depths. I sense he's been careful to keep his legs in close reach of my fingers, so I can pinch him if things get too intense, as we agreed upon earlier. But I love the way he plunges into me, and I let my hand ease against the stainless steel of the table.

The woman unexpectedly strokes the tips of my hipbones with her hands as he fills my throat with his hard cock. I start from her unseen touch at first, but relax as she climbs onto the table, gives me a reassuring brush of her hand, and devours my pussy completely. Her tongue is relatively short, but she more than makes up for it by sucking me deep and licking my clit in firm, upward strokes. The small orb of her tongue piercing drags along the center, making me strain to meet her as I arch my hips as much as I can. The restraints around my ankles are slightly looser so I can prod her with my knee if I need her to stop, but as with the man, I feel completely enthralled by what she's doing. I can't hold back the sounds of my pleasure anymore as I come. They escape, slightly muffled by the man's flesh.

After some time, his angle inside me shifts slightly as I feel him lean forward to meet her. I hear them leaning together to kiss, casting a conjoined shadow over me. I'm here as part of their experience, just like they're giving me mine.

When he stands straighter again, he slips out of me with his own satiated cries before adjusting the top part of the table again so I once again lie flat. His come spatters my face and breasts, rolling into the hollow of the throat he's just fucked. I barely have time to swallow what's glistening on my lips when the woman climbs higher, eagerly lapping up everything I can't reach.

"Warm . . . and wet," she sighs, as she cleans the last of his come from my sensitive collarbone.

"Of course," I whisper, my throat pleasantly chafed from the fullness of the recent guest. "But what *else* might it be?"

I see the realization spark in her eyes and she actually puts her hands to her mouth as she giggles.

"You are a naughty spy, aren't you? We'll just have to pull it out of you, right?"

She nods to where the man must be getting cleaned up and within moments, she's repositioned herself beneath me, kneeling and leaning on one elbow as I hear the man walk behind her. Her face shows that he's started eating her pussy now as she responds with higher pitched gasps and moans. While she writhes, she drives her fingers inside me and progressively explores deeper, taking her sweet time. Her breasts have nearly come out of the top of her latex shirt by now and I savor it all as she reaches the deep place inside me that holds the key. She leads it out by three fingers and, from the look on her face, orgasms again before the man eventually withdraws. Both of them sit back on the edge of the table near my legs. I can partially see the man using a cloth to wipe off the ball that holds the key.

"Well done," I praise both of them, glancing at the blinking red timer on the wall as we all rest for the moment. "It looks like you've beat the record, so you get another session in the room next month like I promised. What do you think?"

They both smile in response.

"That sounds great," the woman says. "What will it be next time?"

"If I tell you," I say, in my best exaggerated spy voice, "I'll have to kill you."

"Maybe if you don't tell us," the man teases, "we won't untie you."

"Do I have to beg to be let go or something?"

The woman leans close to my ear and nips my lobe.

"What do you think, you double-crossing spy?" she whispers, and I can sense that we're playing again, more seriously. My already drenched pussy becomes slightly wetter again in response as I look at the timer and see how much time we still have left in the room. Enough time for them to do anything they want to me again . . .

"I won't beg for you," I say, softer this time.

In response, the woman places the ball with the key into my mouth, making sure that the lines where it splits are parallel to my lips so it won't pop open. I clench it firmly between my teeth, anticipating what they'll do next. I savor the mystery of this, as I hear the man going over to the other table again while the woman brushes my taut jawline with her fingertips.

"You'll beg," she whispers, her face close to mine again. I strain away in mock defiance, determined to be an obstinate brat until I can't resist any longer.

She draws away and both of them stay out of my limited line of sight. Nothing happens for a while and I'm a bit confused. *They couldn't have left without my knowing, could they?* I think. But even though we all know the door isn't really locked, it would still make enough of a noise that I'd hear it.

"When do you think the next thing is coming, spy?" the man says. "Is it torture to wait?"

Some relief comes to me as I realize they're just tantalizing me further. I close my eyes and groan in response, remembering in acute detail all the other things I've okayed them to use on me from the other table. They keep me waiting for a few minutes longer until I really feel myself start to sweat. Then I sense one of them silently stand in reach of my hands again and the other kneeling on the table near my legs.

"Keep your eyes closed," the woman instructs me.

I want to do it, so I comply and nod. I feel her stroke my hair approvingly.

"Now, beg," the man demands.

I'm smoldering with want by now, but I keep acting the part while I still can. I shake my head.

He traces the lines of the ropes beneath my breasts again, then places a clamp on my left nipple.

"Now?"

I'm so glad they chose the clamps—one of my all-time favorites—that I give a soft moan of pleasure from my throat as I enjoy the clamp's sharp bite and its gradual ebbing into duller pressure.

I usually put them on myself, so it's a big step that one of them is doing it to me, but I wanted to try it and it makes me feel so hot to submit to them tonight. When he puts the clamp on my right nipple, though, the pain stays too sharp and doesn't ebb. I give a more frantic cry and pinch the woman's leg.

"Too hard!" she tells him, and he takes it off immediately.

After a moment, he tries again and this time, it's in the right spot. When he asks me if it's okay, I nod and things are fine again.

"And now do you want to beg, spy?"

I shake my head again and the rest of me starts to shiver as I feel him purposefully trace his finger from my breasts down the center of my stomach. He lingers on the rope encircling my waist and I know what's coming next now, just not quite when. I almost beg then, not as part of the role-play, but because I want what comes next so bad.

He waits another minute, teasing my labia with the softest touches that make me squirm. And then he gingerly finds my clit and, after rubbing over it with his large thumb, I feel the last clamp firmly embrace me.

I can't stop myself from gasping even though I knew it was coming. My instinct is to bite down harder on the ball, wondering if I'll leave scratches on the cheap plastic. But I feel one of them remove it from my mouth before both of them walk away from me again.

"You know the word that will release you," the woman reminds me. "Unless you just want to beg for your freedom now."

I know she means the safeword we chose before the session, and I'm grateful for the option. But I stay purposefully silent as I relish the sting of the clamps, the fire of their familiar hold on me, the pressure they impress on my body. The pain makes me feel transcendent, holy in a blasphemous way, taken away to another realm. I'm bound and clamped and at the compassionate mercy of my partners, and that thought alone gets me wet all over again as I imagine how helpless I must look. In about ten minutes, they come closer again.

I open my eyes as the man below me frees my clit. He looks me in the eye as he does it, and I let out a sharp cry before he lowers his mouth to my pussy. He drives his long, unpierced tongue inside me first, then back out around my lips, and finally to my waiting, throbbing clit. It feels completely different than with the woman, but still incredible as I greedily come again.

As he kneads my clit with his tongue, the woman takes off both of my nipple clamps at the same time. I whimper as she puts her lips to one nipple and strokes the other with her fingertips. Between the two of them at once again and the surreal raw scorch on my freshly unclamped areas, I continue to come and twist beneath my restraints.

I'm starting to get tired in the best way, and from the looks of it, they are too. Their attentions to me start to soften into completion. I relax into a final resting comfort while my body still sings with the memory of everything it's enjoyed tonight. I know I'll still feel the sensations on my nipples and clit tomorrow, my perfect secret that strangers would never guess.

"Now would you like to be untied?" the man asks, and his voice sounds more familiar to me.

We're done playing our parts—for now. I answer yes.

They work together to release me. The buzzer goes off with perfect timing as I sit on the edge of the table, trying to get my bearings again and flexing my hands.

I smile at him as the woman comes in to kiss me and carefully massage the rope burns around my breasts. I touch the back of her neck and feel the man kiss the back of mine as I reach my other hand around to stroke the back of his. We make a wonderful triad, I think. We're not spies anymore, but I'm Vanessa again and they're my real life partners Sofia and Aron.

After we leave here, we'll go back to our apartment and share our bed in contented exhaustion. I know the way Sofia tends to kick the blankets off when she gets too hot and the way Aron will inevitably get up earliest of all of us to work out and drink that nasty whey protein powder. We've all discovered how to do these more intimate things through a lot of trial and error these past few years, but it's been exhilarating each step of the way.

Sofia rolls her tongue piercing across my lips one more time before she pulls her mouth away and we all sit together for a moment, holding each other, before we start to transform the room once again into a chaste, fun venue for tomorrow night's real escape room customers. We help each other dress again, pack the implements away in my backpack, unlock the wheels on the tables and roll them into the large hall closets, and lock up the place before starting the short walk home. In the dim night, I walk between them and they both hold either of my hands as we watch the few bright stars we can see beyond the streetlights.

"They're so beautiful," I say, tipping my head upward.

"Yes, we are," Aron says with a playful smile as Sofia laughs.

HAMMERED GOLD

Rosalind Chase

Morgan watched the last bites of cereal swirl around the milk in her bowl. She interrupted the white current with her spoon, stirred the opposite way, watched the bloated grains spin counter clockwise.

Is it degenerative?

It was a man at the gallery the night before. A man she'd worked with off and on for months but he'd only just found out about her disease. He didn't understand. How could he know what he was asking?

How could he ever grasp it?

The invisible nature of it.

The way the disease itself was like a ghost. A poltergeist. Existing only to wreak havoc, spread chaos, keep her up at night.

Morgan thought back. The day she had to leave her last job. The day she started. The day she moved into this apartment. The day she quit going to the support group. The day she joined it.

The day her doctor told her she should get some extra help. The day her diagnosis came down. The day she landed in the hospital.

And there were all the other days in between.

All the moments that melted into a blur of color and sound and pain.

And all the moments that should've been. All the days that didn't happen. The trips she didn't take. The plans she cancelled. The dates she'd shirked.

Were her days getting worse? Was her life getting worse? Was she degenerating?

Morgan opened her phone. Scrolled. Scrolled. Her thumbs ached.

She put the phone back down. Stared out the window. It was full spring now and daffodils and irises had pushed up through the soil in front of the bookstore across the street. The worst of the cold was gone, Morgan hoped, and the warmth of summer would bring a little more ease into her body. Less creaking and cracking and radiating pain. More afternoons with the window open.

But she wasn't there yet. That would be weeks down the line.

Today, it was chilly. Sweater weather. And her body hurt.

The nerves in her fingers lit up, sending a sickening, shiver-inducing pain straight up her arms, through her chest, and down into her belly. Her knees weren't much better and she could feel the hard tightness of her shoulders threatening to follow right behind. She fought her instinct to curl in on herself, to make herself small, to hope the pain wouldn't notice her, would pass her by.

Is it degenerative?

She opened her phone again, scrolled through the contacts, glanced outside. No ice. No driving rain. Just a chill. Would the cold hurt? Yes.

Would it be worth it?

Yes. A thousand times yes.

Now if she could just get him to answer.

She hit the name, Daniel, put it to her ear, let it ring.

She'd met Daniel when she was in her late twenties. That was a decade ago. Before her diagnosis. Her whole life was lumped that way. Before. After.

It rang.

Daniel didn't use a cell phone. He was old-fashioned and English and refused to give up the rotary phone he'd found on the curb when he'd first moved here. He was like that. Always treasuring things other people threw away. Always noticing something shining and beautiful about things that were a little broken.

It rang.

Morgan closed her eyes. How long had it been? Three, four months? Just as the winter had begun to be too much. He'd come to her that day. There was no way she could've gone out. He'd arrived at her door in a hand-knit and hand-patched wooly sweater under an ancient bomber jacket and had shaken the frost from his silver hair.

"Hello?"

"Daniel," Morgan said. "I'd almost hung up."

"You just caught me, love. I've just returned from the market."

Morgan pictured his armload of groceries the way it would be written in a movie, with a stiff baguette poking out the top of a paper bag.

"I wondered if you might have time for me today. I know it's last minute."

She listened to the rustle of paper as Daniel set the bag on the kitchen table, listened to the hard thunk of the glass bottle of milk (where did he get this stuff?) as it shifted against the ancient wooden surface.

"Lucky girl," he said. "Come by in an hour?"

"Yes. I'll be there," Morgan agreed, realized she was smiling.

"Right. See you then."

Morgan hung up and took a long, deep breath. She already felt better. Breathe in . . . two . . . three. Hold. Out . . . two . . . three. It was just how Daniel had taught her. It was how she got through her high pain days. Her regular days. And her sessions with him.

She stood, slowly, and wandered into the bedroom. It didn't matter what Morgan wore, she knew, but she didn't want to show up at his pristine cottage wearing ragged sweatpants and her pizza-stained Emmylou concert T-shirt she'd bought back when she could still go to concerts. She peeled every single thing off and stood in front of her mirror.

She tried to see her long legs instead of the burst veins that spidered under her skin. Tried to see her full breasts instead of the bruises her underwire had left around them the night before. Tried to see a face that was happy in spite of her health, successful in spite of her circumstances, hopeful in spite of her disease. For the most part, Morgan succeeded.

She wiggled into a pair of leggings and a jersey dress, a soft sweater and buttery leather boots. Daniel lived twenty minutes away. She didn't need to hurry but she shouldn't lollygag either. She packed a bag with a change of clothes, her medication (just in case) and, as she was going out the door, the beaded necklace Daniel had given her so many years ago.

A bead for every breath, he'd said.

A circle of beads. Going on forever. Like she would never stop.

"Hello, love," Daniel said when he opened the door. He was

tall and lean. He spent the warm months rowing a single scull up and down the river and spent the cold ones hiking in the mountains. His hair had been white since long before she'd met him and, though she'd never asked his age, she'd loved watching the development of the divergent crow's feet that told the story of his thoughtful life and the deep dents at either side of his smile which hinted at his quietly joyful nature.

"Hi, Daniel."

"Bad day?"

"Not so bad," Morgan said, wrapping her arms around her waist, holding herself close, making sure she didn't fly apart before she could even get into his house. "Good enough to come out."

She let her gaze travel the long length of his body. His worn but well-maintained desert boots led up to soft-looking charcoal trousers and a navy (or, at least, it had once been navy) long-sleeved T-shirt. His skin was perpetually tanned, his snowy shadow perpetually five o'clock, and his mouth perpetually quirked up into a curious almost smile.

"Come on, then," he said and nodded his head toward the interior of his cabin.

She followed him inside and wasn't wholly surprised to see a fire crackling away in the corner. He always made sure she was warm.

The interior of the cabin, all rugged and raw and wooden, was cozy. The space was open, with a little kitchen to one side and the living area to the other. The bedroom and bathroom were beyond the closed door, she knew, but her gaze was pulled, immediately, to the object in the middle of the floor.

Wine leather cushions padded the surfaces of the mahogany bench, which had always looked, to Morgan, a lot like a complicated sawhorse. Its four legs tilted up like twin As and, at front and back, were well-cushioned and sturdy rests for a person to, effectively, kneel on their shins and forearms while their body came to rest against the padded spine of the bench. Each arm and leg rest came equipped with a wide leather cuff to secure the appendages of whoever knelt there.

Morgan realized she was holding her breath at the sight of it and she let it out, through pursed lips, in a long whisper of air.

"Are you ready?" Daniel asked from behind her.

Morgan turned. Her heart was racing. It didn't matter how many times she came here, nor how many years she had known him, nor how long she could possibly keep doing this. Being here, in this room, with this man and his voice and his skill and, yes, her pain, always made her dizzy with want.

She nodded, unable to speak for the lump of excitement in her chest.

"Take off your clothes," Daniel said.

She did. She tugged at her dress, her leggings, her bra and underwear and socks. And Daniel watched. He stood, casually, next to the dining table with a mug of steaming tea in his hand and, simply, watched.

When she started to remove the necklace he held up a hand.

"Leave it," he said.

So she did.

They stood for several long moments. Him—clothed, ten feet away, noiselessly sipping his tea. Her—naked, bare, raw, in the center of his floor, the hearth sparking and warming her from behind, his steady gaze setting the rest of her on fire.

"Go to the bench," he said.

She moved toward it and heard Daniel's footsteps first on the hardwood and then on the carpet as he neared her. He held out his hand and she took it, using it to steady herself as she mounted the bench. It really was like a horse, she knew, and once she'd first figured out how to get situated comfortably on it, she always found it again without trouble.

"Good girl," Daniel said, his voice like velvet.

He knelt by her right wrist and brought the cuff up around her arm, adjusting it here and there until it was neither too loose nor too tight. She couldn't move, but neither was her blood restricted. Instead, she felt secure. Safe.

Daniel moved around the bench, cuffing her left wrist and then both legs, before stepping back to look at her. How did she know that's what he was doing? Could she feel his stare? Hear his breath? Know his desire?

And what was his desire?

Her?

Hurting her?

Healing her?

Morgan shivered within the restraints. Her torso, from pubic bone to sternum, was supported by the leather pad and she was angled slightly so her head was higher than her ass. Daniel had made the pain horse, as Morgan always called it in her mind, on his own. She had never seen the inside of the woodworking shed she knew stood out back but she'd often imagined it. She imagined it again as she rested her cheeks against the massage table style headrest at the front, which she suspected Daniel had installed just for her. She never asked.

What would be the fun in that?

"We'll start light today," Daniel purred from behind her. "What's your pain level?"

Morgan studied the weft of the forest green carpet below and breathed in a long, deep breath, her ribs expanding, her chest pushing into the stiff leather cushion.

"Five to six," she said, breathing out. "It's not too bad."

Morgan knew people—maybe even most people—walked

around at a zero, a one, maybe a two. She thought again about the question the man had asked.

Is it degenerative?

She breathed in . . . two . . . three. Out . . . two . . . three.

With every passing moment was she falling more and more apart? That's what the man had wanted to know. That's what he'd been asking. What would she be like in a year, ten, twenty?

Would the pain have eaten her alive by then?

She heard the long swoosh of leather on metal as Daniel pulled the riding crop from the antique umbrella stand he kept near the fireplace.

"Yeats?" he asked, gravel in his voice as he took a step nearer to her. "Or Shakespeare? Of course, there's always Blake."

"Yeats," she said.

She tried not to brace herself for the first brisk thwack. She tried to let it slide off her like waves over a beach, but she could never help it. She could never relax into the start of a session. And so her fingers gripped tight around the ends of the wooden armrests as Daniel repeated, "Yeats," and let the crop fly for the first time.

It landed against her left buttock with a snap. Not too hard. Not too gentle. It stung and the heat radiated out, through her body, to her curled toes and fingers. Warmer than sunshine. She relaxed a little.

"This is no country for old men," he started. "The young/In one another's arms, birds in the *trees*."

Another snap. This one against her right buttock.

He stepped back. Morgan heard the soft crush of the carpet under his boots as he moved. She imagined him appraising the brief red blossom the leather had left on her skin.

He continued the recitation.

The thwack of the crop wasn't regular, Morgan knew. It

didn't come at the end of each stanza but, instead, wherever Daniel felt it belonged. Wherever a word deserved emphasis.

"Caught in *sensual* music," he said, his voice straining as he brought the crop down hard. It was the first deep hit. The first one that vibrated Morgan to the core. It opened doors in her body, in her mind. She felt the rush of relaxation unlocking her, a piece at a time.

"Sound *clap* its hands and *sing*, and *louder* sing."

Thwack. Thwack. Thwack.

Morgan didn't bother biting her lip, didn't bother gripping at the armrests or digging her forehead into the headrest as she might once have done.

Instead, she gave herself over to it.

Let her body slide from one kind of pain into another. Into this other, more beautiful, more perfect pain.

"And therefore, I have sailed the seas and *come*." SNAP.

She screamed over his next words as the crop bit into her buttocks but she knew what they were.

To the holy city of Byzantium.

They'd tried floggers over the years. Paddles, too. But nothing ever worked so well as Daniel's crop. Nothing ever felt so right. The pure snap of leather against flesh. The reverberating pop through her body. The fireworks that bloomed on her skin and went away just as quickly.

"And be the singing-*masters* of my *soul.*/Consume my *heart away*; sick with *desire*."

Thwack. Thwack. The whisper of his boots on carpet as he adjusted. *Thwack.*

The crop cracked against her thighs and Morgan groaned.

Now she was falling into the warm darkness of her pain. It would take her. She would let it. She welcomed it. She asked for it.

Thwack.

She felt an ache of a different kind grow between her legs, felt the heat of her own moisture, felt the power of her own control.

"I shall never *take*/My *bodily* form from any *natural thing,*/ But such a *form* as *Grecian* goldsmiths make—"

Morgan listened to the hard thump of blood in her ears, the husky rattle of her own voice in her throat, the hot pop of leather against her thighs, close to the backs of her knees.

"Of *hammered gold* and *gold* enamelling."

This was her doing.

Daniel was holding the crop. This was his device on his carpet in his house and it was his voice reverberating through the raw wood walls. And yet it was her choice to be here. Her choice to call him. Her choice to kneel and wait for the delicious snap of the crop. Her choice. Her pain.

This pain wasn't some cruel twist of fate. It wasn't some broken letter in her DNA. It wasn't some failure of her body to protect her.

It was Morgan's pain. It was Morgan who held this power. Power over her body. Power over her mind. Power over this room.

"Set upon a *golden* bough to *sing.*"

The crop's wicked tip met the soft, sensitive flesh just outside her sex.

She groaned and let herself disappear into the mesmerizing rhythm of Daniel's steady speech. Of the mysterious pattern of his stinging hits. Of the warm power that came with the very fact that she was here, naked and bound, because she chose to be.

"Of what is *past*, or *passing*, or to *come.*"

The last snaps came harder, stronger, faster.

Her heart thundered against the leather below and she felt both more and less present than she'd ever been. She was in this moment and she was everywhere. Nowhere.

He reared back for one last blow. She knew the poem well, by now.

She prepared herself without tensing. Without resisting. She breathed into it, her body ready and relaxed as Daniel finally whispered, "To the holy city of *Byzantium*."

Morgan let the pain of the final fierce strike travel the length and depth of her body, let it into her core, her inmost self, let it wrap and curl itself around her fragile heart, shielding it the way thorns shield a rose. This pain was hers. It was her monster and she had tamed it. She controlled it. Her monster, at her bidding, chased away the poltergeist of her other pain. Her daily pain. Not forever. But for now.

It was enough.

She breathed . . . two . . . three. Reveling in this moment that seemed to stretch out forever, made so sweet by the combination of pain with pleasure.

Swoooosh. She listened as Daniel put the crop back into the metal stand. She knew what was coming next and she arched, against the restraints, into it. She could almost feel Daniel—stoic Daniel—smiling behind her back. Amused.

Morgan heard the deep buzz of the high-powered vibrator and, as Daniel pressed it to her clit, it wasn't even two hard heartbeats—not even one and a half—before her body, previously relaxed into a state of pain-induced bliss, wound itself up, twisted itself into knots, as pleasure shuddered through her. She felt the muscles of her vagina clench and spasm and grasp, felt the arch of her back even as she pressed her torso into the padded leather, felt the rasp of her throat as she groaned. She was a tangled, coiled spring. And then she was limp.

She relaxed. Fully.

She was warmth personified.

She hurt and yet she felt nothing. She was oblivious and yet she felt everything.

Every red bloom of every old word that was both intangible and immortal, every abrasion from the leather cuffs against her wrists and ankles, every choice that had led her here to this moment of beauty.

"All right, love," Daniel murmured as he knelt beside her. He unbuckled her wrists and ankles and, slowly, helped her rise from the bench.

"Let's get you in a bath," he said. He gathered her into his arms and carried her down the hall and into the first room. It was a big, open bathroom with a deep porcelain tub and bright copper pipes winding through the whole place. The tub was already full and steaming, smelling a little like lavender and a little like cedar and a little like Daniel.

He helped her step into it and then sat on a wooden bench behind the tub, pushing up his sleeves, as she settled in. The welts up and down her legs stung but she knew they would fade soon, so she cherished them as one does the cherry blossoms. Fleeting. Beautiful. Alive and then gone.

Is it degenerative?

Daniel ran oil through her hair, massaged her scalp and neck and back. She let herself lean into his hands, let herself close her eyes and give herself—again—over to him.

Was this different than what she had felt only moments before?

Was it the opposite or merely the other half?

Vicious whipping. Tender bathing.

Were they not two halves of one whole? Morgan thought they were.

She could never have taken a bath by herself, in her own home. No, there she had a special chair to keep from passing out, falling over, slipping, bruising, breaking, dying. Here, she was safe. Every moment, safe.

Soon, probably in less than an hour, Morgan would be dressed. She would thank Daniel, pay him, embrace him, tell him she hoped to see him soon. She would ease herself into her car and she would drive back home. She would get some more work done and she would crawl into bed and wait for another day to begin. Another day of pain. Another day of pain she didn't choose.

But not now. Now, she was safe. Here, she was in control.

Morgan thought about the question again.

Is it degenerative?

She sighed into the empty space the question left.

Her voice surprised her. It echoed, bouncing off water and porcelain and pipes as she recited, "Consume my heart away; sick with desire/And fastened to a dying animal/It knows not what it is; and gather me/Into the artifice of eternity."

Life is degenerative, she had answered. All life.

All any of us had, Morgan knew, were moments.

And, in this moment, Morgan was free. Free to be in her body, free to exist outside of it. Free of her pain because she controlled it. Free of whatever happened next.

She was hammered gold and her soul sang.

BACK IN THE SADDLE

Page Chase

Vanessa straightened the flogger to lie parallel to the riding crop. Perpendicular to both on the dining room table were a set of nipple clamps and a small bullet vibrator with a wireless remote. The leather on the impact play implements was supple and well oiled. The electronic items were fully charged. After all, it was important to maintain one's equipment. The gears on her cassette, chain, and chainring sparkled like sterling and were sufficiently lubricated, as were her derailleurs. Her frame was the same candy apple red as when she first bought it. She took care of her bicycles as if they were children. But the most important torture device sat waiting nearby.

It was a top-of-the-line smart trainer. She didn't even need a trainer wheel for it; she could connect her chain to a cassette attached to the flywheel. Inside the device were magnets to increase or decrease resistance. It was another expense on top of her remaining medical bills, but she considered it an investment for her future.

As soon as the doctor cleared her for activity, she met up for a group ride. Her body had more or less healed. Now she just wanted to get her fitness back. What she hadn't considered was the state of her mind. After she took her bike off the hitch rack of her car, she stared at it, remembering how its sister looked crumpled on the side of the road right before she faded out. When she clipped in, she slowly pedaled toward the group in the parking lot. A car screeched to a stop at a nearby light and Vanessa hit the ground, shaking. Before she knew it, a crowd had gathered around her and teammates helped her back to her feet. She hated everyone fussing over her, pitying her. So, she strapped the bike back to her car rack and drove home.

For all her bravado telling her friends and family the first thing she'd do was get back in the saddle, just the idea of riding her bike to the store to pick up milk terrified her now. She had climbed mountains and had descended them at eye-watering speeds, for fuck's sake. She had lived for the sprint to the finish line, her heart beating at an inhumanly fast rate. She had rubbed elbows with some of the best regional racers in chase groups and counterattacked her fair share of breakaways for her teammates. She trained through inclement weather, from rain to snow and that one time it hailed. She and the bike were as one before The Crash. But now, the bicycle looked like a torture device, and not even a fun one.

Her non-cycling friends had suggested taking a spin class to ease into her comeback after the group ride incident. Like hell if she was going to grind it out with some suburban Lululemon-wearing hausfraus to shitty remixes of already shitty pop music on a sore-inducing squishy saddle. No, this was much better. Damian with the piercing eyes and steady hand would know what she needed. All she had to do was prepare for his arrival.

When one of her friends had recommended Damian as a ProDom for more recreational purposes, Vanessa was a bit skeptical. She was all the more skeptical when she invited him into her apartment. With his thick glasses and lanky form, he looked more likely to be the guy IT sent to fix the wireless connection than a specialist in "recreational discipline." His soft-spoken reserve seemed better suited to a hipster coffeehouse open mic night.

It felt strange wearing only her cycling bibs. Granted, Vanessa usually did her time on the trainer without a jersey, but she usually had her sports bra on. Still, she followed Damian's instructions to the letter. With her shoe cleats clipped in her pedals and with the nylon ropes tying her wrists to the handlebars, she was tethered to the bike. The ropes were loosely looped, more of a formality, or physical reminder of one fact: Damian would not leave until the job was finished, one way or another. There was no going back.

"Allez!" Damian shouted, striking the flogger across Vanessa's back.

Even though this was a warm-up, Vanessa had to maintain at least a 100 rpm cadence lest she feel the lash. This was challenging, considering Vanessa was always more of a masher than a spinner pre-crash. Still, this was going to be a cakewalk compared to what Damian would put her through later. He circled her like a beast of prey, eyes alternating between her and the data displayed on her cycling computer. There was a time Vanessa would have been self-conscious at being so exposed, unable to hide the scars on her back, chest, and legs from where the doctors stitched her back together like some sort of Frankenstein's monster. Now she didn't care and she knew Damian didn't care. He was there for just one reason.

The leather against her skin stung even harder this time.

Vanessa yelped and looked at the display; her cadence had dropped to 89 rpm.

"Focus," Damian said. "I don't think your head is in the game. Let's see if we can fix that."

He walked over to the table and grabbed the nipple clamps. Even though they had some sort of silicone coating, they still pinched quite hard. Vanessa gasped as he placed them on. He pulled on the chain that connected them.

"Did I tell you to stop pedaling?" he growled in her ear.

"No, Sir." She shuddered, but spun back up to 100 rpm.

Vanessa gritted her teeth and got ready. She had programmed the trainer herself, so she knew that a threshold interval was approaching. Sure, the flogger hurt. The nipple clamps hurt. The nylon rope chafed her wrists. Yet she knew true pain. She knew what it was like to be shattered and reassembled like a goddamn vase. She had regularly done threshold workouts prior to The Crash. This shouldn't be too bad.

"*Allez!*" Another crack signaled the start of the interval.

Now it was no longer about cadence so much as power. She had to maintain 200 W for five minutes. This was easier back when she was fully trained and peaking. She could hold an average power output of 300 W for anywhere from twenty to forty minutes in her prime. Now, after her forced sedentary rest period, this might be harder.

Her eyes were fixed on that 200. Nothing else existed. The nipple clamps were just a vague sensation, like the sound of a television in another room. She felt the familiar increase in heart rate, a rise in temperature followed by the burning of legs and lungs. Five minutes was a lot longer than she remembered.

"Recover," Damian said gently, stroking Vanessa's back as the resistance on the trainer eased.

Vanessa let out a sigh of relief. It would be a five-minute

respite of easy spinning followed by another five minutes at threshold. This would repeat until she had completed five threshold intervals, followed by ten minutes of recovery spinning before she could get off the bike. She noted that it took longer than before for her heart rate to recover, but her legs felt warmed up.

The second interval was fine, as she was now getting to know her own body again. Her legs were warmed up, her breathing and pedaling had fallen into complementary rhythms. Damian decided to mix things up during the following recovery period.

The bullet vibrator nestled inside the chamois of her bibs thrummed against her clit, causing Vanessa to moan.

"Consider this your reward for a continued job well done," he said coolly, pressing the button to increase intensity, not on the trainer, but the vibrator.

"Oh! Th-thANK you, Sir!" Vanessa could barely get out the words, but knew she would be punished if she did not show gratitude.

Eyes stinging from the sweat dripping down her face, she could barely make out the stopwatch counting down to the next interval.

"*Allez!*" A harder thwack followed since she did not ramp up to 200 W in time for the official start of the interval.

Damian had moved on to the riding crop. Vanessa dreaded this one in particular, worrying it would potentially damage either her glutes or her hamstrings. He had assured her that if any marks would be left, they would be skin bruises and not muscle, but if she was uncomfortable with it, he wouldn't use it. She decided that she trusted him as a professional and said the crop would be fine. Besides, it would give her further incentive to stay on target, right?

This third interval was more challenging, given how ragged

she had felt from the previous intervals plus the vibrator. She reminded herself that if she could survive despite her heart stopping in the ER, she could damn well do anything if she put her will to it. The first thing she remembered hearing was the steady beep of the EKG machine in her hospital room. It reminded her of the beep that alerted her whenever—

She heard the leather crop whistle softly in the air before the loud crack as it hit her ass. She had let her power drop to 153 W.

"Concentrate." Damian gave her ass a lighter tap. "Come on, out of the saddle. Hammer!"

Standing efforts. Christ, she hated doing those before, but now having to be prompted in such a humiliating way made her hate them even more. Still, it was a way to boost her power and give her quads a bit of recovery while she let her hamstrings do most of the work. However, she knew that there was no way she could maintain a standing effort for much longer than half a minute and she still had three minutes left on this interval. Her legs burned, but it would only hurt worse if she let her power drop again.

Vanessa almost collapsed in relief at Damian saying, "Recover." She wasn't so certain she could do one more threshold interval, let alone two. It was taking longer and longer for her heart rate to slow down. Without that, it would have been almost like she was going from one threshold interval immediately to another one. She was relieved to not be "rewarded" again, as that would have made it even harder for her heart rate to slow. Damian was a *goddamn* mind reader.

The clock counted down again. *"Allez!"*

She remembered that this interval would be particularly unpleasant since she was supposed to do a standing effort for thirty seconds followed by maintaining the same power while seated and repeat until the five minutes were over. However, the signal this time wouldn't just be Damian's stern *"Allez!"*

She gasped as the vibrator went off and stood up instinctively. She was hit again despite doing it in time.

"Form," Damien chided, tapping her legs and back to guide her into position. "No stomping. Stay smooth with your pedal stroke."

Vanessa was starting to regret being so specific in her instructions about what to target. However, better form meant more efficient energy usage. She closed her eyes and got into the rhythm, moving right as the vibrator went off. She looked at Damian for a moment. Gone was the gangly, awkward gentleman who she'd greeted at the door. She noticed his broad shoulders and impressive sprinter-like quads that filled his jeans nicely. Slim, but well-muscled arms could easily provide strength with every strike, yet with slender-fingered hands that could temper that strength when needed. Cool, impassive eyes gave him a mysterious air.

Yes. Vanessa would definitely fuck Damian, but that was not what she was paying him for. That couldn't stop a woman from fantasizing though. She closed her eyes again, imagined it was his shoulders she was grasping instead of her handlebars. Every thrust of the hips as she stood made her think about what it would be like to have Damian between her thighs, his wrists bound above his head and his cock inside her as she rode him. Since she wasn't watching the numbers on her cycling computer, an occasional strike of the crop would bring her back to the task at hand.

By the end of the interval, she was drained, dripping in sweat, but also more turned on than she had ever been in her life. Vanessa was practically soaking through her chamois. Her wrists almost slid from the nylon ropes.

Damian brushed back strands of hair that were plastered to her face with sweat and looked at her. "Just one more to go. You've got this."

That sudden but gentle touch followed by deep eye contact was almost enough to make Vanessa come right then and there if not for the realization that she still had to make it through one more threshold interval. The lactic acid had built up in her legs to the point they were almost useless. She could barely breathe. Yet one thing kept her going.

"Attack!" Damian's order was as sharp as the sting she felt on her thigh.

One to go. Either way, this was going to hurt. Each subsequent time, it felt like she had to push herself even more to get back up to 200 W. This time, she could practically feel years of her life burning away. Of course, she knew that wasn't how this worked, but it sure as hell felt like it did. Yet no matter how much it hurt, she would never give up. It never even occurred to her to use the agreed upon safeword: *arrêtez!*

It would be the last "fuck you" to the judge who ruled that the driver was not at fault and this was just an accident, warning her to "be more careful" while riding her bike. It would be the last "fuck you" to the internet assholes commenting on the news story of her crash by bringing up cyclists blowing red lights as if that were relevant. It would be the last "fuck you" to every idiot driver who couldn't be bothered to put their goddamn phone down and look at the goddamn road. Not least of all, getting back on the bike and riding again would be the last "fuck you" to the driver who'd hit her. The son of a bitch had passed too close after trying to intimidate her by yelling various slurs and obscenities while coal rolling a thick cloud of black smoke, ultimately running her off the road.

Vanessa was immolated, like a dry prairie struck by lightning. The pain coursing through her was exquisite and terrible. Vanessa was a reborn phoenix. She thought she would completely burn away.

"Recover!" With that gentle hand on her shoulder, Damian brought her back.

Vanessa slumped over her handlebars, gasping. She forced herself to do the ten-minute easy spin, or else her legs would hate her even more the next morning. Her heart rate slowed. She felt the sweat cooling against her skin. She became aware of the nipple clamps again, one of which had fallen off through the course of her final push. Damian removed the remaining clamp, then undid the nylon ropes tethering her to the handlebars.

Once the end workout timer had sounded, Vanessa unclipped out of her pedals, but nearly fell off the bike.

"Easy there. I've got you." Damian helped her to the couch. He handed her a towel and a water bottle, which she gulped down greedily since she had forgotten to drink during her workout.

"Back in a sec," he said, disappearing into the kitchen.

Vanessa started shaking, not from the coldness of her sweat evaporating off of her skin. This also wasn't like the group ride incident. Tears started rolling down her face, but she was laughing.

Damian rushed back in the room with a bottle of chocolate milk.

"Shh . . . shh . . . it's okay." He wrapped the towel around her shoulders and rubbed her over it. "I've got you. It's okay."

Sobbing, Vanessa took the bottle of chocolate milk and removed the cap. She managed to get a gulp down and her shaking slowed.

"I'm sorry, I don't know what came over me. I don't even feel sad. I actually felt euphoric right before this."

"It happens to a lot of people." Damian held her close and stroked her hair. "And I'm not just saying that. It's called 'sub drop.'"

"Sounds like a naval maneuver." Vanessa wiped away her tears with the corner of the towel.

Damian laughed. "Not quite. It's what happens after a particularly intense scene when the endorphin levels drop suddenly. It was probably exacerbated by the energy you spent in threshold."

Vanessa nodded. That made sense. Sometimes after a particularly intense criterium race, she'd be in a funk for a week afterward.

He massaged her legs with oil as she finished the bottle of chocolate milk. She wondered if she had to pay extra for this, especially considering how intimate it felt. It didn't matter. It was worth every penny for how safe felt right now, safe and completely sated. Mostly though, Vanessa felt exhausted.

She awoke wrapped in a blanket, lying in Damian's lap on the couch as he idly stroked her hair. Some show played quietly on the television.

Vanessa yawned. "How long was I out?"

"Not that long. Besides, I was finally able to catch up on this season."

"Oh, shit. I'm not making you late for another, er, engagement, am I?"

"No, you're not making me late for another client." He smiled, twirling a strand of her hair in his index finger. "I make it a point to only schedule one appointment a day so I can take as long as the client needs."

Vanessa felt sheepish. Someone had to fret over her once more. As she sat up, the blanket slid off and she realized she was still more or less topless and sitting in a dirty chamois.

"Geez. I sweat and cry all over you," Vanessa said, wrapping the blanket around herself as she stood. "I don't want to get any further bodily fluids on you."

Damian laughed. "Unless you're into knife play or water sports, I think we're safe there. Even if you were, I don't do those things. My specialty is just recreational discipline."

"And you are amazing at it. I mean, not that I have any other experience to compare it to."

Damian stood and gave her a hug. "Will you be all right?"

She nodded and returned the embrace. "Yes."

"Are you sure?" He pulled back and looked at her face as if to check for signs that she was lying.

"Yes, I'm sure." She beamed at him, still shaking. "As much as I'd love to spend the rest of the day cuddling with you and binge watching things on the couch, I really need a shower."

Damian nodded. "I'll wait just in case."

"Sheesh. I'll be fine," Vanessa scoffed.

Damian grabbed her shoulders tightly and looked her in the eye. "Look, this isn't optional. I don't mean to scare you, but I have to insist that I stick around for a bit longer to make sure you'll actually be fine when I leave."

Vanessa took a nice steaming shower. She had forgotten the pleasure of feeling her pores open up, lathering and rinsing the salt sweat from her skin after a hard workout, but now she luxuriated in it. She also took a bit of extra time spent with the shower massage attachment, no thanks to the intense look Damian gave her as he insisted that he stay. As she put her flannel robe and sweatpants on, she felt human again. She got a couple glasses of water from the kitchen and returned to the living room.

Damian was snoring softly. Vanessa smiled, took a few sips of water, and shifted him into a more comfortable position with a pillow, covering him with a blanket that hadn't been soaked with her sweat. She squeezed behind him to be the big spoon. It was her turn to take care of him now, she supposed, stroking his hair. After all, he had put in quite an effort today.

They woke up with no sense of time other than the popup message on the television screen asking if they were still watching. Rested and certain that Vanessa really would be fine, Damian got his jacket. Vanessa went into her bedroom and returned with an envelope.

Damian didn't bother counting the bills before tucking the envelope in his jacket breast pocket. He knew she would be good for it, which led him to wondering.

"Why don't you just hire a coach?" he asked. "Someone with your zip code could certainly afford to work with a pro. Plus, I didn't know the first thing about cycling until you taught me."

"Been there, done that." She shrugged. "Let's just say I needed extra motivation."

"Next week?"

"Next week." Vanessa smiled.

Maybe she wasn't ready to ride out in the world with her team again quite yet, but it felt so damn good to be back in the saddle.

THE LASH OF A
THOUSAND WOLFORDS

Trystan Kent

They give me power. They transform me from a petite, polite, pretty Chinese American woman to a statuesque, seductive, stunning, don't-fuck-with-me Dragon Lady. They are my not-so-secret weapons for they are always on display; I make sure of that with the dresses, gowns, skirts, shorts, and sometimes nothing else that I wear. With names like Sixty Six, Fatal, Stay Hip, High Heel, Crystal Lace, Paulette, Pure, Allure, Katy, and my favorite, Velvet de Luxe, Wolford pantyhose and stockings do my bidding, and I do theirs. It is a bondage we find mutually beneficial.

My not-so-secret weapons have partners-in-crime. They are the accoutrements to my legwear that complete my seductive mien. A short red or black cheongsam, custom split to my waist so that as I walk the full expanse of my legs are easily ogled, from stiletto heels and trim ankles up slim calves, over suggestive thighs to the lower curve of my buttocks. My victims imagine me as accommodating as a B-girl in a Hong Kong bar; a notion aided and abetted by my never wearing panties with my Wolfords. I sit at a bar on a high stool crossing and uncrossing my pantyhose-sheathed legs. Nursing a champagne flute in my hand, stroking the stem, I raise it to my lips and sip and men flock to me.

I choose my finery to appeal to their generic exotic Asian fetish, a Western male notion of a subservient sex kitten waiting patiently for her savior and master to appear. Judging by the Christmas morning look on their faces as they stare at me from across the room, they are certain I'm their enticing gift, ready to be unwrapped, to please them, to be dominated by their masculinity and used for their pleasure, always ready for more, but as soon as they are spent, quickly left for their mainstream significant others as familial duty nags at their consciences.

Before this night is out, I will have selected my chosen one out of the many approaches I'll receive. Within a few days, weeks at most, through a carefully scripted series of nylon-clad encounters and teasings, they will be my subservient wretch, bringing me expensive gifts so they may be dominated by me and my Wolfords.

I have not always been so bold, nor so predatory. Until a few short years ago my life had been lived in the shadow of men. From the attention and privilege afforded my brothers and not me, to the husband I was unburdened upon by my dutiful parents, to always being overlooked in my career, with promotions and salary raises going to one of the boys' club, I had been raised and treated as if I were an inferior species. In a sexual epiphany, I came to understand that far from being a liability, my demure Chinese American femininity and how men viewed me were assets to be exploited. Unadorned of nylon and heels, I stand a mere five feet and a few inches tall; potential suitors see me as "cute," as if I were a little girl, a delicate hothouse flower to be cultivated and made to serve them in the bedroom and the kitchen. Once I sheath my legs in the flagrant sexuality of contrasting tan and black trim Katy suspender tights and slip on red-soled Louboutins, I feel superhero tall and look it. And I am not cute. Do not dare call me cute. I am beautiful. I am stunning and I am cunning, and the kitchen is down the stairs and to the right. The champagne is chilled; bring me a glass at once and do not spill a drop on the way back up to serve it to me.

I first discovered the power of Wolford as my marriage dissolved. With a husband off being important with another woman, I was curled up on the couch with a bucket of ice cream watching the red carpet parade of stars going to the Oscars. It was the usual "who are you wearing?" fluff. Sigourney Weaver, towering over the interviewer, wore a red gown split to the thigh. Her statuesque black nylon–encased leg angled through the split, inviting a barrage of paparazzi flashes. The obligatory question popped out and without hesitation, Sigourney, a.k.a. Ripley, a.k.a. alien killer who put cowering men to shame, answered, "Wolford!" An astonished look from the interviewer resulted in more gown identity probing but Ripley stuck to her Wolford guns. She was toying with the red carpet circus, men, and the world in general. She was in total control of everything and everyone; that's when I first understood how much I had been controlled and how I could become the one doing the controlling. It was my first glimpse of the power exchange at the core of bondage and dominance.

The next day I called in sick to work and visited a Wolford boutique in Beverly Hills where the knowledgeable sales associate, who was wearing black Velvet de Luxe 60, as she proudly announced with a sweep of her hand, acquainted me with the luxurious pantyhose, further explaining that the number meant the denier or sheerness. I was sold, especially after meeting Katy and Fatal and their cohorts. As soon as I got home, I stripped naked and sat cross-legged on our rarely used marital bed and uncaged my Wolford arsenal. I had bought two pairs of Velvet de Luxe 60, one in black and one in purple, a nude Fatal, a black Katy with black suspenders, and nude High Heels with a black seam. The first thing I noticed—and it was true of every pair, but to the extreme on the Velvet de Luxe 60s—was how silky soft they were on my fingers as I felt them with a careful hand inserted into the inviting sheaths.

Yes, I had done the same thing in the boutique with samples at the insistence of the sales associate as she'd taken me on a crash course in everything I needed to know about stockings, pantyhose, and tights. I'd veritably oozed at how comfortable and sensual the samples felt to my fingers. But here in my bedroom, just me and my Wolfords—*my* Wolfords—there was no sales hype, just us—a woman and her luxurious and expensive hose. I confess, these nylons were as soft as my frequently bathed, often moisturized, always shielded from the sun, babied skin, and yet, as the sales associate had demonstrated, they were strong, Ripley strong, and were not easily laddered, snagged, or torn. They were what I would become.

As I tried them on and strutted around in my various pairs and posed and admired myself in the mirror, I realized they were my second skin, a chameleon carnal camouflage, and like Sigourney and, by default, Ripley, there was nothing I couldn't do in them. My ass was tighter and perter, my stomach was flatter, my pussy was caressed by the crotch, and my legs were longer. The soles of my feet were possessed of a nymphomaniacal spring, and my nylon-encased toes wanted a cock to squeeze and massage into coming or a similarly clad pussy rubbing against mine, Wolford on Wolford. Sigourney Weaver had defeated acid-spitting aliens; the new me was ready to take on the world. That very night I kicked out my shocked, slacker husband. I filed for divorce, and yes, I wore Wolford—Velvet de Luxe 60 in black, and I have never looked back, or looked better.

That is how I learned Wolfords were special—and so was I. Together we unleashed a dormant power that was always within me but had been suppressed by generations of male privilege and my complicity. But not any more . . .

I'm in my bedroom sitting at my makeup table, my gaze ping-ponging from my reflection to the photo of my grandmother in her ornate Chinese opera costume taken at a performance many years ago in Beijing. I'm naked, focusing on perfecting my immaculate porcelain doll visage to match her theatrically exaggerated face, accentuating my black eyelinered eyes and mascaraed eyelashes so they jump out from the red blush eye shadow framing them. A few more brush strokes merge my emphasized eyes with the alabaster powder and foundation covering my cheeks. The blood red glitter of my nails and lips screams in contrast to my pale makeup. My toenails and finger-nails match by design, and in a few minutes my feet and legs will be covered with one of the hundreds of pairs of Wolford tights and stockings that are my prize possessions; so much so that if my home was burning down I would run naked into the streets clutching as many pairs as I could.

My subject tonight has begged for me to wear pantyhose, but I discount my go-to Stay Hips because the crotch is bare, and he wants and needs a gusset soaked with my come. My favorite Velvet de Luxe 60s are what I used to lure him to me in the bar where he fell under my spell—what was it? Two weeks ago. Too short for nostalgia. Tonight requires something special from my Wolford arsenal to complete my dominance of him and make him my slave until his novelty has worn thin and I retire him to Tryst's Home for Laddered and Stretched Pantyhose. Tryst—that is the pseudonym I use with victims. Tryst's Home for Laddered and Stretched Pantyhose is what I call my war-torn basket of Wolfords; I never throw a pair away; they are saved for repurposing and possible use at some time in the future when the right situation warrants a resurrection; and so it is with my slaves. I never throw them away; like those wartorn Wolfords, they are kept where I know I can use them if needed, and they always come when I beckon.

I have given tonight's subject a task to complete before coming to my domain. Because he begged that I wear pantyhose, I ordered him to visit a Wolford store and purchase six pairs in my honor. His selections will tell me volumes about how serious of a pantyhose connoisseur he is. Out of the six pairs he is to wear one all day under his business suit at his executive job. He is to be naked under the Wolfords so that his cock receives maximum stimulation throughout his very full day of important meetings that he presides over while thinking of me and the night ahead I have promised him as a reward for his obedience.

Conventional BDSM wisdom suggests I should wear a black shade of pantyhose to greet him in my chamber, but I rely upon the unconventional wisdom of Marilyn Manson, who in an interview I read considered tan pantyhose to be the most sexual and slutty of legwear. I choose Allure in tan with a contrasting black floral pattern and faux stocking band and garters, casting the spellbinding illusion of wearing tan stockings with a black garter belt and no panties. Black patent Lady Peep peep-toe Louboutin slingback 150 mm stiletto heels add the perfect fuck-me shoes touch. Ass-cheek short, waist-high split, black silk cheongsam with gold embroidered dragons running along the winding button trail from split to high-collared neck is the perfect embellishment to my Louboutins and Wolfords. I apply a dash of Guerlain Idyllic perfume in all the right places and make sure my makeup is as pristine as when I applied it. My dyed platinum blonde hair, piled high above my head with stray wisps falling rebelliously around my face and neck completes my modern-day imperial Chinese seductress fantasy ensemble—carefully crafted to use my victims' stereotypical fantasies against them.

On cue, the doorbell rings and I buzz him up to my penthouse space. I unlatch the door as agreed upon in our arrangement, and I sit in a sex swing across from my four-poster bed, rocking back and forth in candlelit flickering darkness, sipping upon a glass of Pol Roger Sir Winston Churchill vintage *cuvee*. Make no mistake in the tableau I create; I am not a delicate bird in a cage swinging on its perch for your amusement. I *am* the cage.

He enters and closes the door with a soft latch. He announces himself but I do not answer. Silence speaks volumes of erotica in these situations. After a little fumbling in the candlelit darkness he enters my bed space and pauses on the threshold, no doubt soaking in the view of me rocking back and forth from shadow to flickering light. My legs are not crossed but open, the waist-high split of the cheongsam painting the pornographic image he searches the internet for. He holds the white bag with black lettering in front of him.

"These are for you, Tryst. As you requested."

"Put your Wolford offerings on my bed."

He obeys, showing me the contents of the bag as he lays it down.

"Six pairs for you, one of which I have worn all day."

"Which one did you choose?"

"Velvet de Luxe 60. Your favorite. You wore them the first time we met."

"Show me," I command, unfazed by his flattery. He sheds his tie first, pulling the knot aside, dropping it on the floor. He kicks off his Gucci loafers, revealing no socks, just the shimmer of the tights encasing his feet. His many-thousand-dollar jacket and trousers fall to the floor like a discarded chrysalis. He makes no attempt to pick them up or fold them. The tails of his snow-white shirt obscure the bulge of his cock pressing against the opaque crotch. In contrast to the speed with which he discarded his suit, tie, and shoes, he takes his time with his shirt, unbuttoning it slowly, dawdling at the cuffs, the unfettered shirt then sliding off his muscular arms to find its place on the floor. His chiseled body stands before me, naked except for *my* Velvet de Luxe 60s. His cock strains against the stomach panel. I am impressed but I won't show it.

"Pick up your clothes, fold them, and place them on the chair over there."

"As you command, Tryst."

As he bends to do as ordered, I enjoy the muscularity of his buttocks straining against the elastomer of the tights, revealing his bulging balls pressed flat by the stricture of the taut crotch. I press the "play" button on the remote and Puccini's *Turandot* flows from my surround sound speakers. Opera is the perfect accompaniment to my pantyhose passion play; it lasts for hours and *Turandot* especially complements my imagery, telling the tale of the cold, powerful Princess Turandot being wooed by a determined Prince Calaf. Of all the western operas I enjoy, *Turandot* is my favorite, borrowing themes from Chinese operas of the kind my grandmother performed in, and of course, the famous aria, "Nessun dorma," is very apropos of what I have planned for my Calaf. No one sleeps tonight . . .

"Get on your knees and crawl to me. Kiss my Allure-covered toes."

I do not slow my swinging, but outstretch my spread legs, adding to my momentum. He inches towards me on all fours, his eyes locked on my red-soled feet, keenly aware that apart from the view of my tan Wolford covered legs, all he will be allowed to touch with his lips are my toes peeking through the peep toe. He tries to match the motion of his head to the arc of my feet and to avoid the spiked heels of my Lady Peeps but gravity is cruel and physics can't be denied, so it's inevitable he receives a foot to the face more than he is able to deliver an adoring kiss to either foot. As I swing back, I kick off the Louboutins and hit him full force with the warm soles of my Allured feet, knocking him backwards. I launch myself from the swing and stand above him. There is a trickle of blood from his upper lip, but he shows no discomfort, content to lick away the spoils of his worship. I offer no concerned platitudes.

"Get on the bed and spread your arms and legs."

Once he is in position, I step above him, my legs spread above his crotch. The cheongsam rides up my thighs. I aid its ascent with my hands, unbuttoning the dress from split thigh to my neck. I angle my arms backwards and the silk dress slides off my body. I kick it to the floor. I stretch my arms above my head. My small breasts are pert, my nipples hard and bullet-like with large caliber intent.

"Pick it up and lay it neatly upon your clothes. It is silk, and the fibers are doped with my perfume, which will permeate the expensive materials of your suit. You can explain that to your wife and colleagues."

"Yes, Tryst," he says as he takes his time sliding his legs out from underneath my widespread legs, the delicious frisson of Wolford upon Wolford no doubt sending tingles throughout his body, as it does, I confess, through mine. Every time I feel that caress on my Wolford-adorned flesh and hear that spark of nylon on nylon, I flash to the time of my first sheathing and what it meant to me, and I am renewed—invincible, powerful, and excited. My pulse quickens and the first trickle of sexual desire flows.

Once my dress is draped over his suit, he returns and slides back spread-eagled beneath me, repeating the exquisite caress of pantyhose upon pantyhose. I look to my floor-to-ceiling penthouse loft windows and the glittering prizes of the city lights, and I see in the reflection my ass and legs tensed to pantyhosed perfection towering above this statuesque pantyhose-wearing man. So high above the city, we are like gods, fallen angels perhaps, and the sight and notion excite me. My trimmed pubic thatch is pressed flat against the tan gusset, my pussy lips split by the crotch seam, and yes, the trickle of sexual desire from a moment before cascades, soaking the gusset as he craves, making me further wet in anticipation both of what I have done to him and what I will do to him.

I squat down on my haunches and rub my Wolford-covered cunt on his Wolford-covered cock. Paying him no attention, I sift through the Wolford bag, announcing each pair as if it were a guest at my orgy.

"Sixty Six, fishnets, in red. Predictable, hardly surprising. Fatal 15 Seamless in black. Plain but a definite classic. High Heel in tan. Nice, the contrasting black seams are perfect from foot to ass and the black heel emphasis decoration is sexy. Good choice. Paulette—interesting selection in purple. The ribbed seams feel unbelievable against my body and my hands when I have them on and I stroke my legs. Ah, Katy suspender tights in tan too, with black rope-like faux suspenders and a black panty-like crotch. Very appropriate. And yes, the Velvet de Luxe 60s that you have on. Open your offerings for me and then I will open the offering you've been wearing all day for me."

I toss the packages on his chest and he opens each, gently extracting each pair as I press my pantyhose-encased cunt on his pantyhose-constrained cock. After a long day of stimulation throughout which he was no doubt hard more than not as the Velvet de Luxe compressed and massaged his cock with every one of his subconscious movements from walking to meetings to shifting position in his executive chair, my rubbing on him now with the warm wetness of my pantyhosed pussy is too much. He spasms under my grinding, the warmth of his pulses soaking his gusset and adding to the wetness of mine as he groans in pleasure and pain at having come so fast. I adopt a soothing tone.

"Oh dear. What shall we do now? You've soaked my brand-new Allure tights and your Velvet de Luxe are sodden with your come."

He bites his lip, his eyes still closed, his back arched, his toes locked in curled rigor, his fingers threatening to tear through my sheets as he grips the bed, his knuckles white with tension. I take the five pairs of brand-new Wolfords in my hands and work my way up his chest until my drenched pussy mound is on his mouth.

"There, there, we have all night. Lick me clean. Lick your come and my juices from my Wolfords." My soothing tone evaporates. "It's the very least you can do after coming so soon."

The tension from his face and body melts away. He dares a smile.

"Of course, Tryst, I will make amends."

And he does acquit himself more than admirably. He is deft in the oral arts. His tongue laps across the cotton gusset and nylon crotch, and with each lap I think of a cat licking a hand, and it's me that purrs as his tongue probes inside me with surprising strength, pushing the gusset into my sensitized pussy and working it around my sodden walls. I aid his skilled ministrations with a forceful undulation that stimulates my clitoris, producing further creaminess for him to guzzle. I'm close to coming and I know I should stop to maintain my BDSM distance and control, but what's the point of being in control if you can't exert it as you see fit, for your own pleasure and release? I grab his head and pull him into the cradle of my thighs, and rub his face into my pantyhosed crotch in ever-forceful circular motions. His tongue moves the gusset around my clitoris, and he sucks it into the material and massages me to orgasm. I come as the *Turandot* aria hits a high note. I clench his head tight into my sex and squeeze it with my thighs, my arms held high in the air mouthing along—*Vincerò, Vincerò, Vincerò*. Victory, indeed. I collapse forward and steady myself on the bed frame.

Nothing is said for many moments; the only sound in my bedroom is the gradual slowing of our breathing until the opera starts again, and I regain my composure. I reach for the Fatal 15 Seamless in black and knot the crotch around his right hand and the legs around one of my bedposts. I use the red Sixty Six fishnets in a similar manner to secure his left hand. I swivel on his chest and inch down his body until I straddle his waist, my sodden pantyhose leaving a glistening trail snaking downwards. He tries in vain to lean forward to continue his cunnilingual artistry but it's impossible now. His upper body is Wolford bound. I lean forward and slide my Allured legs back toward his head, making maximum stockinged pressure along his torso. I bend my legs at the knee, angling my feet upward and crossing together at the ankles then descending to meet at his eager mouth.

"Suck my pantyhose-covered toes like you sucked my clitoris, as if each one was a clitoris. Attend my feet and toes."

He opens wide for my pantyhose-enclosed size five tiny feet

and toes and shrimps them with gusto as if they were exotic food morsels. It's a delicious, delirious feeling that again stirs my desire, and steels my resolve to complete my pantyhose binding. His cock is already hard and pulsing and demanding as I press my body down on the damp firmness of the Velvet de Luxe 60s and slide back and forth. I use the ribbed purple Paulettes to anchor his right leg to the bedpost. The tan Katy suspender tights with faux rope suspenders are perfect to bind his left leg to the remaining post. He's now spread-eagled and secured by my Wolfords and ready for the culmination of my performance.

I pull my feet out of his mouth and rotate my body on the fulcrum of his cock, replacing my pussy momentarily with my butt. I stand, pressing firmly down on his body with all my weight. He groans as his compressed cock is compressed even more. Breathing deep, I can tell from the wideness of his eyes he knows he's vulnerable. I smirk at him. The powerful executive and upstanding husband relishes his lack of control, and I relish my total control over him. I let him stare at me. I say nothing for several minutes, towering over him, enjoying the feeling of complete dominance, communicating with this pause that what happens next is in my hands whenever I decide to begin the final act.

"I think I'll change. My Allure tights are simply soaked from my pussy to my toes."

He's rapt as his eyes follow the arc of my hands to the waistband of the tights. I ease them off my hips and down, exposing my sodden pubic mound in a silent, slow reveal. I flop down on the bed between his widespread thighs and press my bare sex against his nylon captive balls. I lift one leg and put it in his mouth.

"Help me off with these."

His teeth grip the spaces between my toes. I push the hose

down and pull my leg up and out of the sheath. I repeat with the next one until my legs are free of the Allures.

"Keep your mouth fastened on my pantyhose. Do not let go."

After several more pussy pounds of his balls, I straddle his chest so that I can encase his head in my sodden Allures. I pull the pantyhose over his head so that my sodden gusset is squarely over his nose and mouth. I loop the legs through his mouth as a gag and around his neck to tie them in a knot underneath his chin.

"Now you know how my pussy feels encased in these tights. You can taste me, and you can see through your pantyhose veil that my pussy is bare and my legs are unadorned. This will not do. I shall sheathe my legs in your tan High Heel offering."

I sit on the edge of the bed, performing a show all legwear connoisseurs live for—watching a woman insert her legs into her pantyhose and then stand to work them over her hips, settling the crotch in place with a few sexy hip shimmies. I sit back down on the bed, stretching my legs out one by one with pointed toes, letting him marvel at my lithe limbs. With him hypnotized by my leg show, I reach for a bedside drawer and remove a sharp, pointed pair of dressmaker scissors and turn to face him, snipping together the blades. I slip on my Louboutin Lady Peep stilettos and climb onto the bed, teetering above him with the scissors as my heels sink into the mattress.

"Are you ready for the Lash of a Thousand Wolfords?"

He mumbles and nods his head.

"Are you willing to submit to them?"

More nods and mumbles. I snip the scissors fast and loud down toward his crotch. I place the spike of my Louboutins on his balls and the peep toe at his straining cock tip.

"And you know the safeword is denier—d-e-n-i-e-r—like deny her, which I don't believe you can. If you don't say it, then we stop when I want. Agreed?"

Enthusiastic nods. I kneel between his thighs and begin the surgery, slicing the crotch of the Wolfords down from the waistband, running the blunt side of the blade along his cock as I part the material in long, precise cuts. I continue over his balls, pressing the scissors into his seam as I snip. He tenses, trying not to shake as I angle the blades down to his ass, where I detour around his thighs, turning the Velvets into stockings. I pull the panty area free and roll the material into a crude rope that I knot around his balls and the root of his shaft to make sure his erection stays engorged and demanding.

I step off the bed and enjoy the sound of my Louboutins clicking on the hardwood floor. From a hook hanging in my closet above my basket of Tryst's Home for Laddered and Stretched Pantyhose, I take down a braided whip comprised of strips of Wolford stocking and tights. There are a thousand of them give or take a few, including those adorned with crystals to add unexpected stings. I wrap the strap around my wrist and walk back to my victim, swishing the Wolford lash in the air as I approach. The sound it makes is a threatening hiss, like a snake poised to strike.

I stand on the bed astride his body and let the lash tips flop to his chest, draping them down his torso, dancing them upon his cock with little strokes and twirls designed to make him think this isn't so bad. As pre-come oozes from his purple swollen cockhead, I raise the lash above my head and bring it down full force on his cock. His body arches. He gasps a strangled scream through the Allure gag. I do not pause, working the lashes from head to toe, always returning to his cock, making him come with lashes of a thousand Wolfords, eliciting sobs of pain and joy but no safeword utterance of "denier." So, I don't stop. I place my spike heel on his chest so that my peep toe sits on the Allure gag, my nylon-encased toes teasing him with their proximity. With a backhand sweeping arc I've practiced to perfection the lashes come down hard on his cock from behind my back. He did not expect that. He struggles against his Wolford bonds, but they are too strong, too well made to give in. As am I. And he does not. Another backhand crack and he convulses a long stream of come up his chest, onto his face and my Allured foot. I let him lick his release from my toes in a momentary respite, but I will not let his cock soften. I have more moves in my thousand Wolford lash repertoire to rain down upon him.

The punishment continues until the sun chases away the twinkling city lights. "Nessun dorma" again serenades *Vincerò* from the speakers. My victim is spent and exhausted and I am rejuvenated because I know The Lash of a Thousand Wolfords never ends. Even after this immediate act is over, body memory is permanent. He may think he is released when I finally untie the Wolford bonds, but he will never be free of our influence. It will only take seeing a woman in tights, or even passing a Wolford shop, for a visceral desire to see me, to take control of him. Such is our power, Wolford and me. *Vincerò*.

DAY 730

Rebecca E. Blanton

Seven hundred and twenty-nine days had passed since Cleo had been collared. Her collaring ceremony had been one of the happiest days of her life. It surpassed graduating college, her twenty-first birthday blowout, finding out she was pregnant, and the day she'd met Lou. Each of the following 728 times she'd knelt to be collared by Lou, she thought momentarily of her collaring ceremony. No matter what the day brought, no matter what was on her to-do list, no matter how broke or stressed or tired she was, dropping to her knees to take her collar centered her and brought joy.

   She and Lou had been throwing around ideas for their anniversary. They didn't enjoy the typical romantic nights out. Dinner and a movie usually bored them. Plus, Cleo was a better chef than most of the professionals in their Chelmsford neighborhood, so she and Lou stayed in to eat most nights. They were too broke to do a long weekend away at the beach or in the mountains, so those options were out. Plus, with a one-year-old, they were both always tired.

Cleo wanted something special though. She wanted to reaffirm her commitment to Lou. She wanted to deepen the relationship and push her boundaries. Lou had introduced her to kink. They'd met four years ago at a professional conference in Detroit. Lou was presenting his work in epigenetics and Cleo was presenting part of her dissertation as a poster session. She had attended Lou's panel and was hot for teacher.

At the Saturday night cocktail hour for conference attendees, Cleo worked to catch Lou's eye. She dressed in a low-cut little black dress which hugged her ample curves. She pushed up her large breasts with a pink satin bra which shone bright against her olive skin. She kept tossing her long, dark locks back over her shoulders. When she caught him looking at her, she walked over to ask him a question about his work. She had constructed her question all afternoon. She wanted to blow Lou out of the water with how intelligent and advanced she was for just being a PhD candidate. When she walked up to him at the cocktail hour, all that came out was, "Wow! I really loved your presentation. So smart!"

She wanted to turn tail and run. She'd sounded like a groupie meeting Mick Jagger for the first time. She blushed violently, dropped her deep brown eyes, and prepared to make a hasty exit. Lou noticed her embarrassment and replied, "Thank you. And what are you presenting here?" This began the first of many conversations about their respective work.

Deeply grateful for his grace in the situation, she began to explain her dissertation work. She found herself giving her rote answers as she was distracted by his wide, welcoming smile and large, square front teeth. His looked like the nerdy cousin of the "most interesting man in the world" from the beer commercials but sounded more like Neil deGrasse Tyson. The combination of looks, intelligence, and grace was heady.

Lou taught at a university less than two hours from Cleo. They began meeting for coffee regularly, presumably to discuss career development. Once Cleo defended her dissertation, Lou made a pass. They started dating.

Lou had been in the kink community for over ten years. He had worked with a mentor Dom while he was in grad school and taken his first sub during his assistant professorship. He took his kink as seriously as his academics: attending conferences in both areas, researching what he was interested in, and creating meticulous practice regimens. He moved quickly from interests in bondage and impact to more rarified forms of kink.

On their first date after Cleo finished her grad work, Lou brought up the subject of kink. Cleo was aware of this world, though her only forays into it had consisted of light spankings and hair pulling by an ex. She wouldn't even really classify it as "kink"—it was more just rough sex. Cleo was intrigued and began exploring her more subby side with Lou.

It didn't take long for her to figure out she liked thuddy sensations, disliked super stingy things, liked being restrained, and it always took a little coaxing to try and get her to try something new. The thing she liked most, though, was pleasing Lou. When he would praise her performance, call her a "good girl," or tell her the day after that he'd a great night, she beamed. She would take any hit he delivered with joy if he broke a smile after her yell.

A year and a half from their first date, Lou collared her. It was a simple ceremony with a small group of kinky friends. They had done it at a cabin in the Adirondacks. She prepared a lovely meal, they all ate and laughed. Then they formed a circle around her in candlelight, Lou read their contract, stopping after each clause, and asked her to confirm her commitment and agreement with each statement. At the end, he placed a thin steel band around her neck and locked it on with a small combination lock. Only Lou knew the combination.

In the two years since the ceremony, Cleo worked to develop her submission. She began attending kink conventions with Lou. They joined a local play space. She found an experienced sub to chat with and figure out what kink meant for her personally.

On day seven hundred and twenty-nine of being collared, Cleo was frustrated that she had not figured out the perfect gift to give Lou tomorrow. Stumped, she sat at her computer and Googled "second anniversary gifts." The first site to pop up was Hallmark. *Fuck it. I have no clue*, she thought and clicked the link.

According to Hallmark, the traditional second anniversary gift was paper. The anniversary stone was garnet. The anniversary color was red. That was it! Red. This was perfect. Cleo knew what to do.

Lou loved knife play. Cleo had seen him perform amazing scenes with other bottoms and subs. For Cleo, knives were a hard limit. She had been a cutter as a teenager and feared that knife play would trigger those old habits. Her thighs bore scars of self-inflicted cuts. For her, knives and cutting always represented pain, depression, destruction, annihilation.

But the second anniversary color was red. Here was her chance to push her limits. Here was her chance to do something for Lou that he loved and would please him. Here was a chance for her to explore something for the first time with her lover. She could take a red, a hard limit, and push past it for him. She could redefine what cutting meant to her and give her Sir a very special anniversary gift.

The thought of Lou touching her with a knife made her heart race and her palms sweat. It was terrifying and deeply exhilarating. She found herself taking short breaths and tensing all her muscles at just the thought of him touching her with the tip of a knife's blade. The idea that it could cut her flesh brought about an instant need to pee.

That night, over dinner, Cleo proposed her anniversary gift.

"You know tomorrow's our two-year collaring anniversary, right?" she asked.

"Yes," Lou replied.

"I figured out your gift," Cleo said with a glint in her eye.

"Oh? Do I get to know what it is or do I have to wait 'til tomorrow?"

"I want to do knife play." Cleo felt the words fall out in a rush. If she had tried to pace them, they might have gotten stuck inside her.

Lou looked at her. He knew about her aversion to knife play. He knew why she had this aversion. "Really?"

"Yes, Sir. I think it might help me close an old chapter in my life and open a new one with you. I want to give you something special, something I'll only have done with you."

Lou was quiet as he thought over her request. Cleo stared at him, awaiting a response.

"Have you thought about what this might trigger?" Lou asked.

"Yes, Sir. But it's been six years since I last cut. I've dealt with the issues that caused cutting in therapy. I'm not living with my parents. I feel good about me. I think I can handle this."

"Are you scared?" he asked.

"Yes, Sir, a bit. But I've seen you do knife scenes with other people. I trust you fully. My body belongs to you. I know you will keep me safe. I want to make you happy."

"Okay." Lou smiled. This was an amazing gesture on Cleo's part. Even if the scene ended as soon as he touched her with a blade, he knew this was a true act of devotion and trust on her part.

They finished dinner. As Cleo watched television, Lou formulated the scene they would enact tomorrow night. As he envisioned the different scenarios, he went from pleased to aroused. Without saying a word, he unbuttoned his jeans while still sitting and pulled out his hard cock. He reached over to Cleo who was sitting on the couch next to him, wrapped his hand in her hair and pulled her down on it.

As soon as Lou had started unbuttoning his jeans, Cleo knew where the night was going. Her mouth was wide open before it even reached the top of his hard dick. In one motion, Lou took her from sitting and watching *Hoarders* to pressing his erection deep into the back of her throat.

Lou said nothing while he used Cleo's hair as a handle to pump her face on his cock. Tonight he was taking great pleasure in alternately thrusting his dick into her mouth, forcing his cock deep into her throat and holding it there until her body convulsed with pleasure. That's when he let her up for air before plunging back in.

Cleo felt the top of Lou's cock expand as he grew harder and harder. Finally, Lou pulled Cleo's head up so her face was an inch from his dick and shot his hot come all over her smiling lips, before pulling her back to a sitting position. She smiled and licked his cream off her face with her tongue. Lou used his index finger to get the spots Cleo had missed, then stuck the finger in her mouth for her to suck. "Good girl. Go clean up," Lou instructed.

Day seven hundred and thirty fell on a Thursday. Lou had one class and one lab section. Lab finished at six in the evening. Cleo had two lab sessions in the morning and used Thursday afternoons for her own research. Her last lab section finished at one, which meant she would have to wait in anticipation for at least five hours.

Instead of staying on campus to work after her teaching obligations, Cleo went home. She was anxious and excited. She couldn't sit still. She cleaned the kitchen. Four hours left. She vacuumed the house and dusted. Three hours, fifteen minutes left. She tried to do yoga, but after ten painfully long minutes, aborted the practice for the day. She tried to read a book. When that proved futile, she logged onto Facebook. She texted her mother-in-law to thank her again for babysitting.

When her phone beeped, she scanned the screen eagerly. It was a text from Lou. *Eat a light snack at 5. Shower and lotion with shea butter. Pin your hair up. No makeup. Be naked and ready by 6:30.*

Thank God. She had her to-do list. There was a plan. Lou was in control of this. Her heart slowed down a bit and she was able to concentrate on a streaming video.

At five, Cleo ate a piece of string cheese, a handful of rice crackers, drank lemonade, and finished with two Hershey's Kisses. She showered and meticulously shaved, then slathered on extra lotion. At 6:30 she took the kneeling pillow into the living room and placed it in direct line of sight of the front door. Then she knelt and waited.

At 6:38 she heard Lou place his key in the door. He entered wearing jeans and a T-shirt. She could tell by his smell he had showered at work.

Lou smiled when he saw his girl waiting dutifully for him. He put his messenger bag on the tallboy near the door, kicked off his Converse, and walked over to Cleo. He placed his hand under her chin and turned her face upward, bending over to kiss her. "Happy anniversary, my good girl." He smiled gently.

Cleo's collar sat on the small shelf near the door where it "lived" when she was not wearing it. Lou picked it up and placed it around Cleo's neck. He pulled a new small combination lock from the front pocket of his jeans. He held it in front of Cleo and turned it around. On the back, a small silver plate with a "2" was soldered onto the lock. A huge smile spread over Cleo's face as Lou locked her into her collar.

Lou walked behind Cleo. He placed both hands on her shoulders. "Do you still want to do this?" he asked.

Cleo nodded. "Yes, Sir."

"What are your safewords?"

"Yellow and red, Sir," Cleo confirmed.

"While I want you to try as much of this as possible, I want you to use your words if you are triggered. This is especially important if we hit an emotional trigger. Do you understand?" Lou wanted to make sure Cleo had an out should she need it. He knew she wanted to please him so badly, especially on this occasion, that she might allow something to go wrong and try and push through for him.

"Yes, Sir," Cleo said softly.

"Good girl. Now I want you to kneel on the ottoman."

They had an oversized ottoman they used as a coffee table when they entertained. At three feet square, it provided ample room for Cleo's petite frame. Cleo positioned herself on all fours close to the edge.

Lou left the room. Cleo could hear him in the bedroom closet taking out their two toy boxes. Lou walked back into the living room and placed items on the table behind Cleo. She did not look. Lou had trained her to hold her position. It was a Dom's prerogative to decide what got used during a scene; the sub didn't have the right to inquire what was to be used once negotiations were finished. Lou made a second, and then a third trip. Cleo held her position on all fours.

She heard Lou go into the spare bedroom, then she made out thunking noises. The fucking machine! Cleo blew out her breath. This was a box contraption with a place to attach a dildo to a reciprocating motion bar. This one had options to change the depth of the strokes and the speed. Lou liked to watch it fuck people. He had a range of dildos and altered the size depending on the person and the scene. Lou carried the machine into the living room.

Out of the corner of her eye, Cleo saw Lou go over to the high-backed chair in the corner of the living room. Most people thought this chair was some Gothic revival piece. Its high back was composed of three long slats. Its seat consisted of a small square block of wood and then two long slats. What most people didn't notice was that there were large eyebolts on the undersides of many of the slats.

The chair was actually a carefully disguised bishop's chair. Press a few buttons and the two outside slats on the back clicked into position to form a cross. Unlatch two latches and the two long slats on the seat opened into a "V" position. The eyebolts on the mobile slats facilitated ropes, chains, or other bonding devices.

Lou transformed the chair. Cleo heard him move the fucking machine closer to it. He then picked up something from the table and walked back to Cleo.

A soft rabbit fur mitt touched Cleo's back. Lou rubbed it over her shoulders and neck, down her back, over her ass and to her thighs. He continued to work her ass and thighs with the mitt. Cleo relaxed. The soft touch was reassuring. The rubbing calmed her. Lou used the mitt to pull Cleo's thighs open wider.

Lou had positioned her thighs just wide enough for a slight breeze to hit her bare pussy lips when he swung his hand to spank her wet lower lips. The sensation on her intimate area changed immediately. The breeze felt colder. Her lower lips slid effort-lessly when she shifted her hips. Her nipples were hard too.

She heard Lou pull something from his jean pocket before sharp pricks ran up the back of her right thigh. A Wartenberg wheel! Lou had used this tool on her before, but very briefly. When he used a light touch, she was fine with it. She knew from feeling it outside of play that it could get very painful.

Lou ran the wheel up her right thigh, across her ass just above her little hole, then back down. Tracing the pattern backward, he increased the pressure. When Cleo squirmed, Lou placed a hand on the small of her back to steady her. He took the wheel and ran it hard across her ass cheeks. "Ahhh!" Cleo let out a sound of surprise and a bit of pain.

The wheel pricked her skin in a new and exciting way. It wasn't like the tattoo gun nor was it like a pinprick. Rapid, sharp pokes set her brain racing to contextualize the feeling. The next pass of the wheel pulled her back into the moment. The feeling of tacks being rapidly pressed into her soft flesh led to images of tiny drops of blood rushing to the surface of her sink. With her next breath, she noticed she was wet between her legs.

Lou repeated his attack on her ass. "Ohh, ahh!" Cleo pulled forward to try and move her ass out of the way.

"Uh uh uh! No, you don't," Lou corrected.

Cleo resettled into her original position. Lou left the wheel on the ottoman and walked back to the table. The "click" told Cleo Lou had just opened the silicone lube bottle. Lou's hand was on her ass, then a cold nob of glass nestled against her tight butthole. Lou pressed the toy into her hole—but not enough to enter—and pulsed it a couple of times. On the fourth pulse, Lou eased the first bubble of the glass plug into Cleo's hole.

"Mmhhmhm." Cleo combined enjoyment and effort into the utterance.

Lou reached under Cleo and flicked her clit to help her ass to open more, making her breathing quicken. Lou pushed the next slightly larger bubble into her ass.

Cleo sighed with contentment.

Lou pulsed the glass plug until Cleo involuntarily pushed back to take more of it. When she did this, Lou gave one final push and the last two largest bubbles slid into Cleo's ass.

"Ahhhh. Thank you, Sir." This time Cleo let out a noise of pure pleasure.

Lou wiped his hand on a towel he had tucked into his belt, then ran it over Cleo's lower lips. They were sopping wet. He held her lips open with two fingers and teased her engorged clit. Cleo tried to shift her hips enough to get Lou to slip his fingers into her pussy, but he deftly avoided penetrating her.

Finally, Leo pulled his hand back and wiped it off. "Get on the chair," he commanded.

Cleo moved from the ottoman, clenching the ass plug, and walked to the chair. She took her position on the small seat, legs spread wide on the open slats. The base of the butt plug clacked against the chair as she sat, making Cleo blush.

Lou picked up two leather wrist cuffs from the table. He walked over to Cleo and fastened them to her wrists, then used steel carabiners to attach the D-rings on the cuffs to the eyebolts on the upraised arms of the chair. Cleo relaxed and let her arms hang wide.

This is where she felt most comfortable, like coming home. As she was bound, the need to control her reactions or her thoughts receded. Her breath slowed and tension drained from her face. Lou had control of her now. She was safe and giving into her excitement for the evening.

Lou picked up two leather belts. He attached one around each thigh and through the eyebolts on the bottom of the leg slats. He then took two smaller belts and secured Cleo's ankles to the chair's legs. Cleo relaxed and breathed deeply. She knew Lou had something planned. This would be her only time to enjoy the "calm before the storm."

Lou positioned the fucking machine directly under Cleo, then walked over to the table and picked up a dildo. *Holy fuck,* thought Cleo. The damn thing looked fourteen inches long. Just because the thing was sparkly and glittery did not make it easier to fuck it.

As Lou approached, Cleo's heart rate quickened. Lou was carrying the dildo and their big bottle of lube. He knelt before the chair and started fingering Cleo's pussy. He knew she was already quite wet, so he started with three fingers. He ran all three across her clit and right into her pussy. No resistance. The next thrust was four fingers. Cleo moaned. Lou pulled his hand back and grabbed a pump of lube. Five fingers up to the last knuckle sank into Cleo's dripping pussy.

Cleo moaned loudly. With his free hand, Lou grabbed her nipple and pinched hard. Her pussy pulsed and Lou steadily pushed past his knuckles and felt her pussy wrap around his wrist.

"Oh, thank you, Sir!" Cleo shouted.

He lubed up the large dildo and pushed its head into Cleo's waiting pussy. He then clipped the base onto the fucking machine. Cleo waited for the machine to start. Instead, Lou stood up.

Cleo sat there a little confused. Her ass had a plug in it and her pussy was now filled with a dildo, but no action.

Lou walked to the supply table, keeping his back to Cleo. She noticed he was doing something, but didn't know what.

When Lou turned around and waved, she saw he had put on five stainless steel claws. These had been custom forged for him. The "claw" was a two-inch long rolled piece of steel that was cured and came to a point. They were like eagle talons. Cleo had seen Lou use them on other people, but never on her.

Lou ran the claws lightly over Cleo's breasts and collarbones. Her heart felt like it had leapt into her mouth. Panic gripped her brain with images of the claws piecing her jugular. Struggling to ground herself in the moment she focused on Lou—his presence, his scent, his touch. Inhaling deeply, her panic receded and goose bumps covered her flesh as her nipples hardened and saliva filled her mouth.

He continued to stroke her upper chest and breasts gently. Then he pulled back and tapped her hard right nipple. Every cell in her body perked up, her attention laser-focused on the new sensations Lou was provoking. Lou then took her nipple between the claw on his thumb and one on his index finger and pinched.

"Oh fuck!" Cleo blurted unwittingly.

Lou smiled. He ran the claws across her chest and pinched her left nipple. "Good *Goddamn!*" she shouted.

She glanced at her nipples. She was convinced Lou had just pierced her. But no, not even a drop of blood. Thin red lines emerged on her chest and torso from the claws. She was scratched but not cut.

Lou stroked her inner left thigh with the claws. Cleo liked the pressure and slight scratching. On the second pass from her groin to her knee, he dug in. Cleo yelled. Lou repeated this action a third time. This time deep red lines appeared on her inner thigh.

Cleo looked down, the red lines popped out at her. Lou watched her carefully, taking in surprise, some confusion, and definitely some pleasure. "We still green?" Lou asked.

"Yes, Sir." Cleo nodded.

Lou adjusted his position, then ran the claws down her left thigh. This time he took five strokes before he left any red marks. Cleo was breathing more rapidly, but not panting. Her pupils were wide, her lips parted. Lou checked her pulse. Still in the safety zone.

Lou walked to the supply table and took the claws off as Cleo adjusted herself on the dildo. Her ass ached a bit from the plug but this was the first time she had noticed it since Lou started working on her with the claws. She had actually forgotten her holes were stuffed full.

Lou walked back. He had a silver-dollar–sized piece of cast bronze in his hand. Cleo knew what this was. She forgot about the butt plug and focused on the knife. Lou opened it. A small claw-like blade glinted in the low light of the living room. Cleo made eye contact with Lou, who looked back closely and watched for a reaction. Cleo looked back deep into his eyes. Lou nodded slowly, and Cleo mirrored his movement.

When Lou placed the blade on the top of Cleo's thigh, Cleo felt the tip puncture her skin. Her heart rate tripled. She flashed on her cutting sessions when she'd been a young adult. The body memory of depression and rage hit. Tears welled in her eyes. Then she looked at Lou.

Here was a man she loved. She loved him so much it occasionally bordered on worship. Every morning when she woke and saw him, she internally pledged everlasting love to him. Every time he collared her, she repeated in her mind, *My body is his. My heart is his. My life is his. I serve only him.* Instantly, the direction of her thoughts switched. This scene was her gift and recommitment to this man. This was a deep act of love. This was a man who would transform her. Her cutting was for destruction. His was for love and transformation. She glowed and her heart rate slowed.

As the first bead of blood surfaced, Lou looked at Cleo's face. Her thoughts had moved to him and he saw only love. He ran the knife three inches down her thigh. Cleo yelled out as tears ran down her cheeks. "Thank you, Sir," she whispered as she breathed out.

Lou moved to her other thigh. This cut was quicker than the last, but was the same length and drew blood. Cleo yelled out again, but not as loud.

Lou redlined Xs on the top of each of Cleo's breasts.

"X marks my territory and treasure. You are treasured." Lou looked into Cleo's tear-filled eyes. "You are my most valued possession. I will always protect you."

Cleo's tears fell heavy now. When Lou checked her pulse, it was rapid, her breathing shallow. He set the blade down, running his fingers over her cheeks and kissing her forehead. Her tears were followed by a small sob.

Lou knelt before her, kissed her on the X marks on her breasts. He ran his fingers over her thighs. Small amounts of blood smeared on either side of the cuts. He stood between her spread legs and draped himself on her.

Cleo's sobs subsided. Her breathing slowed. She began to rub her head on Lou's stomach.

Lou stepped back and kissed her on the mouth. Gently at first, then Cleo's lips parted. Lou placed his hand on the back of her head and kissed her deeply, coaxing Cleo's soft moan.

Lou ran his hands over her shoulders and cupped each breast, squeezing them. Cleo smiled and arched her back. Relief and gratitude filled her. Her body had served her, but more importantly it had served her Sir. Her blood bonded her more closely to him. The aches and pain gave way to her desire to be penetrated. A need to climax for a final release began to rise as her pussy swelled.

Lou ran his hands down her stomach and to her thighs. He turned on the machine.

Cleo remembered she was strapped to a giant silver dildo with an ass plug in her tight hole. The machine made shallow, slow strokes. Her pussy felt overfull with the dildo, stretched to its limits. With each stroke, the walls gave just a tiny bit more, taking it in deeper, more easily. Her fluids dripped and lubricated the dildo as it slid in and out of her hole.

Her pussy gripped the toy deep in her until she felt it rubbing through her walls against the butt plug. She arched her back, trying to take more of the toy into her. Her breath quickened as she felt the beginning tremors of an enormous and growing climax.

Lou pinched and pulled on her nipples. Guttural sounds escaped her. She began to laugh at the absurd animalistic sounds he coaxed from her. The contractions from her own laughter made her ass clench around the butt plug before a short orgasm filled her body.

Lou turned up the machine. Strokes lengthened and quickened. The dildo stretched her pussy open and tapped her cervix with each stroke, her inner muscles squeezing the toy with delight while Lou stood and stroked his visibly hard cock through his jeans.

Cleo bent her head backward in delight. Lou turned up the machine. The dildo was now rapidly fucking Cleo, hitting her deeply, the sensation on the border between painful and amazing. Her brain no longer processed any pain. She gave in to the complete pleasure enveloping her body. Tension from pain became the tension of a climax. It grew, beginning in her ass and pussy, filling her from her gut up to her chest until it shook her whole body.

She came, her pussy pulsed hard enough to cause the butt plug to shoot out. It was hanging in by the smallest bubble. Cleo shouted out, "Oh fuck!"

The look on her face was enough to tell Lou that all was very, very good. He smiled at Cleo. "Good girl," he praised.

Cleo came hard with his praise. The plug flew out of her and hit the floor with a thud with the intense pulsing of her pussy. "Oh fuck! Oh fuck! Holy fucking shit!" was all Cleo could muster. Forty seconds into full orgasm, Cleo began to beg Lou to turn off the machine.

"Please, Sir, turn it off. It's too much! I need to stop! Sir, please! I can't keep this up!" Her tone told Lou she was telling the truth. He turned off the machine and lowered the dildo to its resting position. He stroked Cleo's sweaty hair and kissed her. "You were an amazing girl."

Cleo smiled weakly from deep in sub space. He quickly removed the dildo and unstrapped Cleo, then pulled the cashmere throw from the couch and wrapped her in it. "You okay?" he asked.

Cleo nodded as a couple of tears rolled down her cheek. Lou scooped her up in his arms and carried her to the bed, keeping his hand on Cleo's shoulder before kissing the top of her head. They were quiet and breathed in sync. Cleo listened to Lou's heartbeat and lay quietly on his chest.

"I am yours. My body is yours. My mind is yours. My life is yours," Cleo repeated the final part of her contract. She meant this more deeply than she ever had. When she made her vows two years ago, she could not have imagined loving him any more than she did at that moment. Two years into their Master/slave relationship these feelings had deepened in ways she'd never anticipated. She was valued for who she was. This was more than she knew could exist in the universe when she took his collar seven hundred and thirty days ago.

"You are, my girl. I love you. I cherish your gift of submission and accept the responsibilities as your Master. I will protect you all the days of your life," Lou said and stroked her hair as he repeated parts of his vow.

"Thank you for the amazing anniversary present," Lou finished. Cleo kissed his chest.

"You're welcome, Sir."

RESTORATIVE JUSTICE

Alexa J. Day

I am forgiven.

All the weeks of regular apologies for long hours and surprise meetings and emergencies fabricated by people with no time management skills. The phone calls that got further and further apart as I lost control of my schedule. The lurching waves of terror that my girlfriend would realize she could do much better than me. After all that, I am welcome in this narrow bed again, sharing a too-soft mattress with Julia.

She kisses like she has all the time in the world, like she's learning me all over again. Her nails skim over my collar to the skin behind my ear, and when that sets me off, the way it always does, I suck her perfectly juicy lower lip between my teeth. A playful squeak flutters out of her. Her mouth curves into a smile, and I know I'm forgiven.

We'll lose our reservations. The old Mike, pre-forgiveness and new to this relationship, would sit up now and start smoothing his clothes. He would want to rush off to dinner someplace exclusive, eager to prove that his job granted him access to expensive places. Now I know better.

She eases me back into the overabundance of pillows, a pile of fringed and frilly things that smell summery, like her red-tinted black hair. Her forehead touches mine, and I gather up her cascade of curls, baring the back of her neck to my touch. She giggles when I stroke the skin there. Her divine body undulates atop mine. My cock stirs obediently.

"Good to have you back," she says.

"Good to be back." I pull her down for another kiss, tasting her and letting her tease me.

Fuck the reservations.

She hooks her finger into the knot of my already loosened tie and slides it back and forth before I take over. She rolls off me, her weight resting briefly on my hard-on before she hops down from the bed. She unclasps her beaded earrings, and I shuck my pants, awkward like a teenager making the most of stolen time. She grins at the spectacle I'm making of myself while she rolls down the linens.

We're about a million miles away from my place, in every respect. I thought I'd never see this tiny room again. I'd started to miss the way Jeff Bridges and John Goodman looked down at the bed from *The Big Lebowski* poster over her dresser. Nothing in my cavernous gray apartment clangs and hisses like her radiator. My jacket looks like it was made for her worn pink armchair and for the crowd of frilly skirts and artsy-looking blouses in her closet. I drop the horde of pillows, one by one, onto the floor near the bed.

This is when I notice the ropes.

Lying flat on the floral print sheets, one extending from each corner of the mattress, are two lengths of bright red rope. That color and the satiny sheen don't serve a utilitarian purpose.

These ropes are made for tying people up. A chill slithers into my gut.

I lift one of the ropes, pinching it. Softer than I expected. "For me?"

She nods. "If you like."

I have been tied to the bed before. Three times. Usually when the woman of the moment starts to think I'm spending too much time at work. That was desperate stay-in-the-relationship sex. Not with rope like this. That desperation took the form of scarves or something, tied to the headboard, just high enough to make my arms ache. And then it's being underneath them while they try to figure out what to do with me. They're tentative. Or phony, like they're rehearsing lines. Repeating something they saw in a movie or whatever. Inevitably, the knots slide free, and I have to be a good sport and hold onto the headboard until it's over.

They were following pop fiction relationship advice. If you want to keep him from getting away, tie him down. Something from a magazine.

Then again, this is Julia. She spanked me with a paddle a while back for getting mouthy with the hipster bouncer at the tiny club up the street. Three strokes with a wooden paddle she keeps in here, probably in the same place as the rope. I came so hard I swear I went color-blind for a few minutes.

So this is makeup sex. Kinky makeup sex with the woman who's forgiven me. Right?

She perches on the far corner of the bed and undoes the button that holds her emerald green top closed. "You done this before?"

"I have." I don't want to look apprehensive, but my default expression, the one intended to intimidate opposing counsel, isn't right, either.

She hikes up her ruffled skirt and crawls up the bed toward me. Her lips meet mine again, and my skin tingles with heat before she pulls away. "This won't be like that," she whispers.

"I'm sure it won't be," I whisper back at her.

She chuckles and flicks my lip with her tongue.

As I sit up on her tiny bed, I'm noticing that the ropes are not affixed to the headboard as I presumed, but to the bed frame. Neat trick. One that did not come from a magazine or a movie. That shouldn't surprise me after the spanking.

I can't help but smirk as I unfasten my watch. I'm about to unbutton my shirt when she says, "That's fine. Just lie down."

"Little enthusiastic?" It's out of my mouth before I can stop it. Old Mike has found his voice.

"I have a gag in my little bag of tricks, Michael. Do I need to get it?"

Part of me wants to know if the gag is going to be as awesome as the paddle was. But I can read a room. I press my lips together and shake my head.

"Good boy." She opens her hand to collect my watch. "Now lie back."

Her cool voice sends me up in goose bumps. Once I'm where she wants me, she puts my watch on the nightstand between a pair of condoms and a water bottle. She pushes my sleeves up to the elbow. My pulse echoes, muffled, in my eardrums; it's a drum roll in the hollow created by my breath. I think I'm going to have a minute to settle myself down, but the ropes are already looped and intertwined, leaving a neat cuff that whispers into place over my wrist.

I expect her to make quick work of the knots. The lead-up to the spanking was lightning fast. But she spends a lot of time binding me. The rope seems to go on forever, one loop feeding into another. The end going firm, but not tight. The silken texture of it. Her warm fingers slip underneath and wiggle a little, and her expression, calm but intent, reassures me.

I stare at the pattern as she binds my other wrist. Her brace-lets jingle as she works, stacking each coil neatly beside the last. She sits back, straddling me with her hands on her hips as I pull experimentally at the ropes. A playful tug reveals that I am bound quite securely. Wicked satisfaction lights her features.

This is not going to be like the scarves at all.

Julia mistakes the silence for anxiety. She bends to kiss my forehead. "You sure you're okay, babe?"

I reach to pull her down for a longer kiss, but of course, the ropes make that impossible. "Mm-hmm."

"You're sure?"

It's makeup sex. We're back together again. It's good.

I'm lucky to still be here. Lucky to not be having an argu-ment over this. I haven't lost an argument with anyone I've dated since I started law school. The training—and then the job—erodes human decency, and the animal instinct to win at all costs grows in its place like a callus. It's protecting me from fear, shame, embarrassment, and grief, but I'd rather lose an argument to her, and the truth is that I don't know how to do that anymore.

If being tied to this bed is the price I have to pay to stay in it, in her heart, in her life, then I will do it. I will do anything she wants.

"I'm sure."

She kisses me. I love this, when she takes the initiative. I'm open for her, more than willing, and as my tongue meets hers, the ropes recede to the back of my mind.

Until she releases me.

She sways on top of me, her skirt swishing over me. I come very close to asking if she's going to tie my feet down, too, but I don't. It's not even the threat of the gag. Something about being flat on my back, half-dressed, as she examines my restraints has put me in my place. I'm going all the way hard under her.

"How we doing? Okay?"

I nod at her. I can't decide whether or not to smile and it must show.

"Good. Now reach for me. Try it out."

My range of motion is larger than I expected. I can get my hands off the bed and lift up a few inches. I can hear the rope creaking against the bed frame, groaning on the metal. This is not going to slide free while she does what she wants.

She grinds herself against me, making a soft sound of approval. I'm hard enough to hurt. I shift my weight beneath her and she chuckles. "Fight it, Michael. I like when you fight."

She rocks back and forth atop me, unbuttoning my shirt as I buck beneath her. Her nails scrape over my chest through the cotton undershirt. Now that I know I'm tied to the strongest part of the bed, I really give it hell. She asked for a little bit of a show but it feels real for a second.

"Harder. You aren't even trying."

The ropes creak against the bed frame. Muscle burns and aches. But in these ropes, I'm not an average lawyer with pasty skin and a middle-aged paunch, slowly losing himself in an enormous, soul-grinding machine. I feel like a giant. I feel like something that must be restrained to keep it from rampaging over a defenseless world.

I'm hers now. A plaything tied to her bed. A convenience to be used. A well-dressed fuck toy.

"That works," she says.

She rests her palm on my cock. We would be skin to skin but for my boxers, which she tugs down over my erection. I choke on my indrawn breath and push out a low moan, straining up to her as she inches down toward the foot of the bed.

"I don't think so." She shakes her head, amusement on her round face. "I just finished tying you up."

She dismounts easily, leaving my cock jutting upward toward nothing. She reaches for the nightstand, where unseen objects clunk around in the single drawer. With a flourish, she produces a vibrator in the same artificial purple color as grape soda and about the same dimensions as the average porn star. She brandishes it with a grin in front of me. My own flesh and blood cock aches to compete with it. I twist back and forth in these ropes.

Is this it? Did she tie me up here to tease me? I want to stroke myself, to keep myself hard. I don't know how she means to paddle me face up, but I'm hers. It doesn't matter.

She sets the vibrator on the bed next to my waist, where I'm not going to dislodge it with my struggles. She pulls her top off over her head and tosses it at the footboard. The skirt drops next, falling to her feet in a pool of fabric. Her dark eyes meet mine as she slides silky panties down her long legs, and then she mounts me again, wearing only her bra.

She takes hold of my hair, and her fist tightens in it. She's never taken command like this. The sight of her, the lush shapes of her breasts and hips, fires a jolt of arousal into my chest. My arms go limp in the ropes.

"Do you think about me, Michael? When I'm not with you?"

A week's worth of blabbering almost falls out of my mouth. Then I remember the gag and nod.

"I think about you a lot. And you warned me. You warned me about the job."

I warn everyone about the job, the same way I was warned about it. The job kills relationships, my boss said. *Mike, it's like*

*both of you are cheating on each other with the same person,
and then you can't stop doing it because that's all you have in
common anymore. It's inevitable.*

I thought what everyone thinks: that won't happen to me.
Until the job killed my boss in the office I would inherit from
him. That heart attack left him dead and me afraid of becoming
a haggard, desiccated wraith, an unlovable monster who would
die the same way. Alone and unlamented. The night I moved
into his office, I met Julia at a bar. I stopped settling for inevitable that night.

She rears up over me, her strong legs flexing to lift her before
she reaches behind herself to unclasp her bra. The straps glide
down over her arms and the cups fall away, revealing tight,
brown nipples. My tongue slides over my lips. The memory
of her salty-sweet taste arises in my mind. I want my mouth
on her full, soft breast, my tongue sliding around and over her
nipple while my hand claims the slick flesh between her warm
copper thighs. I want her plentiful juices to coat my fingers as I
caress her swollen clit. But she's out of reach. I go a little wild
beneath her.

She smiles indulgently down at me. "You want to touch,
don't you? Looking's not enough for you."

I do want to touch, dammit. I want to touch her and coax
and whisper and growl.

With a click, she activates the vibrator. It makes a tiny buzz,
like the razor we all outgrew from a million years ago. I'm
wallowing in the sheets, trying to work myself free.

"I've missed you lately." She slides the hefty toy over her
mound.

I'm panting now, the harsh sound competing with the vibe.
She pushes the tip of the toy into herself. Just the head, up to
where the shaft curves. A feathery gasp escapes her.

"So I trained myself to get by without you." She takes a couple of inches inside her; the wet sound of her pussy, tightening around it, gives me a rush. "I trained myself for the long nights when you wouldn't be around. I like to think about the night we met."

She'd brought me home with her that night. Looking at the floor, the wall, at anything but her, I'd asked what she would want with me. Pathetic and worn out. On the way down and still miles from the bottom. She pushed me against the front door and ran her hand over my crotch. That, she said, was what she wanted with me.

"The night we met, you were different." Her cunt consumes the vibe's lurid purple shaft and she withdraws it with a slowness that makes me ache. "Like you'd seen your own mortality. The end of the ride. But I knew better."

She starts to really fuck herself now, the hard plastic rod disappearing into her. She takes it all for a few moments, long enough for me to understand what this was like for her. One hand pleasuring herself in this narrow bed, her eyes closed to imagine her absent partner.

I roll my hips up to her. It's not so much not being able to touch her—although that sucks—it's that she won't touch me. Won't stroke my cockhead. Won't lay her nails into my thigh. I am powerless to do more than watch her ride the tacky machine that was there for her when I wasn't.

She's flexing herself up and down onto the toy, her free hand palming her breasts, pinching one nipple and then the other. "I knew who you really were." She sucks in a breath, the sharp sound making me even harder. "I just needed to remind you." She moans my name like I'm not here, starving for her touch.

The night we met, I fucked her on the floor. I pinned her to the carpet and told her she shouldn't have taken a stranger home.

I wasn't that man, until she stroked my cock and convinced me I was.

I rotate my wrists until the ropes cross my palms. I pull them toward me, hard enough to shred scarves, snap those stupid Halloween cuffs like the toys they are. My arms are on fire. Sweat beads on my forehead and my chest before trickling down into my shirt.

Bound, I feel stronger than ever, my muscles flexed hard in my shirtsleeves. I summon the last reservoirs of my strength and feel stronger still. She's pushing harder now, louder, her mass of curls dancing around her face. I'll be damned if she comes by herself with me tied to her bed.

"Untie me." My voice is remarkably level, even to my own ears. But she shouldn't count on a please.

A throaty chuckle between moans. She turns her face up toward the softly whirring fan. "Don't make me gag you, Michael. I'm almost there."

"Come here. I'll fuck you better than you fuck yourself, even with my hands tied down."

She really was close. She's shuddering when she slides that vibrator out.

"Say that again. I can't hear my fuck toy over my fuck toy."

"I said to come down here so I can fuck you."

I hold her gaze, and I wait. I wait long enough for her to catch her breath. I stare into those deep brown eyes.

She disengages the toy. In the silence, the click is loud. She tosses it toward the footboard. Her smile warms the room until the air is superheated. She wraps her hand around my aching cock and I have to work not to close my eyes. I have to work not to pump myself into her fist.

She teases herself with me, running my cockhead over her slit. A sound oozes out between my teeth. Without the rubber, the wet heat is almost unbearable, the sensation strong enough to make my eyes water, but I keep my eyes locked on hers.

She eases herself onto me, my shaft slowly plunging into her. We sigh as one. Her muscles ripple around me, as the wave of pleasure carries me up into her. The condoms forgotten, there's nothing between us now. Nothing to separate us from each other. I need to get my hands on her, to pull her onto my cock until I'm balls deep inside her, to squeeze her sweet, luscious ass, to help myself to her abundant tits. My need to really fuck her flashes over me like lightning, directed down and away from my hands into the ropes.

"I missed you," she says, relief in her voice. She rolls her hips, grinding on top of me before settling into an easy, rocking pace. "I miss the man who fucked me so hard on the living room floor. I miss that guy. Arrogant. Mean. Ruthless."

I push into her, the contact causing us both to groan. "He never went anywhere," I tell her, and I actually believe it now.

No more words after that. No more fear, and no more inadequacy. Nothing but my cock buried deep inside her. The perfect sheath of her body claiming me. The breathtaking heat. The warm, earthy scent of her maddens me, and something base and elemental in the darkness of my brain comes to life, desperate to plow deeper into her, to make her mine and give myself to her, more fully than I have ever surrendered to anyone or anything.

Sensation races through me, impaling me. My back arches up toward the ceiling fan. This is what Icarus must have felt like. Reaching up with his whole body, toward light and heat so intense it would kill him, even as the wax and wings melted and collapsed over his shoulders and down his spine and his hands closed on the air. Needing the sun even as he fell, turning into the cool air, not caring if he met his death against the green unforgiving earth or in the ravenous sea below.

I came back into myself then, taking huge swallows of air as she rode out the last surges of my climax.

I'm returning to normal when the ropes loosen beneath her fingertips, as if by magic. I tug one hand free and then the other. I feel myself sinking into the bed, like something that's melted here being absorbed by the mattress.

She takes my face between her palms and looks into my eyes. For a second, I think she's going to say she's missed me again, but she lowers herself to kiss me. A chaste kiss. My lip between hers. Feather-light pressure, warm and solid. I can get one hand onto her bicep.

"Are you all right?" she asked.

I don't know. I'm bathed in sweat, my clothes sticking to me. The air kisses my wrists where the rope was and makes the skin sing. I'm spent. Completely used up.

Her eyes search mine. I'm hers. I want her arms around me. Her embrace. I'm changed, stripped down and rebuilt.

I nod. I don't know how I am.

"Can you sit up?" I make my way slowly onto my elbows. She lifts herself off my lap as I pull myself up. A warm trickle of spunk runs out between us. She twists the cap off the bottle of water with a ratcheting plastic sound and offers it to me. "Not too fast."

It's room temperature and goes down like heaven itself. It's all I can do not to suck it all down as she takes the vibrator across the hall into the bathroom. When she returns, her hair pulled up and away from her face, she takes the empty bottle from me and sets it next to the forgotten condoms. The vibe returns to its place in the nightstand drawer, and she switches off the lamp.

"Let's get you out of these clothes."

My eyes are still adjusting to the streetlights when she pushes my shirt off my shoulders.

"I'm sorry." I sidle out of my damp shirt. "I haven't been around lately."

She toys with my hair. "Don't be sorry." She helps me peel off my undershirt and drops it beside the bed. I hike my boxers back up. She pulls the sheets all the way up over us both and tugs the blanket free, as if we're going to need it with the radiator on.

"I'm lucky to have you," I tell her. "I know I am."

She pillows her head on my chest.

"I'm not trying to get away from you."

"I know you're not, Michael. I know."

"You're right to remind me, though. All that stuff you said. I'm lucky to still have you."

She's sliding off my chest now and rolling onto her side to face me. I deserve this. I deserve whatever she's about to tell me.

"Is that why you think I said it?"

"Isn't it?"

"No. I called you all those things because it's true. You are arrogant and mean and ruthless. You are." She kisses the corner of my mouth. "I love that about you. I love it when you're all teeth and claws. I love that you're a man whose suit cost twice my rent payment and that you fucked me on the floor the night we met. I love that. Sometimes you forget about that arrogant bastard I like so much. I'm just reminding you."

"Really?" I ask.

"Yeah, of course." Her head returns to its place on my shoulder. "I would never tie you up to punish you, babe. Not for real. That's not a cool thing to do to people." She yawns. "I thought you'd been tied up before."

"I have." I can't find the energy to kiss her, so I settle for putting my arm around her. "It wasn't like this."

"Well, then, maybe you are lucky to have me after all," she says.

"Both lucky."

She snuggles up to me, tight against my body. "That's the spirit," she answers.

LEATHER-BOUND

Elna Holst

This night had been months in the making. Selma could feel the delicious trickle of excitement like a string of pearls snaking through her as she propelled the library cart into the lift in the basement and pushed the button for the top floor. She adjusted the ruffles of her satin blouse and gazed into the mirror to make sure her curly hair hadn't escaped from the rope-twist bun she had arranged it into. As the lift began to move, she smiled ruefully at her own rosy-cheeked anticipation. The plaid woollen skirt chafed at the tops of her thighs where it touched her skin above her sheer, beige-colored thigh-highs. She wasn't wearing panties. They'd only get lost.

Impatiently, she fingered the access card that dangled from a red lanyard around her neck and sported the likeness of Yukiko Tanaka, head librarian, stalwart friend, and long-time supporter of the hand-picked book club Selma and Ed hosted once a month at their small, lower-ground-floor bookshop along a sleepy lane in the Old Quarter. Yukiko was a gem who always came through—discreetly, no questions asked. Selma would owe her, of course. She smiled at her mirror self again, ambiguously, as the lift shuddered to a stop with a ding and the stainless steel doors opened to let her off.

Easing the wheels of the rolling bookcase over the division between the lift compartment and the hardwood floor, Selma pushed her way out onto the library's upper mezzanine, her ankle-strapped spool heels echoing through the deserted, dimly lit space. It was after hours at the city library, housed in a restored castle at the edge of the central park, on the eleventh of May, also known as her wife's fortieth birthday.

Selma reached into her pocket to withdraw her phone and check that her lipstick hadn't smudged. It was silly; she hadn't been this nervous since the early days of their courtship, when they were only starting to learn about each other's fancies and foibles, curiosities and quirks. Selma shook her head at herself in the screen, baring her teeth and rubbing away a minuscule stain of burgundy red. She remembered the young, semi-professional arm wrestler she had met for coffee, nigh on fifteen years ago— just after Edith's twenty-fifth, it had been. When she'd found out about her recent birthday, Selma had dragged the slightly dazed and—really—mouth-wateringly muscular woman to her favorite LGBT-friendly jewelry shop and presented her with a small silver pendant in the shape of a lambda. It had been a spur of the moment thing. She had never been in the habit of handing out tokens of affection on a first date. But Ed—well, Selma couldn't help herself. She'd been smitten, and that was the truth of it. Right from the start.

She guessed it had been mutual, though Edith had later confessed she'd been a tad taken aback by the gift. Of course, she still wore it, in a black leather thong around her neck, up until this very moment, fifteen years down the line. Her fortieth birthday, in the sweet and merry, innocently blossoming month of May.

Selma turned off her phone and pocketed it. She didn't want to be disturbed. Last year, when Ed turned thirty-nine, they'd held an Alice in Wonderland–themed tea party with the book club. A classic, verging on the kitschy, but Edith had loved it. She was such a geek, her partner in business and in life. Selma knew her wife would have been perfectly happy to receive a rare edition of some out-of-print and half-forgotten tome, with a stern admonition to curl up in bed and read for the rest of the day, but Selma had other plans.

It was her fortieth, after all. She wanted to make it special. It was a tradition of hers.

"Can I invite my siblings?" Edith had asked four weeks ago, to which Selma had answered with an emphatic *no*.

Ed had pouted. Selma had pinched her cheek.

"Invite them for the weekend, if you must, though do we need to have all of them?"

Ed looked aghast. "You want me to choose between my brothers and sisters?"

Selma had sighed, conceding defeat in advance. "It's just that you have so many. It gets—cramped."

"I love you," Edith had replied gravely, meaning: end of discussion. It wasn't that Selma didn't adore Ed's sibs, which she did, each in their own way. But when the six of them got together, all at once, with their significant others and the children—all those nephews and nieces and whatnots—dear God.

She'd ordered catering and booked the shared courtyard round the back. Edith would make it up to her, would appreciate the effort, would make it worth arranging a minor festival, and then some. She always did.

The floor on this level creaked, ever so slightly, as she went along; Selma had never noticed before. But then again, she had never before had the privilege of visiting the public library when it was completely devoid of—well, the public. It was a fantasy come true.

It was Ed's fantasy come true.

Beaming beatifically, Selma passed another section of book-cases, arranged in neat rows along the tall-windowed eastern wing of the building. Edith had nearly fainted when she had brought her up to the main entrance, a scant two hours ago. Selma had let her loose with all her heart, vicariously relishing her wife's childish delight as she ran pell-mell, helter-skelter, delving deep into the behind-the-scenes. She had followed the conveyor belt where returned books passed along during the day right into the very heart of the off-limits, exclusive-to-staff part of the library. She had filled up her own cart of random, yet-to-be-shelved returns and dashed from here to there and back again, putting them up in their assigned places, looking like nothing so much as Curious George gone berserk. Selma wasn't fooled by appearances, however. She knew very well Edith could rattle off the classification system by heart. The old and the new one. She was a fountain of knowledge where all things book-related were concerned. It was how Selma liked her women: clever, with a touch of nerdy zeal.

And endearingly submissive. With a dollop or two of chal-lenging brat.

After a little over an hour, Selma had clapped her hands together, and Edith had responded promptly, loping up to her with a big grin that threatened to split her face in two.

"This was the best present ever. Thank you, thank you—"

"Take your clothes off."

Ed just about keeled over. Just about.

Selma's pace had quickened. There was a din in her ears at

the mere thought of how her darling had looked, nude but for her lambda necklace and the two tan leather cuffs with brass rings around her wrists, which Selma had gifted her with in the morning, over tea and pancakes in bed.

As she'd stood stark naked in the empty central hall of the library, Ed's eyes had been glossy with conflicting emotions: embarrassment at her outré get-up in this familiar place turned unfamiliar; a budding arousal as Selma raked her gaze over her; a vague fear of security personnel stopping by on their rounds of the city's municipal facilities; and trust. Above and beyond, first and foremost. Forever trust.

Selma had opened the voluminous handbag she habitually carried and brought out two things: an intricately twined length of leather rope, perfectly matching Ed's new cuffs, and a powder-pink butterfly vibe, fully charged, straps and all, to which Selma carried the remote in the pocket of her skirt, subtly bulging over her lower abdomen—a bulge that had earned her more than one furtive glance from her partner over the course of the evening.

"I know it's your birthday, pet, but this is for me," Selma had said, effectively releasing her wife from any sense of obligation, laying the foundation for the entertainment *de nuit*. Edith's fair skin pinkened. Selma crouched down and helped her step into the straps, sliding the vibe into position over Ed's groin, snug against her clit.

As was to be expected, Edith had already been moist, her slickness brushing Selma's fingers as she arranged the thigh straps, pulling them tight; Christ, but she felt divine. Fifteen years and going and Selma still found it difficult to withstand the temptation of dropping everything and burrowing her face in that lovely, luscious, eminently lickable cunt right then and there, plans and gear and setting and literary devices be damned.

Edith had moaned softly. Oh, she could read her mind only too well.

Pursing her lips, Selma had stood up. On cue, Ed presented her wrists, held together, palm- and brass rings-side up. Selma gave her a curt nod of approval and attached the leash.

"From here to eternity, Prew," she trilled and tugged her gorgeous, stripped, and restrained birthday girl toward the winding stairs. On the second landing, she slipped her hand into her pocket and pushed the remote, thrilling in the concomitant whirr of the vibe and Ed's sharp intake of breath.

She turned her head to see the glimmer of pleasure in her captive's eyes and her lips twisted wryly as she reminded her:

"By the way, you can't come until I tell you to."

Finally, Selma again stood in front of the door to which she had led Edith less than an hour ago. It was a white, nondescript flush door, keycard protected and leading onto a tiny room in the southeast turret. In fact, it was exclusively keycard protected, as there was only a single access card around that could be used to open it. Selma glanced down at Yukiko's blank, professional mien on said card and bit her lip, biting back a chuckle. She definitely owed Ms. Tanaka. How she would deal with that remained a question for another night.

Flashing the card in front of the reader, Selma shivered as the door clicked open. It was time. Showtime. At long last.

Edith was tied up for her fortieth. Figuratively speaking and literally: she lay with her legs spread-eagled, her arms flush to her sides, on a red velvet divan in a little nook of the city library of whose existence she had had not an inkling in all the forty years preceding. Between her wide-open legs the lepidoptera-shaped vibrator hummed, patiently, insistently. She was physically and mentally worn down from holding the impending orgasm at bay.

To do so, she had focused on the familiar scents of lit candles and old books around her: parchments, mothballs, half-French and French bindings—she fancied she could even smell a vellum-enclosed manuscript or two. She was off her rocker, most likely. Being continuously stimulated could do that to you. After this, she had turned her attention to the sensation of the broad leather belts that held her in place on the cushiony divan; their presence under which seemed to startle even Sel, for the space of a breath, before she summarily embraced them.

They were supple yet sturdy, and the feel of them against her skin, checking her, containing her, hemming her in, brought Edith so perilously close to the edge she had to bite her cheek, her tongue, anything to prevent herself from toppling over—from breaking the golden rule.

She never came without her wife's permission.

It gratified them both to no end.

Even so, as she heard the faint click of the door signalling Selma's—she sincerely, fervently hoped—return, she let out a sigh of relief.

She had no idea how long her lover had stayed away, or what she had been up to, but tears of gratitude, of sheer, vulnerable joy stood in her eyes as she turned her head and saw—

It was the librarian. The made-up librarian of her naughtiest, most pervasive fantasy: a pince-nez perched on her pretty Romanesque nose, her hair pulled back severely, her royal blue jabot blouse shimmering in the candlelight as she moved. She was pushing a cart in front of her, loaded with a selection of reading materials, a clipboard, and something—something more.

"So, Miss . . ." The picture-perfect apparition snatched up

the clipboard, tapping it with her steel-tipped pen. "Edith, is it?"

Ed's neck tingled. She cleared her throat as the librarian's gaze swept down the length of her, lingering for the merest sliver of a moment on the way her tits swelled between two of the firmly secured belts.

The woman's eyebrows arched. "All comfortable, I take it?"

Edith forced herself to speak.

"Yes, Miss. Thank you, Miss."

"Good, good." The librarian shifted and the drone of the vibe abruptly died down. "I don't want you to be distracted, Miss Edith. Now, don't be upset, but I'm afraid I've got a score to settle with you on this library's account." She rapped at the clipboard again, sharper this time, and a rush of exhilaration went through Ed. "According to our records, you got your first library card with us when you turned ten. Is that correct?"

Edith licked her lips. She was stupefied, her mouth dry, her sex *throbbing*. She braced against her bonds, as the librarian tilted her head, the toe of her shoe drumming the floor. Edith was transfixed, in every sense of the word.

"Is that correct?" There was a note of warning in the librarian's modulated voice, a sharpening of consonants that made Ed's exposed skin prickle with goose bumps.

"Yes," she wheezed, trying her best not to swoon. "That is correct, Miss."

The librarian smiled and leaned in over her, her lily-of-the-valley perfume overpowering Edith's senses. She whimpered. The backs of her thighs slid for a hundredth of an inch against the padding underneath.

"Happy anniversary," the entrancing creature lilted in her ear. "You've been a library cardholder for thirty years, pet. To show our appreciation, I've decided to let you fuck me, here, in the head librarian's hideaway, surrounded by her very private bibliophilic collection. Would you like that?"

She couldn't think. Her brain seemed to have disconnected, leaving her stranded, turned into a blob of jelly—a trembling, liquified mass of want. From the recesses of her addled mind she conjured up the phrase required, pronouncing it huskily, half stuck in her throat:

"Rilke."

Which meant: Yes.

Yes. *Now.*

The librarian pecked her primly on the forehead. Then she righted herself and there were dimples in her cheeks, a stray curl of hair feathering her slender, achingly beautiful neck. Edith wanted to touch her so badly, so badly—but she couldn't. Her heart beat against her constraints.

Kneeling, the librarian took up a wooden box from the lower left shelf of her cart, opening it with a small brass key and displaying the contents to her like a salesperson at an upmarket department store.

It was a wooden dildo, streamlined, lacquered, in the exact same brown-reddish wood—rosewood, that was it, *Dalbergia nigra*—as Selma's fiddle, back home. The librarian stroked it appreciatively.

"From your wife. She's got great taste, hasn't she?"

"Impeccable."

The librarian smirked and lifted it out. It was already attached to a harness—which alerted Edith to the fact that she would not be allowed the use of her hands after all.

"Let's see how it fits, shall we?"

Ed lifted her head, straining her neck to catch a glimpse of how the quick-fingered woman pushed the deactivated butterfly down until it nestled over her slit instead and placed the hard, unyielding wood over her battered nub. She hissed through her teeth, but the librarian paid her no heed as she fastened the new straps on top of the old.

"There we go." The librarian glanced up at her, and she was a sight for sore eyes: red lips, half-lidded gaze, her pince-nez a smidge askew. She caressed the shaft of the dildo, grinding it against Edith's swollen clit in the process.

Ed bucked her hips, which proved entirely ineffective. She clenched her hands into fists.

The librarian kissed the tip of the wood, then kicked off her heels and bunched her heavy skirt up around her hips, revealing the lacy, rubbery edges of her stockings.

Edith groaned, bucking again, with the same poor—make that non-existent—result. She swore roundly. The librarian's eyes flashed.

"You're too loud, love. This *is* a library. Here, let me help you."

She should have seen it coming, but she didn't, not until she was encircled by silky thighs, the thick wool cloth falling about her, damp folds tickling her lips.

A bolt of red-hot passion shot through Ed as she felt her mistress's hands in her hair, clutching, pulling, as her soft, muffled voice urged her on: "Eat me. Yes, fuck. Eat me like you mean it."

She did mean it. She meant every sweep of her tongue, every nibble of her lips, every lick and swallow and dart as she was smothered in cunt, eager and sopping, pushing her deeper into the cushions, pushing her clear into another dimension, a spaced-out world of submissive bliss.

The thighs on either side of her head juddered, and she wanted to grip them, but more than that: she wanted to hold onto this moment, be forever suspended, forever on the cusp, her arms pinned to her sides, her painfully tight breasts popping between leather belts, her clitoris elongated into erect wood.

Tears streamed down her cheeks—happy, ecstatic, out-of-her-head tears—and any second now she would—

"Not. Yet."

Her world slanted to the side, or rather her librarian mistress did, and for an instant Edith felt so bereft she could have cried out loud, but a cool digit touched her lips to hush her; burgundy lips mouthed, "Soon."

The librarian straightened her pince-nez, her blouse dishevelled, her face flushed. She bent to flick one of Ed's contracted nipples with the tip of her tongue, smiling at Edith's gasp even as she locked her eyes onto hers.

She didn't say anything; she didn't have to. Her gaze was an open book, brimming with pride, pleasure, raw emotion as she shimmied into position and slowly, inexorably lowered herself onto Ed's wooden length.

Edith could swear she felt her lover's inner walls tightening around her, and she wanted it—wanted her: Selma, the librarian, her wife, her partner, her gentle, loving Domme—so fucking much, she just about tore herself loose.

Just about.

Because she couldn't.

Sel shook her head once, vaguely, as if to say *don't be silly*, but then the wood hit home, and she gulped and rocked her hips, every minute twitch of her cunt translated and multiplied onto Ed's pumping need, her juices trickling onto her between the straps, her head thrown back in ardour.

Edith stared up at her helplessly, and she would erupt, explode, disintegrate, any moment now, as she watched her librarian-for-the-night effortlessly work herself toward a mounting climax, a *coup d'éclat*, on top of her, with her, through her.

"Selma," she pleaded, her voice jangly and scattered, like so many bits of tinfoil caught in a thunderstorm, "for the love of—"

"Yes, do."

The response was so breathy, so close to the peak itself, she could almost not make it out; but what she could make out was the vibrator suddenly coming alive beneath the strap-on, its plump, smooth end poking at her, thrumming, as Sel pushed down hard and came for her. Edith roared.

"Ms. Tanaka?"

"Edith! How nice to see you—happy belated birthday!"

Yukiko fell about her neck, smacking loud kisses a hair's breadth from her cheeks, French style, and Ed inwardly cursed herself for her telltale awkward formality. They'd been Yukiko and Edith since forever and a day, but after Selma's epic treat for her, two days ago, she felt … different about the head librarian. The tips of her ears burned.

"I—Selma asked me to return this to you, with her compliments."

Yukiko accepted the access card in its red lanyard, hanging it around her neck with a nod and an indulgent grin at a gaggle of primary schoolers heading to the children's books section. Her eyes slanted slyly toward Edith.

"So, how did you find the library after hours, sweetheart? Was it everything you'd hoped it would be?"

Ed's face warmed afresh and she began to suspect exactly why Sel had insisted she should be the one returning the card today. Her torso was still garishly polka-striped underneath her shirt, and when they had packed up to go, she'd noticed that Selma didn't take the belts along with the rest of their stuff, but simply tucked them back under the divan. Yukiko's divan.

Exhaling a long-held breath, Edith decided to roll with it. It was what Sel would do.

"It was immensely enjoyable. Surprisingly so."

Yukiko's gaze fluttered down to Ed's new leather cuffs, the brass rings jingling conspicuously.

"Would Selma ever . . ." The librarian's voice trailed off, and she shifted her stance, her hand digging deeper into her pocket.

"You'd have to ask her yourself," Ed said sweetly, imagining her wife's dismay at not being spared this conversation. She would be paying for this. "Though I should warn you," she relented, meeting Yukiko's eyes above the rim of her reading specs, "she's not in the habit of sharing her toys."

TABLE FOR TWO

T.R. Verten

If he had to pick the thing guaranteed to humiliate him beyond words, it would be this. But the whole point is that John isn't allowed to pick.

It had been her idea. 'Course it had.

John is so used to it that he can usually anticipate when it's going to happen. Weeks can pass by without either of them mentioning it, and then the next thing he knows they'll be out, on a date, all three of them, one of their usual spots, John might catch her smiling in Seth's direction, the inside of his mouth going dry, because he can just sense that they're both thinking about him. Him, and what to do with him.

He hates it.

His flaw is that he's too eager. John knows this, knows her to be genuinely displeased when he tries to anticipate, whereas Seth—

He'll take her side, when she's there.

But if she isn't?

If she isn't Seth only pretends to be disappointed. John can tell by the way one side of his mouth lifts in a smile, the way he says *oh John* in the most pleased tone.

He's not permitted all that often. It's in his nature to get too overwhelmed, too quickly. They won't even tell him in advance, because should he know what lies ahead, then he'll simply try to anticipate that, too.

Which is why Seth has put the blindfold on him first thing.

And Christ, how he wants to second-guess them then. Do they want him on the bed? The floor? Where should he put his hands? Questions bubble up but he can't find the right way to ask them. It's already so much, too much. Straightaway.

But he can hear *her* through the anxiety, her voice sharp and to the point, hear her tell Seth to undress him down to his underwear, to assist him down to the floor.

"John?" It's Seth, Seth's hands on his shoulders, Seth a comforting presence.

His breath whistles through his nose but he manages a fierce nod.

He really does hate this. Hates how much he needs them.

There are fingers on the side of his face (*his*), a tug on his hair (*her*).

"Arms up," Seth says, and John holds them out at once with his wrists already crossed. Anticipating, like he's good at.

Nora laughs, not unkindly. "He's done it again," she says, her voice coming closer as one of them—*him*, John thinks, shorter fingernails, heavier hands—moves his arms until his wrists are close in to his chest, pressed against one another side by side and the other one—*her*, it must be then—touches his neck.

The item against his skin is cold, heavy, and, he realizes with a guilty shock, rigid. Already he's fighting the urge to wriggle against it as he hears three distinct clicks, and then his shoulders are pulled forward and his upper body goes taut from the constriction.

Immediately he feels about ten times more at ease. This is what they want from him, then. This is all he's meant to do.

"Sit up," she says, a little less kindly. John wants to be good for her, he does, but he moves too fast and sways there on his knees. Then there's a hand on his head using him for leverage as she climbs onto the bed, a shift from behind him, a squeak on the mattress, a dark, pleased noise from Seth. He must be close by—must be on his knees, too, by the way she's sounding all of a sudden.

That they let him listen at all fills him with guilty excitement. For whatever reason this is a million times worse than when he listens from the hallway when they're together in their room. It thrills him to think of them, that they might know—Jesus, *of course* they know, they know everything he thinks, wants, before it's even become conscious thought for him—that he's out there.

Listening.

Keeping their sounds tucked away to ruminate on. When he's walking to work, doing chores around the house. Reminding himself how much better they are than him. How he doesn't deserve one of them, let alone both of them. Berating himself for thinking he could ever be the same to them as they are, to him.

John sags, his sweaty wrists slipping against the metal. The weight yanks his shoulders down, a dull ache already building in the sockets. This he knows. This he can do.

"Are you finished?" Seth asks her, once they've checked in with John.

He's dizzy with how excited he is from this alone. Hard, in his underpants, and it's beginning to hurt in a not unpleasant way. He shudders when he realizes that, a full-body shiver climbing up his spine and ending with him shaking his head side to side. The metal slides cold and protective against his overheated skin.

John wants to go forward onto all fours so his body isn't as noticeable, but he's prevented from following through by the device fastened round his neck. Instead he squirms, the aluminum rigid, slick against his wrists from where he's strained against it. If he keeps at it there will be marks there tomorrow. He bruises too easily for those things to pass by without incident. That thought excites him, too.

"Hardly," she answers. She puts a hand on his shoulder, heavy, as she gets up off the bed, slightly dislodging his blindfold—an intentional move. From that opening he can now see a small corner of the room, Nora in her bra facing away from him.

Seth looks over at John as she's putting a towel down, which reminds him that he's knelt barelegged against the scratchy carpet, that there's sweat built up in the creases of his knees, where his thighs press against his stomach. Once more he's compelled to lean down, bend over, give in, surrender, but manages to bite the inside of his cheek and give Seth a tight little nod instead. It takes all his energy and courage, that nod. Seth, the handsome bastard, grins right back at him before reaching across and pulling the blindfold up over his eyebrows and up into his hairline. It's down low enough that he can look away should it be too much.

It feels like it might be too much.

But he looks anyway.

He can see it all happen, the way Nora is caught off guard when Seth grabs her by the waist. He observes as she kicks out sharply with her leg, grazing John in the process.

"You absolute dick," she yelps, and bangs her fists onto his broad back as he pins her to the ground on top of the towel.

John shivers. How can he treat her like that, so cavalier, inconsiderate? He would never. He could never.

"Whose dick?" he asks from atop of her, his tone all cocky and self-assured.

"Mine," Nora gasps out, swinging a leg over him. "If you're not careful."

John looks for the floor, because that's a safe place to focus his attention, only he can't see much past his hands. He can see what they're doing, what Seth's doing, if he cranks his head a certain way, despite the cold press of metal, but when Seth looks back over his shoulder John flinches on instinct. He shouldn't look, he shouldn't want to look, but he wants, so much, to look.

"On who?" Seth teases. He grinds into her and she moans. "On me?"

"Sure," she manages. "Or maybe—" John can feel his balls draw up against his body, tight and hot inside his boxers. Her tone makes his stomach muscles tighten up as well. They're good, together. They're perfect. Maybe after this one of them will touch him. Maybe Nora—

"—maybe I'll use it on him," Nora says through clenched teeth.

"And leave me out entirely? Goddamn it," Seth swears. "You're such a bitch."

"Fuck you," she says, and punches him lightly in the chest.

"Ow," Seth says, and looks back over his shoulder, his handsome face all pouty. As if that really hurt. Despite his build, Seth isn't great with pain. John sits up a little straighter, pleased with himself. There are a few things he's better at than Seth, pain and its tolerance being chief among them.

He moans again when she does, straining forward in his excitement. His shoulders burn but it's the only way he can see what's going on, the way she flips and straddles him, the way her hands press hard against his chest until they're both finished and lie there, side by side, gasping for air.

Nora rolls off Seth, who is eyeing the unmissable tent in his boxers.

"You poor thing." He brings his hand up to touch. It's damp underneath his palm, and now it's John's turn to moan.

"What do you think?" he asks Nora, who is leaning on her hand, her elbow cocked, scrutinizing him in a way that makes him wish he didn't have to have a body at all.

"I think he might want to see a little better," Nora says, with a horrible, mischievous glint in her eyes. If John could bring himself to so much as fathom the thought, then he'd definitely hate her.

She reaches over Seth's body to push the blindfold up over his forehead. It pushes his hair back in a way that must look stupid, girlish, but he can't be bothered worrying about that because she's got a hand under his chin and Seth's untucking him from his boxers, putting his mouth on John's balls, the underside of his cock, not that he can see, with his hands, forearms, elbows in the way.

Nora asks, "Do you want me to let you go?"

He wants to look, he wants to see, but he needs to be held up, otherwise he'll crash straight to the ground, and Nora knows him, knows him so well that though he can't make words, can't say what it is he needs her to do, she knows.

His words are dry clicks when he tries to speak. She shushes him.

"All right," she says, "then that's what I'm going to do." He wants to thank her for understanding, for giving this to him, but there aren't words. She unlinks the little padlock; three short clicks release him. Blood floods into his arms and they tingle like his cock does as she drags him to his feet, kicks his legs apart so he's just about level with Seth's face. Seth is kneeling once more, only this time John can see everything, and he can't, he shouldn't, he mustn't. Seth is flushed pink down his neck, his slick mouth right there, and Nora says, "If you can make him last another five minutes I'll let him finish on your face."

"Deal," he says, before sliding his big hands up the outsides of John's legs, coming to settle just below his waist. The hair on the back of his neck prickles. The sweat that had built up behind his knees feels cold now that his legs aren't folded in on themselves. Seth gets one wrist, holding it steady against his thigh, and she pulls on the other, until it's bent behind his back. His shoulders ache from being held up for who knows how long.

"You wanted to look." Nora's got her hand on the nape of his neck. She shakes him, hard, and John heaves from his stomach up to his chest. Shit, shit? Is he crying? She won't be pleased with that at all. But she merely sounds firm when she says, "The least you can do is be considerate."

"I am working very hard." Seth grins up at them, delighted with his efforts.

"Work a little harder," Nora says, to which Seth just laughs. John isn't too far gone that he doesn't wince at that. John would never do something like laugh aloud; he doesn't have it in him to be insolent. Nor is he shameless like Seth, Seth who's performing for them—for her—with a hand on his dick and his tongue tracing wet circles all over the place. John twists in his grip, away from the sensation, but she's there to stop him from running off entirely. Seth's free hand covers John's own, pressing it into the front of his thigh. Their hands are moving, back and forth, up and down, working together to reduce him to the nothing he knows himself to be.

"Seth," Nora says, and doesn't have to say more than that. He just knows. He lets go of John's hand only for her to take it up in her own, then arrange it behind his back until his forearms are clasped together. Again he feels calmed by his own obedience. She hums a pleased noise that only intensifies his pride.

"He's good at that, isn't he?" Nora says against his shoulder. The verbal answer is just beyond his reach. He knows it's there, can feel the shape of it, but it's no use. He doesn't mean to sag but he must because she's pushing him to stand upright and straighter, straight back into the hot dampness of Seth's mouth, the roving heat of his hands across his stomach and thighs. With an aching flash John feels himself lurch closer to orgasm, to coming in front of them. The absolute humiliation of that possibility becoming certainty turns to fright, bleeding into excitement, then anguish.

Nora lets out an exasperated sigh and holds her hand up in front of his mouth. He preemptively sticks out his tongue, does it before she tells him to. He can't help it; he wants to be good but he can't stop himself from trying to know what she wants from him. But instead of being cross, she merely murmurs against his ear, "You must really need it, hm?"

He hates needing it. He wishes, more than anything, that he didn't need anything from her, anything from him, that he could simply exist in their world, as inconsequential as an end table. His body wants things that he would never deign to ask for. It's up to her to puzzle them out, to them to turn them into reality. Still he is mired in the hot shame of it all.

His response is to lick her palm until it's damp, and then to whine, high in his throat as she wraps her hand around his wet, aching dick, and says to Seth, down there on the ground, "Stay still, you greedy little thing." Seth grins again, like it's a normal thing to want a person to do in front of anyone, let alone on them.

It hurts, in his balls, in his stomach.

Someone curses.

Someone screams.

Seth winces, once, and then he parts his lips as John writhes, tries to look away, but Nora is right there, her own small hand finding him and pulling root to tip until his eyes water. Seth's mouth follows her hand in the opposite direction, John's come rolling into the hollow of his cheekbone and then down the side of his face.

He sags against Nora. "Fuck," John hears someone say. "Oh, fuck."

When Seth's top lip bumps against the sensitive tip of his dick, John wonders what would happen to him if he screamed, right now, if he flung himself against a wall, but then Nora is there saying, "It's okay, John, it's all right." Seth bends forward again, sucking once, hard, like he's trying to make certain he's got everything.

There's come on Seth's flushed face. John's come, the shameful evidence of it obvious to everyone. He did that, that awful, awful thing. Shame bubbles up from beneath the haze of orgasm. Why must he be like this? Why can't he simply be satisfied with that?

"You're so good," Nora tells him. "Look how happy you've made Seth." Seth does look happy, filthy and smug. John basks in that momentary praise until he becomes painfully aware that she only said Seth, she didn't say anything about herself.

She helps him into the bed and stays there with him until Seth comes back, his face scrubbed pink and clean, with a water for him and a whiskey for them to share.

"All right?" Seth asks John, his hand rubbing gentle circles between his shoulder blades as he drinks the water, nods violently. There's a warm, blurry prick behind his eyes. He coughs, wetly, against the glass. "You're all right."

"Seth," John manages to say.

Nora hands him a tissue, helps him wipe the tears off his face.

John repeats himself, stupid beyond measure. "Seth," he blurts out again. If he cries now he won't be able to stop for a long, long while.

Seth puts the glass down on his bedside table. He smells of whiskey and soap. The familiarity comforts him. "It's fine, it's all right."

Nora turns him onto his side so he's facing Seth, her own compact body pressed close against his own.

"We love you," Nora murmurs and John chokes out a sob. Where do the tears keep coming from?

"It's true," Seth says, and kisses John on the tip of his nose, his forehead, his hairline, his jaw.

"Seth," John says again, sleepy and numb this time. His toes are tingling.

"Shhh," Nora says, and throws a leg over them both.

HEADSPACE

Evan Mora

It's take your girl to work day. That's what Daddy said.

He was being funny, I know, because *take your girl to work day* is whatever day he says it is. Like Tuesday. Or all the odd numbered days in the week.

I keep my eyes down as I walk through the tall glass doors, past the wide reception desk and the two matronly women seated behind it. Some days I can meet their eyes, even nod a polite *hello*. Daddy told them I'm a consultant working with him on a new project. I even have a messenger bag with a laptop inside slung over my shoulder as proof.

But Daddy also told me that I was never to walk through those doors with anything on beneath my clothes, and today, that means the white linen shirt he bought me (*leave the top three buttons undone*) tucked into the tight, summer light denim jeans he favors. I'm conscious of the way my breasts sway as I walk, and the fact that my nipples are tight behind the thin material. I imagine the raised eyebrows, pursed lips, and knowing glances the matrons share and move quickly past them, a flush of pink staining my cheeks.

I hear the deep tenor of Daddy's voice through the solid mahogany door as I knock lightly and let myself in. He knows it's me because he told me to come at three, and I would never, ever be late. He's on the phone, finishing his call by the sounds of it. He waves me in and I lock the door behind me.

For a moment, I just drink him in, still as starry-eyed over him as I was the first time we met. He's a fox, my Daddy. A sexy silver fox who outfoxes all the rest. Tall, lean, and refined, he's every inch the business magnate from his Ted Baker top to his Ferragamo soles.

He hangs up the phone and hits me with a smile that makes my breath catch and sets my pulse racing. It's hungry and confident, the smile of a predator who knows his prey is already won. He pushes his chair back from his desk and pats his lap.

"Come say hello," he says, and I do.

I climb into his lap and feather little kisses along his cheek, his jaw, and on the corner of his mouth. He makes a satisfied sound and slides a hand beneath my hair, cupping the back of my neck and angling his mouth over mine. His kiss is as hard as mine is soft. I melt into him, giving everything he asks, loving the feel of his tongue stroking mine.

He breaks the kiss and looks at me, a knowing smile pulling at his mouth as he takes in my tousled hair and parted lips and the haze of arousal already clouding my eyes. He cups my ass with his hands and stands, lifting me as though I weigh nothing and setting me down without ceremony.

"Take your clothes off," he says, crossing the room to the credenza that sits below the bank of windows on the other side.

I dither a little, reminding myself not for the first time that no one can see us through that big wall of glass, or through the frosted panels on either side of Daddy's door. But I'm still conscious of all the unseen people on the other side of these walls, brokering deals and making trades with their designer suits and practiced smiles.

"Was that unclear?"

"No, Daddy." I jump to the task, shivering a little at the coolness of the air against my skin and the heat in Daddy's gaze.

He slips something into his pocket and after a moment's deliberation removes a riding crop from the credenza drawer. He taps the leather end against his open palm as he closes the distance between us, making my nipples harden into tight peaks in anticipation.

"So pretty," he says, tracing the curve of my breast with the crop. Daddy loves playing with my breasts.

He drops back into his chair and lays the crop on his desk. "Come here," he says, making space for me between his legs. This time he traces my curves with his hands. I love Daddy's hands. They're strong like he is, long-fingered and tanned, and equally skilled at delivering pleasure and pain.

He settles his hands at my waist and captures a nipple with his teeth, drawing it deep into the heat of his mouth and making me moan. I thread my fingers through his hair, holding him to me, desire curling through me as he teases me with his tongue. One hand slides down between my thighs, urging them apart, and then he's inside me, his chest rumbling with approval at the wetness he finds.

He works me with his fingers and mouth, thumb stroking my clit, teeth grazing my nipples. It feels so good I close my eyes and let my head roll back. As the sensations wash over me, the beginnings of an orgasm tighten low and deep in my belly.

Then his teeth clamp down and my body goes rigid and it's all I can do not to cry out aloud. His hands are like a vice at my waist, holding me still while his teeth grind my tender flesh.

"Please, please, please . . ." I plead, but I don't ask him to let go; I know better than that. My hands tremble as they stroke his hair, holding him to me when my body is screaming to push him away. He stays locked on for so long a sheen of sweat breaks out on my skin. I'm not sure how long I can hold on and then suddenly, the pressure's gone.

"Ask me to bite the other one," he says against my skin, trailing kisses from one breast to the other.

I don't want to ask.

His hand lands on my ass with a sharp crack.

"*Ask.*"

"Please, Daddy . . ." I whisper, letting the words trail off.

He slaps me again, the sting blooming into heat.

"Please bite the other one," I force myself to say; he bites down fiercely. Fire races through me from every point of contact. It goes on forever, or feels like it does; when he releases me, I sag against him in relief.

"Look how beautiful that looks," he says, tracing the marks he's made. They're like perfect circles around each areola, the imprints of his teeth so deep and red they're almost purple.

He picks up the crop and catches me on the nipple, a swift strike that makes me flinch. He does it again and my hands rise instinctively. It's too soon, and the sting hurts like the dickens. He raises an eyebrow at the hands covering my breasts, but I'm slow to lower them, which earns me another swat on the ass.

"Behind your back," he says.

I do as I'm told, clasping my hands together so I'm not tempted to move. He brings the crop up to my mouth, nudging my lips apart with the tip. I open up and he runs the flat of the leather against my tongue.

"That's it," he says. "Nice and wet."

Then he begins.

He's good at keeping me off guard, switching from one breast to the other, one stroke on the tender side of my breast, the next directly on my nipple. I don't need to see the color of my skin, because I can feel the flush rising in my chest, and it's getting harder and harder to stay still. There's no sound except my erratic breathing and the crop hitting my skin, which seems absurdly loud to my ears.

The next stroke hits the very tip of my nipple. I bite off a yelp and twist my body to the side. He waits until I turn back and does the same thing again; this time I can't stop my hands from rising and I back a step away.

He lays the crop down on his desk and rises, his 6'2" frame dwarfing my 5'4". He cups my chin in his hand and raises my face to his.

"I think you're forgetting who's in charge of this game."

"I'm sorry, Daddy," I say.

"You want to be the boss?" His smile makes me shiver. "Why don't you sit in the boss's chair."

"No, Daddy, I— "

"Sit." There's an edge to his voice I dare not ignore.

I sit in his chair, conscious of my nakedness, of the wetness between my thighs meeting the supple leather beneath me.

He's back across the room, rummaging through another drawer in his credenza.

"A-ha!" He raises a triumphant fistful of multi-hued computer cables and electrical cords and marches back over to me, dropping them on the desk. He rests his hands on top of my wrists on the armrests of his chair, lowering himself until we're eye to eye.

"You're not in the right headspace right now, so I'm going to help you out."

Blue cable around my left wrist.

Purple around my right.

I tug at them to test their strength, but the bonds are secure; Daddy's good at this sort of thing. He's right about where I'm at too, and the funny thing is? Once I know I can't move, I feel such relief. When he binds me like this it's like his arms are around me and he's holding me tight, telling me to let go and sink into the sensation.

He's got two more cords to fasten, but these are more for aesthetics than restraint. With more time and in another place, he'd make a pretty rope harness for my breasts and chest, but for now a thin black cable crosses the swell of my breasts, and a second crosses just on the underside. He pulls them tight, forcing the cables nearer to one another, compressing my breasts in between.

I moan a little, feeling the blood pool there; feeling my pulse in every indent of the bite marks that ring my areola; feeling my nipples harden to the point of pain.

"Better?" he asks.

I nod mutely, already sinking under his spell.

He unfastens the buttons on the cuffs of his shirt, then removes his tie and starts on the buttons at his neck, working his way down. The pale blue shirt makes his hazel eyes a brilliant blue. Each button he opens reveals more of the tanned, well-muscled chest beneath. I want my mouth on him more than anything, and his smile says he knows—but this is part of it too. Having him this close but not being able to touch him is a pain all its own. I shift on my seat as arousal thrums through me.

He picks up the crop. This time, there's no turning away. No shielding myself, no sidestepping.

"Count it off," he says.

One . . . two . . . three . . .

I feel every stroke. Every sting. Every bite.

. . . eight . . . . nine . . . ten . . .

I tug at my hands, trying in vain to lift them, to cover my aching breasts, but I can't. There's muffled laughter coming from the boardroom next door and I wonder if they hear us. I wonder if they know.

. . . nineteen? Or was that twenty?

I'm losing track. They're bleeding together, one into another, as the fire in my breasts spreads throughout my body, warming me. Heating me. Carrying me to a place where there is only this moment. This feeling.

His open hand hits my breast with a powerful blow. All the breath leaves my body and for a moment it's hard to breathe. Another on my other breast and now all of my attention is focused on him.

"There you are." Daddy's smile is knowing. "How do you feel?"

I feel like my smile is ten feet wide. Words seem far away, but I manage a murmured, "Good."

"That's my girl."

Daddy unties my wrists, but leaves the binding around my breasts. When he removes a set of clover clamps from his pocket, I let out a strangled moan, though I'm not even sure if it's in protest or anticipation. He attaches them to my nipples, the connective chain dangling between them. I bite my lip at the sweet downward tug on my nipples, at the burn of the clamps squeezing them tight.

He helps me from the chair, then bends to kiss me. It's slow and deep and I slide my hands into his open shirt, pressing my tortured breasts against his chest, loving the feel of his skin against mine.

He lifts my chin so I meet his eyes. Such beautiful eyes. I could look into them forever.

"I have some emails to return, so I want you under my desk taking care of me, okay?"

"Mmmhmm."

I crawl into the space beneath his desk, feeling the darkness, the press of solid wood all around me. There's hardly room to lift my head, but when Daddy undoes his belt and drops his pants, sliding his big leather chair up snug to the desk, I don't think of that at all. I don't think of anything except taking him into my mouth, loving him with my hands and my tongue, showing him what a good girl I am for him.

He's hard already, and I love knowing that the way we play arouses him as much as it does me, but I want him even harder. I take his shaft in my hand, run my tongue from the base of his balls to the head of his cock, dip my tongue into his slit and taste the pre-come that's already there. For a while, I work him with my hand and mouth together, reveling in the sounds of pleasure he can't stop himself from making.

But it's not enough. I want to be closer. I want him deeper.

I move in so close that the soft hair on his thighs brushes my cheeks. I take him in slowly, inching down his cock until I can feel him pressing into my throat. I breathe in the heady mix of his clean, masculine scent and our combined desire, wanting him so badly I ache. I ease back until I'm holding just his head between my lips, then take him in again. Fully. Deeply. Over and over, until I'm falling into a rhythm as old as Eve and there is nothing in the world but the two of us and this space.

Then suddenly he's gone and I want to cry out at his loss, but then he's lifting me up, bringing me back into the light, settling me on his lap and pressing kisses to my forehead, my eyelids, anywhere he can reach.

"I need to be inside you," he breathes against my mouth.

"Yes." It's less a word and more a plea. Then before I know

it, the thick head of his cock is at my entrance, pushing into me until we're bound together as deeply as two people can be.

I rock against him instinctively—it's not even conscious thought. I have to move. I have to feel him.

"That's it babe. Come for your Daddy." His hands are on my hips, guiding me, urging me on, the chain from the clamps swaying between our chests, mesmerizing us both.

"You look so fucking beautiful."

And I feel it.

Through the heat and the pain and the arousal, I see how I look in his eyes and it ignites me. My body clenches around him as my orgasm burns through me. He's right there with me, caught in the same fire, and when he closes his eyes and empties himself into me, I think he's beautiful too.

UNICORN

Jacqueline Brocker

She was leaving and she wasn't coming back. That was what Cara told herself as she swept up her bag and short cape and marched out of the office, away from her boss's closed door, away from the ringing phone, away from the shout of "Cara, you getting that?"

Fuck him, she thought as she hit the cool autumn air outside.

Why it had taken three little words—"the coffee's cold"— from him to make her do it surprised her. After all, this had been the year of slammed palms on her desk, tantrums when she'd been photocopying down the corridor when he'd wanted to speak to her immediately, and snide remarks on her choice of clothing. The coffee being "cold" wasn't the worst of it, but it was the final insult that cut deep enough to spur her to action.

Fuck him, she thought again. She'd go back to her flat and— she winced. The reason she'd hung on to the job was because it was a mere ten-minute walk from her flat and paid to keep her there. She loved it so much. Just how rent would be made now . . .

Cara shook herself. She'd gotten out of a shitty situation. That was a good thing. Now it was time to regroup and think about the next step. She couldn't be afraid. She had to take charge. Not that she was very good at that. Probably why she'd let the bastard walk all over her. But not anymore. From now on, she was the princess who'd stormed out of the castle seeking adventure.

She had a notebook in her handbag, perfect for getting her thoughts out. The fear of overdue rent made going home less attractive, so where. . . . Of course. The park. She'd pass through it anyway to get back to her flat, and it was a lovely afternoon, bright and sunny despite the autumn chill. Cara smiled.

The park had plenty of green open spaces and small fenced-off patches of lush shrubs, autumn gladioli, and ferns. There were a few large oak trees and an avenue of limes at the far end, close to her place. She entered through the low gate and up the path; she noticed a female police officer ambling up the path away from her. Cara was always pleased to see women in roles like that—she'd never have had the guts to do that job herself. But maybe now ... maybe now she could speak to her about it?

The officer took another route. Cara decided that was a silly idea, and stuck with her original plan: to go to the lady and the unicorn fountain and find a space to sit and ponder.

When she reached the green expanse that surrounded the fountain, she was dismayed to learn that the good weather had brought many people out—families with toddlers, couples canoodling, people in suits having late lunches.

Cara gazed longingly at the overcrowded area. There was no way she'd be able to squeeze herself into a gap without invading someone else's space. A shame, because she wanted to be able to sit and look at the fountain.

The white, faux marble carving in the center depicted a woman in a flowing dress sitting tall and noble. Kneeling beside her was a unicorn, whose horn jutted to the sky while it stared adoringly at the woman. A collar graced the unicorn's neck, and the woman held a leash attached to it. Cara had always loved looking at it, and today, she needed inspiration from a woman who had so much control.

She glanced about the space for somewhere she could sit. Her eyes drifted back up to the path she was on, to the fenced-off ferns.

She came to a dead halt when she saw the man.

He was up against the low fence, an eye-catching barrier made of wrought-iron thigh-high rails topped with fleur-de-lis spikes. He was tall and wore his hair spiky short. It looked like he was stretching his arms behind him, palms pressed to the top of the fence. Like he was preparing to do a yoga pose, or was holding one. Cara made that imaginative leap judging the clothes he wore—sky-blue yoga gear. A T-shirt that clung to his well-defined biceps and across his broad chest, and drawstring yoga pants that hung loose at his ankles, lapping at his bare feet. Around his neck was a thick silver chain that hung just below his collarbone.

A breeze blew. He shivered, but kept the position. The hairs on his arms raised and he made no attempt to smooth them down. His clothes must have been thin too. The breeze swelled, and Cara drew her cape closer. He closed his eyes, shivering.

What the fuck is going on? she thought.

A large fern was just to the side of him, partly concealing his hands from her view. She took a few steps closer. That's when she saw the handcuffs.

They were clamped on just below the upper bar of the fence. He could have slid down to sit or squat on the path, but he'd have trouble getting up again. His arms flexed the couple of times he seemed to be testing the hold. The cuffs looked real enough; he wasn't getting out of them soon.

Cara's eyes kept going back to the cuffs and his taut arms, then to his face, which was straining to conceal his stress. Cara did her level best to ignore the little flutter in her chest and what that meant. He was in trouble. What kind of person was she to get . . . *turned on by it?*

She retrained her thoughts on the actual situation. This was a prank, for sure. A stag do. Some college kids mucking around, though he looked a bit old to be a student. She couldn't have freed him, but maybe she could help. That desk at work—her old work!—had felt like it had chains on it, and she'd had little comfort this past year. At least she could offer it to someone else.

She came up right next to him.

"Are you okay?"

He started at her words, stumbled, and had trouble righting himself. The chain clinked. He stared at her, like he couldn't believe someone would speak to him. Heat coursed through Cara. He had gray eyes, like tumbled river stones, and a luscious lower lip. She had to crane her neck a touch to look at his face. She wondered what sort of person would have been able to get him like this; he looked like he could fight back and win, if he wanted to.

"I'm . . . yeah. I'm fine."

"Really? I mean, do you want me to call someone? Fire department for bolt cutters—"

"No! I mean, please don't do that." The panic was real, and it took Cara aback.

"All right, I won't. But . . . what happened?"

"That's none of your business."

She heard an undertone of her ex-boss's voice. And since he was now her ex-boss, Cara wasn't going to put up with it. Her hands went to her hips and she used her best "you'd better damn apologize, mate" voice.

"Hey, you're in trouble and I'm trying to help!" she snapped. "A bit of bloody gratitude would be appreciated."

The look that flashed across his face wasn't what she'd expected. His pupils dilated and his breathing became sharp and shallow. He swallowed, and seemed to take a few moments to compose himself. It was an odd reaction, Cara thought, to being told off.

"Sorry . . ." he whispered. He swallowed again, and straightened up. "Look, it's not what you think. Really, I'm all right, and if you stay, I'll get into more trouble."

Cara relaxed her stance, sympathetic once more. "In trouble from who?"

His gaze went across the open grass and then he hastily looked away. "I can't say . . ."

Cara looked across the grass, toward the fountain. There wasn't anyone looking at him as far as she could see. No set of students sniggering, that was sure. Everyone else was occupied with their picnics, their children, their friends, and there was one Goth-looking young woman sitting on the edge of the fountain reading—

Cara took another look at her. She stole a quick glance back at the man. His eyes were back out across the park, and yes, they were definitely on the woman.

Cara didn't like her at all. Raven-black hair—dye job, had to be!—spilling all around her like a pool of ink, the kind of clear porcelain skin people gushed about that probably had no freckles to speak of, and bright red lips—they weren't natural either—that were right then biting into a green apple. Like she was some innocent fucking Snow White. She was definitely not innocent; Cara had known enough women who could feign it to spot it in seconds. To cover her shoulders, she wore a red velvet cape draped down her back and down her front. There was a gap where the material didn't quite meet on her chest, and beneath . . .

Her breasts were completely bare.

Cara took a step back, bumping against the fence. She'd not have seen it if she wasn't looking for it, but the woman was naked from the waist up under the cape. The sides of her tits were briefly exposed for all when she shifted her arms to put the apple down, but then the material magically settled back, and it looked far more like she had a top on that just happened to allow for revealing cleavage.

And the woman wasn't even looking at the man. She was engrossed in her book, and with whatever her hand was doing . . . straying past her breast and "accidentally" brushing a nipple. It looked so absentminded, but it had to be deliberate. Him at the fence wouldn't be looking so fascinated if not.

The man pressed his legs together. They were trembling. Cara's gaze dropped to his crotch and her hand flew to her mouth. There it was. The stirrings of a hard-on, and he was straining to hide it. Did anyone else notice? Was that woman even aware? She must have known, but didn't care to acknowledge it. . .

Cara had to clench her fists to keep herself controlled. She stared at Snow White and went red with jealousy. Not just because she had this really hot guy getting hard for her, but because . . . Cara didn't want to think it, but because he'd *let* her cuff him to the fence. He probably *let* her do all sorts of things to him, and he *liked* to obey her. That was what was going on, and dammit. . . . Damn them for having it.

But she couldn't walk away now. Not after he'd looked at her like that. Was he into the fact that she'd gotten bossy? That intrigued her too much. Besides, she had to tell him about the woman officer. That's why she was staying. Really.

She stood right in front of him, not caring if she were blocking his view of Snow White. He stared at her, frowning.

"What are you—"

"Look, I've seen her, I know what's going on. So you can look at her if you like, but I'm going to stand here so no one else sees that you're . . . you're . . ."

She couldn't say "turned on" or " getting hard" out loud in public. He smirked, realizing her dilemma, and said, "You noticed. You like looking at my cock?"

His insolence startled Cara, and an impulse to put him in his place came over her.

"Don't talk back."

His smirk vanished and he shivered. "I'm sorry. I was trying to embarrass you so you'd leave. Please . . . if you stay, she'll be so angry."

Piss off Snow White? With pleasure. Cara leaned in a lot closer, and whispered with as much heat as she could, "Oh, then what? She'll have to bend you over her knee and spank you? And you'll just *hate* that, won't you? That's not going to turn you on *at all*, is it?"

He bit his lip, and bent his head, trying to hide his blush.

"Thought so," she murmured. She pulled away. "Besides, I think you'll want me to stay like this. There is a female cop in the park. You want to get arrested?"

He blinked, and muttered "shit" under his breath. He said it a couple more times.

"I can go and explain to her—"

"No! If you do that—"

"*She'll* be really angry?" Cara rolled her eyes. "Come on, that's hardly fair."

"I know, but . . ." He sighed, shook his head. "You wouldn't understand."

Cara wanted to say "try me." Really thought about asking why this was all going on, to see if she was kind of like Snow White—damn her—but right now she felt too scared to ever try and be her. Like she'd been scared of her boss for a whole year before she'd walked out this afternoon, claiming her dignity again.

"Fine. Maybe I won't. But we've got to do something."

"Like you said, just stay there. Wait until she's come and gone, and then go. That okay?"

Cara shrugged, because this was a perfectly normal conversation to be having. "Yeah, that works."

They said nothing for some long moments. Cara wasn't sure what to say, then figured there was one bit of information they could share.

"I'm Cara. What's your name?"

"Michael."

Cara supposed she could have asked Snow White's name, but decided she didn't really care, and quite liked thinking of her as something out of a story. A little less real.

Michael started to say something when Cara shushed him. She'd spotted the officer coming across the grass.

She was strolling with a smile. She looked ready to tip her hat to gentlemen and wink at children. Cara couldn't help staring at her with fear.

The officer glanced at them, then kept looking, and frowned, puzzled. Cara looked away quickly.

"You saw?" she said to Michael.

"Yeah. It probably looks a little odd," he said. "You standing there in front of me with your hands in your pockets."

Cara took them out, but wasn't sure what to do with them now. She was picturing the officer coming up to them, and tried to think what kind of explanation might be acceptable.

"I think you need to come a bit closer . . . " Michael whispered.

"I'm doing what I can," she muttered back.

"Maybe if you put your arms around me . . ."

His blush suggested that he was well aware this would mean she'd be pressed right against his hard-on, and that he didn't really want to ask, but didn't think there was much of a choice.

"If you're sure—"

"Yes." The word was a sharp breath out.

Cara tilted forward, and found herself almost hanging off his neck, pressing against him for support. The pose made her think of rom-com film posters—the woman flinging herself at the man, arms swept around his neck as he caught her. Only this one couldn't catch her, so she was forced to lean up against him a little more than she would have. Her arms brushed the cold links of the chain, and she wondered if it was heavy on his neck. He stifled a sound, something that sounded like a plea and also arousal. As if he couldn't bear her eyes on him yet relished it all the same.

Cara's chest swelled with heat. This close, she could properly discern the color of his eyes—yes, they were gray but with a hint of iridescent blue, and how his lips were red and flushed and he, unlike Snow White on the fountain's edge, didn't need anything to enhance them. He looked tough with the spiky cut, the strong features, and with her arms laid across his chest and around his neck, she could sense just how strong he was. But now she could also see more than a hint of vulnerability, and just like that, she knew why Snow White wanted him like this. So everyone could see all of him, not just the big strong man he appeared to be.

"Will your . . . will *she* mind?"

"Probably. Definitely. This was meant to be a punishment for forgetting to buy flowers for her this morning."

Cara was stunned. "That's just . . . that's so damn petty."

He shrugged, lifting her hands a little on his broad shoulders. "That's how it works."

"You said so before. But . . . why do you put up with it?"

He gazed back at Snow White over Cara's shoulder. "She's beautiful."

Cara bit down at the back of her mouth, wishing the words were for her.

"Well," she said, aiming for flippant but sounding petulant, "you like her, that's what matters."

The corners of Michael's lips lifted a little, and she thought he was going to tease her for her jealousy. She thought about pulling away, telling him to sod off and deal with the officer alone so she could go back to her flat after all and come up with some kind of plan for a better job, when he said, "I like you too. I . . . liked the way you spoke to me."

Their eyes locked. His cock was now right against her stomach. The thin material of his yoga pants couldn't hide how hard and large he was, and her own skirt was far more flimsy than she'd recalled. She found her thighs wanting to part, and had to force herself to be aware of her body so it didn't do anything stupid of its own accord. That made her hyper-aware of how her nipples were hardening against her bra, how she was tingling right to the soles of her feet. This close, if she leaned up just right, she could have kissed those lips, and he couldn't have stopped her.

But she couldn't do that, not without asking. She met his eyes again, about to speak, but no words came. The hint of blue was on fire, and Michael breathed in. Almost imperceptibly, he nodded. Like he'd read her mind. Cara's lips parted, she pressed the balls of her feet down as hard as she could to make herself as tall as she could—

"Behave, you two."

Cara turned sharply to see the police officer stroll past, hands behind her back, winking at the pair of them, before moving out across the grass. Cara craned her neck around to watch the officer disappear behind the fountain. Beyond that was another exit. She was gone.

The moment had snapped. Cara stumbled back off Michael, and he exhaled.

"I think we got away with it," he said.

"You. You got away with it, because I was here. You owe me!"

"Yeah, I guess I do." His eyes dropped to his groin, and back to her. "You want to help me out?"

It took Cara a good long minute before she was able to hiss, "Here! Are you crazy?"

"No—I feel like I'm about to burst."

The swelling had grown; he was fully hard and the strain against the cloth couldn't be hidden without her.

"It's not like I can 'help you out.' You're with her."

"We're not exclusive."

"*Oh, I see!*"

He gave her a pitying look. "Don't knock it 'til you've tried it. And you don't have to do anything you don't want to. You just got me out of trouble, and I'm grateful." He smirked. "And you seem like you want to 'help.'"

They were, she realized, the words of a man used to being cuffed and bound. He may have given up his power in one way, but he could still taunt. Irritation pricked at her cheeks, but then she thought of the serene lady with the unicorn on a leash.

Be that lady, she told herself, a plan forming.

Cara leaned up to his ear. "Beg me."

Michael twitched. His cock hardened more. Cara smirked, and waited.

"Please . . . touch me."

His plea was so sweet and poignant. So damn sexy that she considered crawling onto his lap and dry humping him that second.

She held herself in check. *Focus on the plan.*

Cara let her lip curl cruelly. A puppy-dog eagerness came over Michael, but Cara instead reached up and grabbed the chain and dragged him to her. The thick, heavy links felt good to grasp. He yelped and scrambled as she bent him forward so she could whisper right in his ear.

"I *could* touch you right now. I could undo that drawstring and rub it up and down your cock, maybe wrap it right around and tug it. I could do *anything* I liked to you and you wouldn't be able to stop me. Isn't that right?"

"Yes . . . fuck yes . . ."

The desperation in his voice drove her on. "But isn't that a very naughty thing to ask me to touch you in public? Isn't that a very bad thing? Especially since I was so nice and stopped you from getting arrested?"

"It is, it is! I'm so sorry, I'm just so turned on right now and . . . you're really pretty. I couldn't believe it when you spoke to me . . . I'm sorry!"

And damn her if that didn't send jellyfish flashes up her spine and make her neck burn.

Not letting go of the chain, Cara leaned away from Michael. His eyes were wet with sincere apology. She relaxed her grip a little, and he exhaled.

Looking down, her cape was skirting the tops of his thighs, and in fact would have hidden her hands as well as his cock.

Cara ran a thumb across his jaw. "You're sweet when you're not being cheeky." She dropped her hand, hovering just above his crotch. "Ask again."

"Please, Cara. Touch me."

He'd not used her name before, and it was delicious to hear him say it while begging.

Her free hand ducked beneath and found his dick. Michael gasped. His cock was raging with heat and straining hard against the thin material.

She squeezed, slow and intense, moving her hand down to the base and back to the head. His eyelashes fluttered, he tilted his chin up and made a low humming noise, his Adam's apple exposed and bobbing.

"Good then?"

"Yeah, yeah . . . God, I want more, but . . ." his eyes opened, his full lower lip plump as he bit down and met her eyes. "That would be—" He stopped moving.

"Shit. She's coming over. She's seen us."

Not him, but "us." Cara hadn't meant it to be an "us" but now it was.

Cara stepped away from him. Michael straightened up.

The woman approached with a sense of regal grandeur; even holding a pair of men's sandals, she looked elegant. Head high, almost haughty, walking in a straight line. People shifted out of her way. Her eyes were piercing right through both of them, and she wore a smug grin. As she got closer, and the beauty of her features became clearer, Cara knew exactly why Michael was afraid of her, why he was terrified of upsetting her, and why he'd allowed himself to be chained to the fence.

Snow White, Cara thought, was wrong. She was the Wicked Queen, and enjoyed being wicked.

The Queen stopped before them. She first looked at Michael,

who hung his head and said nothing. She then turned to Cara. Probably expected that Cara would back away too. And Cara did shift her feet, and tilt her body away instinctively, but she held her gaze.

That grin didn't leave, but slithered into a gleeful one.

"I can see why he likes you." She held out the key to the cuffs, dangled them just out of Cara's reach. "This was supposed to be his punishment, but I can see that it hasn't worked. So if you want him so much, bitch—" She flung the key into the ferns behind. "Go fetch."

Cara gaped as the Queen winked at a horrified looking Michael, flung his sandals on the ground, and simply walked away, stately and calm and visibly refusing to give a single fuck about what she'd just done.

"Um . . ." Michael said.

"I'll get it, I'll get it!"

Somehow Cara managed to get over the fence without spearing herself on the row of barbed fleur-de-lis. She tried to remember which fern frond shook as the key flashed past it and into the mulch and wood chips.

"Thank you—"

"Shut up!"

When crouching wasn't effective, she ended up on her hands and knees, feeling her way. She wasn't sure how long it took, but eventually she spotted a glint half-buried in the dark soil.

She flung herself back over the fence, grumpy and irritated and now messy from crawling on the mulch and wood chips. Michael smiled sweetly at her, full of gratitude. It didn't dispel her anger, but it softened it. She found the lock, and wrenched the cuffs off him.

Michael rubbed his wrists, exhaled with relief. His hard-on had deflated as well. The cuffs in her hand, Cara wasn't sure what to do with them, so she shoved them and the key in her handbag.

He put his sandals on, and looked up at her with a grin.

"Thank you. Really, thank you."

That did it. Cara went right up to him, anger spilling out. "You better be bloody grateful! I stopped you from being arrested, came this close to getting you off, and then had to spend ten minutes scrambling to find the bloody key to let you out because you and mistress are playing games!"

"And you didn't have to do any of it. But you did. So thank you."

Cara groaned, and threw her hands up. "Well, you're out now. I'm going. I've got to change my clothes."

"I could make it up to you."

His voice was gentle, deep, and full of promise. Cara fidgeted. Yes, that would be good . . . but what to say?

"You did say I owe you . . . and as I said—"

Cara said, "You say you're not exclusive, but you'll get into trouble if I ask you back to my place."

"Lots of trouble." He winked at her.

Cara groaned. "I'm still second fiddle to her."

"We've only just met; of course you are. You also don't know what she knows." Michael grinned. "I think you could learn. Be even better than her."

She was sure he'd just said that to convince her of his plan. The sod, but it worked.

Cara beckoned and started walking away. Michael followed, keeping in step but a little behind as if they were walking separately rather than as a unit.

He followed her to her apartment a few streets away. She paused at the front door. Now was the time to choose. She glanced up at him over her shoulder. There was an eagerness to him that hadn't been there in the park, the fear and arousal replaced with a keen pleasure.

Sexy as fuck.

She let him in, led him upstairs to her flat. Once in the living room, she said, "You like it when women give you orders, don't you?"

"Um . . . um . . ."

Cara grabbed his jaw, forcing him to look at her. "Yes or no?"

His hard-on reappeared as his eyes widened. "Fuck . . . yes . . ."

"Then take out the drawstring and hand it to me."

She let go of him, and he looked down to obey her, tugging the drawstring out from the waistband. It came free, and he held it out to her.

Taking it from him, she threaded it around her fingers for a minute or so. He was looking, waiting, his cock sitting back up to attention. Cara grabbed either end and snapped the taut string between her hands.

"Take your shirt off."

He did it slowly, purposely, and let the shirt tumble to the floor. He stood, proud of his taut and sculpted body. The chain caught the light spilling in through the window, glinting like treasure. Cara let her eyes rake over him but didn't touch him. Her hands itched to do so, but she could wait a little longer.

"Turn around."

He did. She took his wrists, freshly freed, and crossed them, using the drawstring to bind them together. He sighed as she tightened and tied the knot.

She made him face her again. "You like this, don't you? Being handcuffed, tied up?"

A vigorous nod.

"And you like doing as you're told?"

"Sometimes I like it. Sometimes I don't. But I do it anyway, for my mis—"

Cara pulled him closer to her lips, as she stood on her toes, and hissed in his ear, "I'm not your mistress. I'm your fucking *queen*, and you will kneel in front of me right now."

Yes, *she* was his queen. Even if just for a little while.

Michael didn't wait. He dropped to his knees, eyes up at her, waiting for her next command. Cara tore off her dirty clothes, flinging the cape aside, whipped away her skirt and pulled her knickers down. She had known she was wet, but just how much wasn't clear until her cunt was exposed to the cool air. Michael licked his lips.

"What do you wish, my queen?"

Cara cupped the back of his head, and guided him toward her labia. "Lick me until I come."

Michael smiled and kissed her cunt. As his tongue and lovely lips teased and delighted her, Cara decided that while she no longer had a job, and didn't know what was happening next, *taking charge* was the best bloody thing she'd done in a long time.

BALLAD OF DESIRE
AND SACCHARINE MELODIES

Sonja E. DeWitt

Talia's fingertips danced across the black and ivory keys, the notes growing quieter as she reached the final rolled chord. A silence washed over the stage hall and she brushed her carmine tresses back over her shoulders before turning to Dimitri, who sat in the front row of an empty audience.

His legs were crossed as he leaned against the arm of the auditorium chair with his cheek pressed against the palm of his hand. His eyes were closed, and he let Talia suffer in the quiet a moment longer before finally looking up at her. He clapped as he rose from his seat. *"Magnifique, ma chèrie."* Dimitri trotted up the steps to meet her on the stage. "Your technique is much improved."

Talia could tell he had more to say when he looked away from her. "But?"

"But you lack charisma." Dimitri sat beside her on the piano bench. "You're stiff . . . plain to watch. I must close my eyes to imagine the piece as it should be played. Unfortunate, no?"

"What does it matter? You're supposed to focus on the music, isn't that the point?" Talia flipped the score back to the first page.

Dimitri caught her wrist and forced her attention back to him. He stared intensely into Talia's green eyes as he spoke. "No, Talia, this is about you." He gently touched her cheek with the backs of his fingertips. There was a smokiness to his soft voice that she found captivating. Dimitri's melody was one she could listen to forever. "The audience seeks a show. If I wanted to listen to Chopin played to perfection and nothing else, then I would listen to Chopin."

Dimitri turned and held his hand out to the empty seats. "They want more than just technical excellence; they want to be moved, and it is your job to invoke that emotion." He brought his attention back to her. "You should want for them to see you . . . to enjoy all of you, not just a piece of music. It would be a shame for them to close their eyes, no?" His dark blue gaze left hers and he focused on her mouth as he brushed his thumb along her bottom lip. "Considering your beauty." He glanced up at her and she looked away, her face flushed. "I will not stand for such tragedy, ma petite minette."

"If I focus on showmanship then I'll get distracted and mess up the piece." She glanced at Dimitri from the corner of her eye, still too embarrassed to face him fully. It didn't matter how long she'd known him or how many times his lips had met hers, she still found herself shy in his presence. Dimtri intimidated her . . . as a pianist, a teacher, and lover, but she welcomed every moment.

"Impossible *n'est pas français*." Dimitri stood and pulled his brunette, shoulder-length hair up into a quick ponytail. "You could play this piece blindfolded." He loosened his cerulean tie that mirrored the blue depths of his eyes. "And if you can do that, then you should have no problem performing properly." He stood behind her and draped his tie over her eyes, blindfolding her. He whispered in her ear, the warmth of his breath kissing her skin as he finished tying off the silk, blackening her vision. "Play it again . . . just as before." He slid his hands down her shoulders and guided her hands to the first set of chords, his chest pressing against her back. "I trust there will be no mistakes."

Talia inhaled and let her hands rest in place as she visualized the keys in her head. She knew every note, but she always kept the sheet music in front of her, second-guessing herself. Dimitri knew that. He was testing her, forcing her to see her gift as he did, and he wouldn't let her fail. She'd get it right, perfect, like every time before, or he'd force her to play it again until she did. She wouldn't disappoint him. She couldn't.

She pressed her fingers to the ivories and let the music take hold. Every note rang true and though she couldn't see him, she was certain Dimitri was watching her, smiling. He was right; her technique was perfect. After months of preparing for that night's recital, Talia had mastered Chopin's *Fantaisie-Impromptu*. When the final note dissipated into the quiet, she pulled the tie covering her eyes down to her neck and turned to face Dimitri, who stood beside the piano.

He smiled. "See? Perfection."

Talia wanted to return his smile, but she couldn't be satisfied until she was confident in all aspects of her performance, and according to Dimitri, she lacked personality. "Yes, I suppose you were right, but what good is my playing if I bore everyone?"

"The solution to that is simple." Dimitri leaned toward her and placed his hands against the bench on either side of her, forcing her to lean back. "Show them passion, ma chèrie . . . that same look of fantasy you give me." His lips brushed against hers, stealing her breath before he turned his attention to her neck. He drew at the flesh above her collarbone and slid his hand up her shirt, beneath her bra, so he could caress her breast. He waited for a sigh to escape her before pulling back. He looked down at her flushed face with a grin. "Oui, just like that." He cupped her cheek. "Absolutely captivating."

Talia diverted her glance and placed her hands on his chest. She tried to focus on her breathing and ignore the tension mounting in her core with Dimitri's knee pressed between her legs. "I couldn't . . . it's too embarrassing. Besides, it's not that kind of song."

"Oh, it is, I assure you." He rose and took her hands in his, pulling her up with him. He held her against him. "Allow me to show you." Dimitri traced the skin of her inner thigh with his fingertips until he found her center.

Talia pushed away, startled. "Dimitri, we can't." She looked around the stage hall. She knew she was blushing by the heat in her cheeks. "Not here."

"I am afraid this lesson cannot wait, Talia." A smirk crept across his lips as he approached her, backing her up against the piano. "The space is ours for now, but should someone interrupt . . . Well, I do enjoy an audience." He wrapped his arm around her waist and brought her hips against him as he took her mouth with his.

Talia surrendered. She draped her arms around the back of his neck and parted her lips so his tongue could meet hers. She wanted him and Dimitri knew it. She was his from the moment he'd first kissed her three years ago and with every new taste she fell harder, deeper, until she'd given him complete control.

Dimitri parted from her, allowing her to catch her breath. "You will grow wet each time you hear *Fantaisie-Impromptu* once I am done with you." He ran his fingers through her hair until they were just below the base of her skull. He gripped a handful of her locks and pulled her head back, turning her back to him. He shoved her against the piano and bent her before him, then hiked up her skirt to see the red lace underneath. He was powerless against her, weak. To Talia, he was in control, but in truth, she consumed him. Dimitri ached for her and it was all he could do to avoid coming undone. He needed her, but first he wanted her to mirror his trembling passion. He grabbed her hips and pulled her ass against his erection, letting her anticipation build. He pressed further, the weight of his chest against her back as he cupped her breasts. He thrust against her once, teasing the penetration he knew she longed for. He could see her ache in the moisture gathering between her legs. He could feel it in the way she arched against him, and he could hear it in her voice as she pleaded for more. He understood her desire because his was the same, and he wouldn't stop until he'd played every chord. Her ecstasy was his aria. He kissed just below the back of her ear and whispered, "Wait here," before pulling away, slowly, inch by inch.

Talia nodded and waited for Dimitri to disappear behind the curtains before she straightened and adjusted her skirt. Though he was only gone a few moments, her need made it seem painfully deliberate. She squirmed to try and quell her eagerness, but once Dimitri lit her fire there was no escape, not until he filled her with his own lust.

When Dimitri returned, he was holding a small black carrying case. He beckoned her over to the bench where he sat with his back to the grand piano. He unzipped the case and opened it across his lap. Inside was a tuning kit with a tuning hammer, wrench, awl, and tone tuning fork, but it was a red temperament strip that he removed before sliding the kit across the stage. He placed the temperament strip beside him and crossed his legs. "Strip."

Talia gave a sheepish nod as she stepped out of her heels. She knew the difference between Dimitri asking something of her and commanding her to do it, and with sex, Dimitri never asked for anything. It was always an order and Talia submitted to his want willingly, always satisfied in the end—always in ways she'd never been before. She unbuttoned her blouse, one black button at a time. She focused on her hands, glancing at Dimitri from time to time. His gaze was transfixed as he rolled up the sleeves of his dress shirt, taking her in. She let her shirt slide from her shoulders onto the floor. She did the same with her bra before moving to her skirt, letting it fall to her ankles before stepping out of it. Dimitri stopped her before she could remove the last bit of lace.

"No, leave them on." He curled his index finger in toward himself, calling her to him. He stood to meet her, the red felt temperament strip curled in his hand. He placed one end of the strip on the inside of the piano, along the far edge, before closing the lid, locking it in place. He turned back to Talia and tapped his finger against the smooth finish. "Up here, mon amour. On your back, with your hands above your head."

She was hesitant, realizing again that they weren't in private . . . that any moment someone else could walk in, find her lying naked on the symphony's grand piano. She found it both exciting and embarrassing, but she couldn't deny him. The longer she took to follow through, the longer he'd make her wait to feel him. She stood on the bench and crawled over the keys onto the cool surface of the lid. She lay back as Dimitri instructed and he grabbed her wrists, placing them close together before binding them tightly with the felt strip anchored beneath the lid.

He walked around the side and helped Talia raise her head so he could reapply his silk tie to impede her vision. "I want every note pressed into you, so you may relive the sensation each time you play." He removed the wearable, pulse-vibrating metronome he kept like a watch on his wrist and parted Talia's legs. He slipped the band beneath the front lace of her thong and adjusted it so the metronome nestled tightly against her clit, causing her to squirm. He forced her thighs together and removed his belt to keep them that way so her movements wouldn't undo his work once he started.

Talia's heart raced as the ache between her legs washed over her body. She didn't know what Dimitri had placed against her, but she twisted against her restraints, wanting more—desperately. She longed for release, but Dimitri viewed pleasure as the perfect crescendo: slow, gradual, until the melody overpowered all else. She couldn't take it. Her want was torture. "Dimitri, please, it's too much."

Dimitri programmed the metronome through the app on his phone to set the pulse vibration to the song's time. "Sweet, Talia, petit a petit, l'oiseau fait son ni. What have I told you about practicing patience?" He placed the phone next to the sheet music in front of him and took one last look at Talia as she suffered the anticipation. "We have only just begun, so you will need to plead harder than that." He pressed his phone to activate the metronome as he struck the first chord.

Talia felt the chord move through her, from the vibration of sound against her back to the metronome pulsating between her legs, keeping time with Dimitri. A moan escaped her as she writhed against the melody. She didn't have to see Dimitri to know that his focus was on the piece. She'd seen him play enough times to know how easily he succumbed to the music, how passionate he was with every note, in every movement. Dimitri *was* music, and that only made her want him more. The melody was a piece of her too now, and she was beginning to see things as he did. The piece was more than just sixteenth notes against triplets; it was a tale, one of longing, desire the initial kindling of a flame before it settled into a season of warmth, love, and an everlasting, burning, passion.

Talia neared her breaking point as the piece crept back into presto. She cried out to Dimitri between heated breaths. "I can't take much more." But his focus remained on the music, until he gently hit the last Picardy third, holding the chord until Talia climaxed. Her back arched slightly and her legs shook as she felt every note thrust into her. The mounting pressure in her core released into a pulsing ecstasy . . . each wave a new chord, a new progression of pleasure. It was harmony.

Dimitri paused the metronome and released his hold on the last C♯ as Talia's sighs softened into hastened breaths. He stood and traced his fingertips along her quivering thigh. He undid the belt holding her legs together and slowly removed the metronome, which was wet with her excitement. Dimitri smiled and pocketed the wristband. "Is it safe to say you see my side now?" He lifted the tie covering her eyes and she looked up at him, still feeling the ecstasy of her bondage. He stroked her cheek. "There it is; that look is intoxicating." He removed the felt binding her hands and helped her sit up and slip off the piano lid.

Her legs were weak, and she fell against his chest as her feet touched the ground. "I think I get it now."

"Oui, I knew you would. You have always been an exceptional student." Dimitri placed his thumb beneath her chin and lifted her gaze to his. "However, we are not done here." Dimitri grinned. "Put on your heels . . . quickly."

"Of course." Talia stumbled forward slightly as she regained the strength in her legs. She still longed for Dimitri and until it was with him, no orgasm would be enough. So she slipped on her heels and hurried over to him.

He pushed the bench aside and welcomed her next to the

keys. He stepped behind her and faced her toward the piano as he had before, only this time Talia was forced to hold onto the piano top and her breasts brushed against the cool keys, causing her to gasp. The chill ran through her, heightening her need for Dimitri's warmth.

Dimitri slipped the last piece of red lace down her legs, revealing her heat. He placed his palm on the inside of her thigh as he crouched below her. "Spread your legs, ma chèrie." He waited for her to do so before straightening slightly. He ran his tongue along her opening before tasting her fully. She shuddered as he dipped his tongue inside her, causing her breasts to fall against the keyboard, creating their own chord. His own need began to be too much. He wanted to be inside her, sending her over the edge again and again until his lust was satisfied . . . and with her, it was never enough. He always wanted more, needed more . . . from her and only her. He was addicted the moment he first kissed her and there was no going back.

He let his fingers follow his tongue's previous path as he stood. He continued to feel her, letting his fingers sink deeper with every reentry as he unzipped his pants. He shifted his hand to the small of her back, forcing her to lift her hips.

Talia sighed and her hand slipped from the piano top onto the keys. The mixed chord rang out and masked her increasing moans.

He pressed the head of his cock against her clit before tracing it along her center. He was slow to enter her, savoring her warmth before finally pushing into her fully. He wrapped his arm beneath her lower waist to help her maintain her arch so she could take in all of him, touching the deepest parts of her.

Talia gasped as he filled her emptiness. He drove into her with quick, hard thrusts and tangled his hand in her hair, pulling her head back slightly. "Dimitri, don't stop, please."

This time, he'd let her have her wish, but only because his desire was the same. He continued pumping into her until her legs began to quiver. She was close. He removed himself from her and quickly turned her to face him. He hooked his hands behind her knees and lifted her up onto him. He leaned her back against the piano, his hand separating her back from the hard edge above the ivories, and propped his foot up on the piano bench for the leverage he needed to thrust into her the way they both desired.

Talia threw her head back and she gripped Dimitri's shoulders tightly as she came a second time. The throes of her pleasure were rhythmic, a pulsing between her legs to her toes and up through her body. It was a gradual melody, growing until it was overpowering: Dimitri's perfect crescendo. The warmth, electric and euphoric, consumed her.

Dimitri continued his stride, not letting her pleasure cease until they could do so as one. "Kiss me, Talia."

She pressed her lips to his and as their mouths opened to taste one another they lost themselves to each other until neither had anything left.

Talia finished buttoning her blouse as she sat beside Dimitri on the piano bench. She leaned against his shoulder once she was finally dressed and he kissed the top of her head with a smile.

"So, then, mon amour, are you now prepared to truly embody the piece?" He draped his arm over her shoulder and squeezed her gently.

She nodded and kissed his cheek. "I think so."

"*Très bien!*" Dimitri quickly rose to his feet. "Then let us see." He was already hurrying back down the steps into the audience before Talia could object.

She waited for him to be seated before she turned back to the piano. She took a breath and closed her eyes.

Dimitri watched in earnest. As always, she hit every note, only this time he knew she could feel them too. He was absolutely captivated.

ACTIVIST

Sienna Saint-Cyr

The bark dug into my bare flesh as I struggled against the rope. A strange mixture of emotion hit me as I realized the predicament I was in. *I'd signed up for this.* In the pit of my stomach, I sensed I was going to regret agreeing to Nikki Sinclair's protest. "Save the trees," she'd said. "It'll be fun," she'd said. If only her sweet candy scent and plump crimson lips hadn't been so mesmerizing.

Birds chirped and sang a joyous song in the pre-morning hour. They mocked and reassured me at the same time. I couldn't see them, but I heard them as they flittered about in the evergreens above.

Nikki smiled a deviant smile and snapped the rope circling my breasts as though it were a rubber band.

"Ouch!"

Her smile widened. Her fair skin seemed to glow under the artificial light. The red hair curling around her cheeks looked almost surreal.

"Come now, little Jess, surely you've been bound before. You did give that wonderful presentation in class about BDSM and all the ways in which you find bondage lovely." Nikki's words were thick with implication, *and temptation.*

I swallowed. "Yes, but . . ." My words faded. I couldn't respond.

"But what?"

"This is . . . different," I said as her finger circled my nipple.

"How so?"

Is she really asking me that?

"I, well. . . . My play has always taken place in a dungeon. This is . . . *not that.*" My voice was shakier than usual. It cracked. Each time, Nikki looked into my eyes as though searching for meaning.

She pressed into me, her white sweater soft against my skin, pushing through the crisscross of the ropes. I breathed out hard and squirmed. My nipples hardened under her pressure and my squirming ass rubbed against the bark. It stung as it tore at my flesh, but felt so good too. I wanted more. I leaned forward enough to let my lips touch hers, but she pulled back.

"Not yet, eager little Jess." Nikki backed away and cleaned the mess of excess rope she'd left. She stuffed the extras into a large black bag and laid some safety scissors at my feet.

"At least you came prepared," I said.

Nikki laughed. "Of course I did. This may be a protest, but safety first."

"This isn't *just* a protest though, right?" I squirmed again. "I mean, you did ask me out for the purposes of play. We negotiated terms."

Nikki didn't answer aloud. Again, she cast her wickedly seductive smile. She had too much power over me, and I loved it.

Sun peeked through some trees as the light of early morning

lit the area. Nikki extinguished her lamp and tucked it by the bag. The more the sun penetrated the dark woods, the clearer my surroundings became. As I looked around, I saw an area to my right where so many trees had already been cleared. Cut down to stumps. My heart ached at the emptiness. To my left, I saw thousands of trees still standing. Tall evergreens that seemed to touch the skyline.

I looked back at Nikki, completely silent. I understood what she was doing. During our cultural studies class, we'd all shared something that was important to us. For me, it was the kink community. They had embraced me in my queerness when no one in my small town had. For Nikki, it was stopping the clear-cutting happening on the outskirts of town. No one knew why it was happening, but many were trying to stop it. Nikki was giving me something I wanted, and she was getting something she wanted in return—my naked body tied to a tree long enough that the judge could sign a temporary order to stop the clear-cutting. Even a temporary order would be progress.

Nikki circled the tree and pulled on the ropes from behind. I gasped. The rope dug into me, leaving lines of red, tender skin after she'd let go. I felt so exposed as my bare breasts pushed through the rope.

"Now it's time for your legs," she said. "Spread them." Her tone sharpened as she moved to my front side again, and she slapped my inner thigh.

I did as she ordered but my stomach twisted. "Um, Nikki?"

"You have a safeword. You sent it as part of the negotiation. What is it?" She kneeled before me and pulled the strangest spreader bar I'd ever seen from the bag. She kept working as she awaited my answer.

"I don't want to say it or you'll stop," I said.

"So you don't want me to stop, then," she said as her hands

worked the rope tighter around my ankles and through a loop on the spreader bar.

"I mean, I know my safe is s.p.a.r.k.l.e," I spelled it out so there would be no confusion about my use of the word in the moment, "but this isn't about you stopping. I've just . . ." I hesitated.

"Yes?"

"When I said I liked exhibitionism, I meant the consensual kind. How are these workers going to consent?"

Nikki stood and looked directly into my eyes. I pictured her pale blue and my chestnut brown eyes intertwining in that glance, creating some sort of meet cute for our souls. It was sappy and hot. My heart beat faster, skin warming under her steady gaze, and I suddenly felt like a goofy kid with a first crush.

"Naked protests are a thing, little Jess. Anything I do to you," she leaned into me again and reached for my clit, "will be done before the workers arrive."

"Oh." I wanted to say more but as her finger circled my clit, sensation distracted me and all I could do was close my eyes and feel her.

"I can't just have you standing here naked, after all. That won't distract the loggers long enough. They'll just move to another area or cut the ropes. If I want them to stay here and ogle you, I've got to make sure you're so wet and enticing— glowing with the aura of a girl that has just come her brains out—that they can't help themselves. Are you up for that?"

"Yes, please, Miss Nikki," I squeaked.

"Good little Jess," she whispered into my ear as she pinched my clit.

I let out a moan and yelp at the same time, as though my slut body couldn't figure out what it wanted—pain or pleasure. Maybe both.

Nikki kneeled again and finished tying my ankles. I tried to move but she had me tied much tighter to the trunk now. The bark was rough and dug into me, causing the perfect amount of discomfort. Just enough to make me wetter for her.

I pulled against the ropes, eyes closed, and felt a strange kinship with the trees around me. They too were stuck. They could not run away from their fate. Yet they stood tall and proud, unafraid of what was about to happen. I pictured their wisdom pouring into me as I squirmed against the evergreen's skin.

Nikki had risen and stood before me again, but I only knew because I felt her breasts pressing into mine. Her *bare* breasts. I gasped and my hips swayed as much as they could under the restraints. My ass rubbed into the bark and it scraped into my flesh, causing me to moan again.

"My, my," Nikki said. "I'm not even making you come yet and you're already enjoying yourself. Are you a dendrophile, little Jess?"

"I have no idea what that is, Miss Nikki," I replied slowly. The sensations were building like a fire inside me as I rubbed my ass against the bark harder.

Nikki reached for my cunt.

"A dendrophile loves trees. In a . . . *sensual* sort of way." She rubbed my clit harder now and my eyes closed tighter.

"I . . . what? I don't know, I, it just . . . feels—" I couldn't say anymore as Nikki pressed her lips to mine. Her plump, luscious lips.

I pushed forward greedily, reaching for her, but she had all the control. Just far enough away to build my desire, yet close enough to let me taste her.

"Please, Miss Nikki, come closer," I pleaded.

Nikki ignored my plea and lowered her head. Before I could

ask what she was doing, I felt her lips sucking on my left nipple. My cunt rushed with moisture and I cried out as she bit down on my tender flesh. She worked her tongue in circles around my nipple at the same time as she shoved two fingers into my ready cunt. My inner muscles tried to tighten around her, pull her in deeper, and she bit down again on my nipple.

I moaned and gasped. Pulled against the ropes. I wanted her . . . needed her.

But I was helpless.

Once again, I felt a kinship with those trees. Knowing what their fate would be, what was coming for them, but being helpless to do anything about it.

Nikki pulled away from my nipple and ran her tongue down my stomach. Slowly, menacingly, down, down, down, until she reached my clit. She sucked in my wetness as she too was greedy with need. She circled her tongue over my clit as she shoved a third finger inside me, pushing deeper as she did so. I pulled against the ropes, trying to shove my cunt into her face, then pushed back into the bark for another scrape of delicious pain.

She fucked me harder, so deep inside me that I felt myself stretching around her. Making room for whatever she wanted to do to me. The fire grew hotter, moving to other parts of my body until I felt about to burst. Nikki's tongue circled faster—fingers fucking me harder and deeper—then the rush of release hit. I cried out so loudly that the singing birds were silenced with my wail of pain and pleasure. My inner muscles tightened without my control this time and Nikki responded by biting my clit.

I cried out again, this time feeling a flood of wetness leave my orgasming cunt. I couldn't slow the sensation had I wanted to. I craved her too badly. Wanted to wrap myself around every inch of her and suck her into me. All of which added to the rush of pleasure moving through my body.

Nikki pulled her fingers from my moist cunt and stood. She pressed into me again and this time, crushed my lips with hers. I tasted myself on her, her flavors and mine mixing as she thrust her tongue deep into my mouth. This time, I was able to kiss her back with a force of my own. She seemed to like it as I felt her squirming against me.

We kissed long and hard, until I felt Nikki's hand between us. At first I thought she was reaching for me, but I quickly realized she'd slipped her hand into her own panties. I felt her fucking herself, just a thin layer of clothing between our bodies, and she kissed me harder—faster—as her own sensations seemed to build. Nikki moved her hand faster until she pulled back enough to cry out. Her body tensed and jerked against mine, her pleasure causing me to come again.

I didn't want her to stop, but I heard a low growl in the distance. At first, I thought it was an animal, but this noise was different, mechanical almost. As the sound grew louder, Nikki pulled away. Dazed from the experience, I could hardly meet her eyes.

"Why?" I had to swallow and take a deep breath. "Why stop?"

"Because the workers are almost here. Right on time." She tapped her watch with her moist finger.

"Oh, the mechanical animal," I said, then closed my eyes again.

Nikki laughed loudly. "What?"

"I, oh never mind." I laughed myself and forced my eyes open. "Now what?"

"Now, I finish stripping as well and grab some rope so they think I too am tied to a tree. Then we will both be squirming and smelling of sweet sex as they approach. We only need to keep them distracted until Tamara gets here." Nikki began pulling off her remaining clothing as she spoke.

"I don't know Tamara," I said.

"My friend from the courthouse," she said like it were common knowledge. Then she backed into the tree to my left and loosely tossed some rope around herself. She really didn't look tied down but I suspected folks would be too distracted by our projected desire that they wouldn't notice.

Several trucks pulled up, stopping about thirty feet in front of us; folks hopped out and began grabbing tools and chainsaws. They were dressed warmly, covered with layers, and that was the first time I realized that it wasn't that warm out. *Nikki* had kept me warm.

The realization caused my body to respond and my nipples hardened again. Without conscious thought, I pressed back into the bark and let the memory of Nikki's fingers and tongue take hold. One of the workers, a seemingly younger man, turned just in time to see my hips sway slightly.

"Holy fuck!" he shouted, dropping his chainsaw. "Um . . . boss?"

The young man turned back to the truck and an older man looked up. He had a rough unshaven face and looked a bit like Bradley Cooper. I felt a sudden pang of regret as he approached. But it wasn't me he was focused on. The man walked straight to Nikki.

He shook his head, but with his own sort of wicked smile. "I see."

Nikki grinned with meaning in her eyes, as though that were answer enough.

"I see you found a new toy," he said.

Nikki laughed. "Yes, and hopefully I'll bring her to a party sometime soon."

Clearly, they knew one another.

The man shook his head, but with a mixture of annoyance

and a deep, appreciative smile. He walked back to his truck and rallied the workers.

"Looks like we're at a standstill for a while. Kick back and relax for a bit," the man said, then looked straight at me.

"Nikki," I spoke soft enough for only her to hear. "Who is that man?"

"He owns the house I play at. They've got a pretty fancy dungeon. Sometimes I tie him up." She met my eyes again and smiled wider.

"I . . ." I wanted to speak, but suddenly this was all making sense. She knew the boss, knew he wouldn't push past us, knew he'd be a good little boy and wait. He also likely knew what we'd been doing, even if the others hadn't. Her plan was brilliant.

I faced the man again. He was still smiling at me with all kinds of hidden meaning behind his eyes. The noises of the workers mixed with the returning chatter of birds, but I hardly absorbed any of it. My symphony was of a different sort. A realization that Nikki was a badass and I'd be her little activist anytime she asked me to.

DARK DREAMS

Posy Churchgate

Gail gathered Roger's things into a carrier bag, placing them with finality in the car to transport to a charity shop. The sadness she felt that their six-year affair was over mixed with surprise that his presence in her life occupied such a small space.

Being the other woman, or mistress, created a very one-sided life. All her friends were settled by now, with husbands and families, or careers. Gail worked as a real estate agent. She enjoyed the job, but evenings and weekends dragged now without sexy secret liaisons with Roger filling her time. It wasn't easy starting again at her age. Available guys around forty had baggage: failed marriages, workaholic attitudes, or commitment issues.

In her new single state, Gail found comfort in reading. She'd discovered a wealth of erotica on the internet. She dabbled with social media, following authors whose work she'd enjoyed. She had several virtual friends.

One friend was Charmaine Chastity, a blogger who penned

lesbian erotica. Gail enjoyed Charmaine's fiction. They DM-ed each other at the day's end.

Hey Gail, sipping a G&T.
Hi, Charmaine. Nightmare day, need a drink!
Babe!
I ditched Roger's things today ...
Good riddance.
Don't be like that. He was good to me.
He was a fool.
Thanks—that helps.
Time to get back on the horse.
I'm not bothered. Men are too much trouble.
If you ever want to change teams ...
No, darling. I love you, but I'm straight!
Do you follow Her Master's Voice?
No, does she write good stuff?
It's a guy writing BDSM
I haven't tried BDSM stories.
Well, his have a dark appeal <smiling devil emoji>
Thanks, I'll check him out.

Gail settled on the sofa, cozy in pajamas with eighties radio playing music from her youth. She was soon engrossed in a short story by HMV, the author Charmaine had recommended. She was surprised by how sexy she found what he described. Reading the story made her feel quite warm. She browsed his site for another.

She found a storyline featuring a schoolgirl who misbehaved frequently to earn punishment from her stern headmaster. The disclaimer termed it fantasy-based with all participants over eighteen, so Gail's imagination ran with the action. She lost herself in their power dynamic: a charismatic principal and a student who was alternately in awe and bratty.

Her Master's Voice wrote eloquently, stirring such passions that Gail continued to open each new episode of the adventure, aware her panties were becoming slick and her breasts heavy with lust. She'd never felt an interest in spanking and caning before, although she was proud of her own curvy rear. She grazed a hand over one nipple, feeling shocked when an intense bolt of sensation travelled to her core. Slipping fingers between the buttons of her pajama top, she fondled her breast, tweaking it so her pussy spasmed.

Gail devoured the serialized story while stimulating the bud of her nipple. Her breathing sped up. An orgasm built steadily within as she read until she abandoned the plot of punishment by authority figures. Instead, she concentrated on pleasure, pinching and pulling each nipple, she thrust her hips until she came. A powerful nipplegasm suffused her, leaving her throbbing against her gusset.

Returning to her senses Gail blinked with surprise at the intensity of her response. She left a glowing comment to the author. She stated how much she'd enjoyed the story, remarking that he'd converted her to D/s. That night, vivid and arousing dreams filled her sleep. Her pussy was wet when she awoke.

Another busy day ensued. Gail was glad to get home and kick off her heels, after a light supper she opened her laptop.

A DM was waiting from Charmaine.

Darling, how was your day?

Gail typed: *Busy. Yours?*

Reviewed a fabulous latex corset.

Was it comfortable?

Hardly relevant—it's for BDSM lovers! <laughing emoji>

Speaking of BDSM, did you try Her Master's Voice?

Loved his writing!

You got into it?

Yes! In more ways than one!
Tell me more!
Modesty forbids. <blushing face emoji>
Enjoy!

Gail browsed social media, but felt restless and unsatisfied, where previously she would've enjoyed reading short stories. Tonight the plots felt too tame. She had a strong urge to visit HMV's blog to read more about bondage. She opened his next installment. It was as exciting as she remembered. When the tale came to its conclusion she selected another series. This one featured a Dominant called Sir who referred to his submissive as His Toy. Their adventures were thrilling, particularly as Gail found the submissive female a character to whom she could relate.

Sir, a rich businessman, met up with His Toy in a city dungeon. Within its specialized facilities, he teased and punished her, training her to climax on command. This storyline was both exciting and alien to Gail. Her body responded powerfully to the various scenes.

Gail's earlier sex life had been vanilla, which didn't mean it wasn't fun. What became clear, as she devoured the stories, was that there were things she was curious to try. A submissive role-play was now top of her list. She also intended to purchase some sex toys to satisfy her needs and explore further.

Stroking her fingers through the moisture gathered between her thighs she pictured intense eyes watching her. A shudder of desire coursed down her spine imagining his commanding voice: "Come for me."

In play obedience, she rubbed and pressed her moist folds until her body spun out of control and she came hard.

That night, Gail's dreams were full of the dark sexual encounters which had aroused her the previous night. She awoke heavy-limbed and throbbing, needing a cold blast under the shower to shake off her languid state. As she dressed for work that morning she fantasized about undressing for a Dom—*her* Dom—later. To play along she chose her outfit with care: a white blouse which could be unbuttoned and a dark pencil skirt to hug her curves and hobble her steps.

Imagining that she had a stern master to please boosted her mood. Gail was decisive with clients, applying some extra pressure to those inclined to dither. After setting herself a list of objectives and tighter deadlines than usual by which to achieve them, she felt her day at the office had been productive. When she got home she remained in work attire, simply slipping off shoes in the hall.

She cooked a meal before settling down with her laptop. Keen to continue reading about Sir's toy training, she logged in, discovering a new message waiting. It was HMV replying to her comment.

Good evening G@1L,

Thank you for taking the time to leave feedback, your response was so positive.

I'd be interested to know what you liked best about the story. Was it the punishment or handing over control to another? What was your response when the schoolgirl disobeyed her headmaster? Were you anxious or excited when she broke the rules?

You say you're new to BDSM. How did your parents or teachers punish you? I hope you don't find my questions intrusive.

HerMastersVoice

Gail's heart beat faster. She felt compelled to respond immediately. With tension pricking her fingers, she answered his questions honestly.

Good evening HMV,

I loved your story, in particular when the girl is instructed to bend over the desk and be ready for punishment. I like the submission. The power is hers to make it a short or long punishment, by complying or disobeying.

I felt anxious when she disobeyed her headmaster's instructions. I longed for her to be good. My parents never punished me for disobedience, but I was grounded for coming home late. One lover used to hold my hands above my head as we fucked, which felt exciting.

Currently, I'm reading your series Tyrannical Toy Training.

G@1L

Having talked with HMV online, she imagined that he was watching her as she read more of his stories.

His Toy was tied to a spanking bench with restraints holding her in position, limiting her movements but tilting her buttocks up so her soaked and swollen pussy was on full display.

Gail felt a sympathetic throb of arousal in her depths. She reached inside her pencil skirt while she read, dragging her panties down and completely off. She examined how damp they'd become, breathing in her spicy scent.

Sir started slowly with hand-delivered spanks, alternated with rubs, on His Toy's peachy behind. Soon her warmed skin bore a rosy glow. Sir changed implements to a leather paddle. Its impact was harder, deeper. Soon His Toy's tears began to flow, even as the heat and arousal built within her, causing her head to swim.

Gail was fascinated by the floaty feeling of subspace described. She stroked herself as she read, becoming sticky with arousal as her interest grew.

Sir knew that His Toy required further punishment. Before delivering stripes with a crop, he fondled her chest, then moved to grasp her nipples in a pincer grip. His sub was unable to wriggle away, yet this wasn't an issue. She groaned and gasped with pleasure, begging her Dom: "Please Sir, please may I come?"

Gail felt fevered from the vivid passage. She hastily unbuttoned her blouse to free her breasts from the confines of their satin cups. She felt shameless sitting with one hand up her skirt and her tits exposed, but playing into her fantasy that she was being watched, it was thrilling.

She pinched each nipple hard. The intense sensation, equal parts pleasure and pain, caused further throbs in her pussy. Alternating between each nub, she maintained fresh triggers of sensation. Bolts of lust raced from her chest to her pussy. Gail imagined her dominant lover commanding she torment her tender flesh as he watched her squirm.

She was aware that her liquid arousal, which coated the plump flesh of her pussy, had trickled downward, tickling her butt crack. She'd never experienced such a copious flow until she'd begun reading about restraint and dominance.

In the story, His Toy was struggling to hold back her climax. Gail's own hips were straining and tensing in sympathy.

To delay His Toy's gratification Sir instructed her to change position. He fastened her bound wrists to the dungeon's winch, cuffing a spreader bar between each ankle. With her legs pushed wide apart by the bar, there was no disguising the evidence of His Toy's arousal. Lines of her lubrication stretched until they snapped, dripping puddles on the hard floor.

"You love this, don't you, you dirty bitch?"

Sir's English accent was heavy with apparent distaste. His Toy simply nodded with a mixture of lust and shame.

He cranked the winch up until His Toy could only just stand on her tiptoes. With arms and shoulders pulled taut, her breasts and pussy were on full display.

"Let's see how much you can take," Sir growled, clamping a clothespin on each of His Toy's already swollen nipples.

Gail bit her lip. Despite how agonizing that would surely feel, her own slit moistened even more.

"Six stripes. Count please." Sir's commanding voice was emotionless.

As he rained strokes across the flesh of his submissive's buttocks, she yelped. Trying to remain in place, she counted. Her voice cracked with the sobs she was holding back.

Sir flung the crop aside to grasp His Toy around the waist, drawing her toward him while lifting her at the hips to position her onto his engorged penis.

"Don't you dare come," he demanded. Then he used one hand to brush both clothespins off her trapped nipples.

"Sir! Pleeeease!"

His Toy squealed with pain as the blood rushed back to the fleshy pinpoints.

"Come!" Sir roared before rubbing each nipple tip in turn. His Toy bucked and thrust wildly on him, her juices running free. Her pussy pulsed and throbbed around his length. Using her bound arms for leverage, she rode her master like he was a bucking bronco on a dude ranch.

Gail was now thrusting three fingers into her soaked pussy, administering pleasure combined with brutality. Shocked and excited in equal measure, the intensity of sensations she felt had her thrusting knuckles-deep inside herself. Her swollen clit pulsated in time with the squeezing of her pussy walls.

These stories seemed to unlock a different kind of passion in her, one she'd never experienced. She was discovering they unleashed a hunger in her body, the embers of which continued to glow even after she'd climaxed. They never completely cooled, so she'd find herself with aching nipples or a slick of moisture coating her pussy any time she recalled the stories she'd read.

Gail wondered if this change was because she was missing regular sex? Liaisons had never been exciting with Roger— nothing like what she'd experienced from reading HMV's stories. Rather, it had been comfortable, a way to show affection and relax.

The next evening, she went online to order sex toys. Gail chose items aimed at beginners. Her virtual shopping basket contained a soft, silicone vibrator, curved to reach her G-spot, a small rose gold bullet vibe and a glass dildo, which was textured with twists that were tinted red and blue, making it beautiful to behold. Once she'd paid, she checked her email.

A direct message was waiting from Charmaine.

Hi Gail, how are you?

I feel energized! How about you?

Busy. Where's this energy coming from?

Not sure but I keep feeling horny! <devil face emoji>

Gail's fingers hovered over the keyboard. Should she discuss this with her friend? They hadn't met but in a month's time, they'd attend an erotic conference together. She decided to keep her own counsel a little longer.

I've just ordered some sex toys.

Go, girl!

<blushing face emoji>

Having regular orgasms is self-care. I'd go crazy without them.

You are crazy!

Crazy in love with you!

Flirt!

A list of conference delegates was just shared. Her Master's Voice is attending!

Gail's stomach did a somersault as she composed a reply.

I confess, his stories are very arousing. Will it be weird to meet him?

You're too chilled for that.

What if I go all fangirl? <sweating face emoji>

Trust me, Gail, there's nothing a writer finds more flattering than appreciation for their writing.

As they chatted, Gail saw a new email from Her Master's Voice appear, making her pulse pick up. She itched to open it but wrapped up her conversation with Charmaine first.

Good evening G@1L,

I hope you're well. I wonder if you continued to read "Tyrannical Toy Training." It's my favorite series. I feel it depicts the ideal D/s relationship. A Dominant who is strict but nurturing, a submissive who wants guidance and care. Together they learn and explore.

There are many facets of BDSM, as you will find. If you want advice on reading matter I'd be happy to make suggestions.

Her Master's Voice

Gail was charmed by his gentle questioning. Her subconscious painted him in the image of the considerate but masterful Dominant from his stories, although she knew the truth about online personas. Itching to read more about Sir and His Toy, she clicked open the next episode.

Once again her hands crept into her panties, trailing teasing strokes across the taut silk as she read. Soon her yearning was such that she pulled the fabric aside for direct access. The fictional action was so compellingly erotic that she almost immediately strummed herself into a starburst of orgasmic fireworks. The power dynamic of surrendering one's needs and desires to another's control had tapped into her sexual core.

The next day was such a blur of activity she came home deeply tired. She cautioned herself against obsessing about HMV and his writing. Without Roger in her life, time felt heavy on her hands. But knowing the sex toys she'd ordered had arrived energized her. Gail opened the package in her bedroom, marveling at the soft silicone of the black G-spot vibrator. The smaller bullet vibe, with its high shine finish, was pretty. It was shaped like a lipstick with its top cut off at a blunt angle. It promised to deliver pinpoint accurate vibrations to her clitoris, a very appealing idea. She hefted the weight of the glass dildo in her hand and admired its twisting colors before storing it safely in a drawstring bag.

Responsibly, she decided to sate another appetite first with dinner. The whole time she was cooking, Gail's mind excitedly flitted back to the toys upstairs. Like a child who'd peeked at her presents under the Christmas tree, she could hardly wait for the moment she could play!

After making quick work of her meal, Gail got into bed naked, the bullet vibe, glass dildo, and a bottle of lube beside her. She familiarized herself quickly with the controls of the bullet before beginning to tease herself, moving it lightly over her mons and labia. Its tickle was delightful so she closed her eyes, enjoying the pure sensation. Gail spread her legs wider, becoming more aroused. She stroked a finger through the cleft of her pussy to gauge her wetness. The dildo was girthy, so for comfort, she drizzled lube on its tip.

No previous experience had prepared her for nudging her hot lips apart with such a thick, chilly protuberance! It was cold in contrast to the heat of her skin, and she shuddered with delight as she ran it up and down her slit. The dildo slid between her folds, a knife through butter. Gail teased herself with shallow insertion and withdrawal. Each thrust pressed incrementally deeper until she was moaning aloud with satisfaction, welcoming its insistent penetration.

When she looked down at her pussy she gasped to realize how much of its length she'd taken. She felt euphoric, proud to have accommodated its girth. The dildo's textured shaft dragged at her labia, stimulating them with ridges and nodules. She smiled as she noticed her creamy fluid coating its glossy surface each time she eased it out.

"You love this don't you, you dirty bitch?" she said to herself, suppressing a throaty chuckle. She held the bullet vibe against each nipple in turn, stiffening them to swollen points.

"Don't you dare come!" she rasped aloud, pressing the bullet vibe against her clit. Imagining she was being dominated by a man who knew how to nurture her darkest desires propelled her toward the abyss. Almost instinctively she slid the column of glass in and out of her pussy. A hungry yearning within her core drove her to climax, and she submitted to it—as if she could have disobeyed. Behind her closed eyes a brooding presence watched her lewd display. A voice in her head instructed: "Come for me."

The domination fantasy tipped her over the edge. She pressed the glass dildo hard against her G-spot and, with a few jerky thrusts of her hips, she came.

The date of the conference approached fast. Gail had as many questions for Charmaine as she had butterflies in her stomach. Her first was about dress code. Her friend explained street clothes were fine, although people dressed up for evening socials. Gail breathed a sigh of relief, having imagined feeling intimidated if all delegates were wearing fetish gear.

As she packed a suitcase, Gail was more excited than nervous. She hoped to meet Her Master's Voice. They now emailed regularly. He'd introduced her to further tales of BDSM. The scenarios varied, from period to modern, but the reaction she had to them didn't. They made her hot, wet, and throbbing.

She tucked her bullet vibe into her makeup bag. She treated herself to an orgasm most days now, kinky erotic stories served as her foreplay. This regime energized her. Even the lingerie she'd packed for the conference was sexy, to help her feel the best version of herself. She grabbed keys and phone, then wheeled her case to meet her taxi.

A train journey took her to the hustle and bustle of the city. At their glass-fronted hotel, which was also the conference venue, she and Charmaine recognized each other, hugging and air kissing. It took no longer than the journey to their room to feel like old friends.

"What are you wearing?" Charmaine's voice drifted out of the bathroom.

"A wrap dress and some boots. You?"

Charmaine appeared, clad in high-waisted panties, a corset, and thigh-highs. Over these, she buttoned a double-breasted coatdress.

"That's stunning!" Gail admired.

"Thanks, I love your look too." Charmaine reviewed Gail's outfit. "Try this with it?" She offered a black suede choker with a scalloped edge.

Gail hesitated. Not quite a collar, the accessory would look edgier than her usual gold chain.

"Okay." She giggled, holding her hair away from her neck for Charmaine to fasten the jewelry.

A few minutes later, Gail entered the busy conference room with Charmaine. The delegates were even more colorful than she'd expected. She did not, however, feel out of place in her dress.

People recognized Charmaine from the picture on her

website, so it was easy, standing beside her, to meet a stream of friendly people. All of them wore names on lanyards. As the room got more crowded, Gail was reduced to nodding and smiling. No matter, people watching was great sport, and this gathering offered much to entertain. She tried to guess whether her fellow kinky conference-goers were submissive or Dominant, single or with a partner.

A tall guy in a nearby group caught her eye, so she smiled. Charmaine and an editor were taking a selfie but getting the giggles. Gail didn't want to be in any pictures so she stepped away, accidentally bumping into the tall man she'd smiled at earlier.

"So sorry!"

"My fault," he responded. "I've spilled your drink."

"No, don't worry. It's only ice water by now."

"Could I get you another?"

She hesitated, glancing at Charmaine, who was laughing. Gail knew her presence could be spared.

"Thanks, that would be nice," she answered.

"Follow me. Maybe it's quieter near the bar."

It was lighter there and she noticed his intense blue eyes, their outer corners webbed with laugh lines.

"I'm Gail." She looked up at him curiously.

"Hello, Gail, I'm Adrian." The confident way he said it made her study his name tag. She was startled to realize this was Her Master's Voice. His eyes were bright with amusement; he'd already made the connection.

"What are you drinking?"

"Rum and Coke please."

Adrian ordered her drink plus a G and T.

"So, it's you I've been swapping reading tips with?" she teased.

"Yes. It's been rather fun educating you."

There was an undercurrent of mutual admiration while they discussed her job and his work as a photographer.

"It fits my dominant nature," Adrian theorized. "I tell the models how to pose and I boss my assistants around!"

"When did you first discover that domination was your kink?"

"I've always known, from my first sexual forays. I'd say what I wanted and girls would obey. I can usually recognize a submissive girl at a glance."

Gail felt a flutter. "Am I submissive?"

"Do you think you are?"

Gail looked away, a blush rising in her cheeks. "I'm not sure. Reading about BDSM excites me more than other types of erotica. But do I want to surrender control, be bound and beaten?" She glanced back at him.

"There are many ways to submit which don't involve pain."

"Yeah, I get that."

"Had you thought of watching a scene?"

"I'm not keen on porn." She wrinkled her nose.

"Not porn, real." When he gazed into her eyes, her stomach flipped. "I'm staging a scene in my hotel suite tomorrow night. Come and watch."

Gail's emotions swirled erratically. "That sounds intense."

"It will be, but I assure you the submissive will enjoy herself. She loves an audience."

"What if it's too much? If I don't like it?"

"I think you'll cope just fine. If you're worried, stand by the door."

Adrian called a couple of women over.

"Gail, meet Rhona and Mandy. Maybe you know them as Saucy Sub and Unicorn69? I've invited them tomorrow."

Both women seemed friendly.

"I wouldn't miss it!" laughed Rhona. "Who's your sub, Adrian?"

"It's a surprise, but ladies please reassure Gail about tomorrow. She's a D/s newbie."

"Oh, Gail," Mandy exclaimed, "that's so exciting! I think you'll love it but I can imagine it's a daunting first step."

"My first scene was at a munch," Rhona announced.

"Do you know what that is?" Mandy asked kindly.

Gail shook her head.

"It's a gathering of kinky people, part social and part play. Newbies can go to a munch to get the feel of what happens or to meet potential partners."

"I went to my first with a submissive who I befriended online," Rhona chipped in. "I was in awe of all the Doms. Simultaneously terrified and drooling."

"You're always drooling!" teased Mandy.

"I know. I'm a greedy slut." Rhona gave a blissful smile.

"Do come tomorrow, Gail. I'll look after you." Mandy touched her wrist, making Gail feel she'd made a connection.

"I'll screw up my courage," Gail responded.

"I'd better find my roomie." She suddenly felt tired. "Adrian, it was lovely to meet you, but now I need some sleep."

"Ditto, Gail. See you tomorrow." And with a flash of his eyes, he was gone.

Gail needed time to think about HMV's offer to watch a BDSM scene. She wondered what it would entail. Would it overwhelm her to be so close? she pondered while she brushed her teeth. She'd talk to Charmaine tomorrow.

When she broached the subject, Charmaine was all for it.

"What a great way to test if it's your kink!" her friend exclaimed the next morning.

"I'm worried it might upset me."

"You can duck out if you hate it."

Gail mused while they ate breakfast, and by the time she'd finished her coffee, she'd decided to grab the opportunity. When Adrian ran into her later, she told him shyly that she'd be there. He looked pleased, supplying his room number.

She saw Mandy in a kinky workshop, where she whispered, "See you at six."

Mandy gave her a hug. "He likes you!" she confided.

"Who, Adrian?" Gail's insides lurched, secretly thrilled.

Gail knocked at Adrian's suite at six. The door opened and she was relieved to spot Mandy. The conversation was muted; people stood on the peripheries. Her gaze was drawn to a curvy woman in black underwear and stockings who knelt in the middle, head bowed, hands behind her back, in the classic submissive stance.

Adrian stood on the far side, talking to friends. Tonight he was all dominance: wearing black jeans and a leather chest harness. He caught her eye, his smile was charismatic, but she felt a chill to see him so focused.

Mandy joined her. "Are you looking forward to this?" She seemed excited.

"I'm nervous. I'll stay near the door."

"I'll stand with you. It's starting."

A hush descended. All eyes were on the submissive. Adrian strode forward to stand in front of her.

"What are you?" His voice resonated with authority.

"Your slave, Sir."

"What are you here for?"

"Your pleasure, Sir."

"Give me your hands."

The submissive complied, holding her arms out, for Adrian

to bind them together with silk rope which was a vivid shade of purple. His looping and fastening of the rope were swift and skilled. He created an intricate, latticed web, securing her wrists and forearms as one limb. She was trapped yet somehow her beauty seemed enhanced by the tight bindings. A small sigh escaped the sub, indicating her happiness to be subjugated clearly for her audience. The tension in the air was palpable. He reached for a chair, which he placed in front of his sub.

"Rest your forearms on the seat, but stick your bottom out. Everyone wants a good view of me punishing your backside."

"Yes, Sir." She arranged herself correctly.

"What's my favorite number?" Adrian circled like a shark around the kneeling girl.

"Twelve, Sir." There was a collective sucking in of breath.

"Twelve swipes with the paddle," Adrian confirmed.

Almost immediately Adrian struck the first blow. A thwack resounded, the impact shocking to Gail in the silence. He continued to strike, his arm swinging back to follow through, reminiscent of a tennis forehand. As the blows rained down, his sub began to gasp, discomfort building.

Gail surveyed the room, observing the guests. A couple held hands, a woman bit her lip.

When Mandy turned to mouth, "Are you all right?" Gail nodded.

"Now you're warmed up," Adrian announced, "but I think you can take more. Can you take more?"

"Yes, Sir, if it pleases you."

There was a tremor to the submissive's voice. Her cheeks were flushed and her bottom must have been burning. Discarding the paddle, Adrian selected a whip. It looked vicious, its tails long, its handle plaited leather.

"Twelve again." A statement not a question.

Gail's tummy flipped with nerves for the bound submissive, yet her panties dampened. Guests parted behind Adrian, nobody wanting to obstruct the swing of the tails. He began, with lashes so controlled his style was graceful. Although the traces were long enough to hit the ceiling, his strokes were carefully placed, the first few just slicing through the air to build anticipation. Gail imagined their presence felt like a breeze on the prone girl's warmed skin. The lights picked out goose bumps on her back.

"One!" Adrian broke the spell when his first lash bit her skin. The sub let out a tiny gasp she couldn't suppress.

"Two!" He continued, the traces landing on the alternate cheek.

As he whipped, she counted, while the audience collectively held its breath.

Gail wasn't sure what she felt. Watching didn't excite the same responses in her body as reading. The slaps and smacks conveyed a thrill, but to counterbalance the sensation, the sub's groans tied her stomach in knots.

At ten strikes, the submissive said, "Amber."

Adrian immediately stilled the whip and crouched close to her. Master and sub talked quietly, his voice soothing while he stroked broad hands down her back, gentling her like a frightened horse.

"Stop or continue?" he asked her, no longer controlling.

"Continue," she replied in a small voice.

"Be sure," he warned. The audience was on a knife edge to know.

"Continue," she said, her voice stronger.

"Eleven, twelve." He wielded two strikes in quick succession, placing one on each cheek of her rear before laying the whip aside.

When it was over he embraced her. After wrapping a blanket around her, he scooped the sub into his arms.

He called her his "good, brave girl." She was carried to a bed in the adjoining room. Guests gave them privacy for aftercare.

The conversational murmur swelled. People circulated, sipping drinks and comparing reactions.

"Well?" Mandy's eyes on Gail were bright with excitement.

"Powerful, intense." Words were an understatement, but they were all she had. "You?"

"Oh God, I loved it!" Mandy's breathlessness revealed she was a spanking devotee.

Gail realized she felt buzzing, euphoric, remembering what she'd watched. In a while, Adrian appeared beside her, looking elated and perspiring slightly.

"That was so hot!" Mandy congratulated him, before moving away.

"What did you think, newbie?" He smiled down at Gail. His blue eyes pinned her, forcing her to be honest.

"It was intense. I can see you love it."

"But did *you* love it?" He focused on her, which was unsettling in a good way.

"I don't think I'm really one for watching," she hedged.

"Would you try it?" A smile crept over Adrian's face.

"If you're willing to show me, and go slowly." Gail looked up at him. "I would."

TRADE SHOW

D. Fostalove

Tara nudged me with her elbow, jarring me from my stupor. "You're sitting there looking like you just stepped off the set of *The Walking Dead*."

I chuckled. "That's how I feel."

"Long night?"

I nodded. "Our plane was delayed a few hours because of a medical emergency. When I finally arrived and checked in, I couldn't settle down. I ended up tossing and turning the entire night."

She adjusted a few products on our table and spread out company brochures for easier access.

"You could have sent me a text to let me know you needed to sleep in," she said as she sat back down beside me. "I could've handled things until you were ready."

"Thanks, but I'll be fine." I took a quick sip of the energy drink I'd purchased earlier from the lobby vending machine and slipped it back underneath the table.

"You sure?"

"Yes."

I glanced down at the screen of my phone, momentarily blinking as I scanned the limited early morning crowd of industry professionals perusing the vendor displays situated around the convention center. I unlocked the phone and saw a message from a Baltimore number. Although I had flown into the city for a three-day trade show, I didn't know anyone from the area and the only call I'd received from a 410 number belonged to the hotel when they confirmed my reservation.

WYD? the text read.

I started to delete the message but a second one came through asking if I could talk. I typed back, *I think you have the wrong number.*

Moments later: *Nah, I got the right number. WYD?*

I looked up to see a pair of representatives from a large rehabilitation center in the region as they stopped in front of our company's booth. Tara immediately engaged them about the latest medical supplies we had to offer. I adjusted in the plastic chair and responded that I was working.

Same here.

Do I know you? I asked.

Nah. Not yet.

The mysterious stranger piqued my curiosity with the insinuation we would eventually make each other's acquaintance. I looked up from my phone to see the two reps Tara had been speaking with navigating away from our booth and through the increasing clusters of people milling about.

Who is this?

Quincy.

Like he said, we didn't know each other. I didn't know anyone by that name.

What's your name?

Reluctantly, I tapped out my name. *Katrina.*

That has a nice ring to it: Quincy and Katrina.

Tara interrupted me from the random chat to ask if I was talking to Demarco. I shook my head and held up the phone so she could see the brief conversation. She lifted the eyeglasses from her face and glared at me. I knew what she was thinking without her having to say a word.

"You're not really entertaining a complete stranger. Are you crazy?"

I didn't have a response. I wasn't entirely sure why I had continued on with the conversation. Maybe it was my lack of sleep the night before, the flight delay, or the long day that lie ahead for us. Needing something to keep me awake was the best answer I could come up with.

"Block him."

"Why? I don't see any harm in a little mindless texting. I'm not going to meet him or anything."

Tara frowned before reminding me what an incredible, attractive man I had back home who loved and adored me. She didn't understand why I would be interacting with a total stranger when women would kill to have half of what I had in Demarco. I attempted to quell her frustration but she continued by reminding me how her ex-husband had cheated on her relentlessly.

"I shouldn't have shown you."

"You know what? You're right. You shouldn't have." She took a deep breath. "I'm taking off my friend hat right now and putting back on my coworker hat."

I excused myself to use the restroom and compose myself from the minor spat. When I returned, Tara was in a discussion with four people standing a few feet from our booth, all holding our brochures and other marketing materials. As I sat back in my seat, I felt the phone buzzing in my pocket. I pulled it out and saw I'd missed a call from Demarco. The vibrations had come from the voicemail he'd left.

"Hey babe, just wanted to hear your voice before I started my day. I'll call you back around lunchtime. Have a great day. Love you."

I found our last text exchange from the night before and pecked out a quick message to him. *Sorry I missed your call. Didn't hear the phone. It's so loud and busy here. Looking forward to your call this afternoon. TTYL.*

When I minimized Demarco's text message box, I saw the notification that I had two unread messages. I brought up the text window from Quincy. *Are you there? I didn't scare you off, did I?*

I typed back, *No. You didn't scare me off. Busy with work. Good.*

Tara stood suddenly, saying she needed to find something to snack on. When I looked up to acknowledge I'd heard her, I could see the disapproving glare as she stepped around the booth and vanished into the crowds. Maybe she was right. I needed to end the conversation and focus on work. A chime notifying me of a new text message pulled me from my thoughts.

What you look like? The first message read, followed by, *Send me a pic.*

I don't know you.

He sent a smiley face emoji back. *Thought I'd try. Describe yourself then.*

I told him I was 5'6", brown skinned with shoulder-length locks. I added I grew up in the Caribbean and when I got excited, traces of my accent could be heard.

You sound fine AF.

I smiled at the compliment but it faded when Demarco crossed my mind. *I have a boyfriend.*

A few minutes passed before a response popped up from Quincy. *Just making convo. Not trying to be your man.*

Okay.

I thought to ask what he looked like but decided against it when Tara returned with a small bag of pretzels in hand and two women in tow. She began pulling marketing materials from the table and pointing to supplies we had on display. I set the phone down and stood as an older man approached. He extended his hand, announced the company he represented, and I went into my spiel.

Seated back behind the booth twenty minutes later, I grabbed my phone and found three unread messages. The first one came from Demarco. He informed he wouldn't be able to call during lunch because he'd forgotten about a scheduled afternoon meeting with a client. I replied that I understood and I'd speak to him after work.

The two remaining messages were from Quincy. The first was an image, a headless, bare-chested caramel-complexioned mirror selfie. A half sleeve tattoo covered his left arm and one of his nipples was pierced. The accompanying text read: *What you think?*

I held the phone up to Tara as she chomped on pretzels.

"I think catfish," she said plainly and continued snacking. "He's probably some scrawny teenager with bad acne having the time of his life with y'all's juvenile conversation."

I let out a sigh.

"Who even does headless torso shots?"

The one-sided conversation ended when someone approached our booth. Tara jumped into action while I responded to Quincy's question.

Nice.

A moment later, he replied, *Just nice? Lol.*

Yes. Nice. I thought to ask why he'd chosen to send a headless photo but decided against it since I hadn't given anything but a brief description.

Okay. I'll take that, he said, followed by, *How's work going?*

It's going . . .

One of those kinda days?

I looked up from the phone to see if Tara needed any assistance. She didn't. *Kinda.*

At least it's almost lunchtime. Got plans?

Usually Tara and I would randomly pick a place within walking distance from the venue we were working in but I wasn't too sure if we would eat together or do our own things for lunch. Quincy didn't need to know any of that though. *I'll probably pick up a salad or something quick.*

Cool, Quincy said. *They got this new sandwich shop down the street from my job. I think I'm about to go there.*

I recalled the front desk agent at the hotel mentioning a new sandwich shop a block away when I asked for restaurant suggestions during the check-in process. *Do you work near the Inner Harbor?*

Yeah.

Someone told me about a place that sounds similar to what you're talking about.

Tara cleared her throat. I glanced up from my phone.

"I'm about to take off for lunch. You want anything while I'm out?"

I shook my head, telling her I'd pick something up when she got back. She grabbed her purse from underneath the booth and disappeared. I returned to the conversation with Quincy.

You heard about it all the way down in Charlotte?

Actually, I'm in Baltimore right now for business.

Fifteen minutes passed before another message came through from Quincy. The first was an apology for the delay in response. He had gotten busy with work. I let him know it wasn't a problem.

That's funny tho.

What's that?

You being in Bmore, he wrote, followed by, *What they call it? Serendipity?*

If you say so.

Another ten minutes passed before Quincy informed me that even though he was enjoying our impromptu chat session, he really needed to take care of some things at work.

I understand. I should really get back to work as well.

I know you probably gonna say nah, but want to have a drink after work?

I thought of Demarco and felt Tara's disapproving presence in the air. *Thanks but I don't think my guy would like that.*

He got you under lock and key like that?

Lol. No.

It's just one drink. In a well-lit, public space. I promise I'll play nice, he followed with, *I just wanna see who I been chatting with all day.*

I thought about it for a long time. *K.*

Cool. He sent the name and address of a place I'd actually walked by on the way to the convention center that morning. He told me it was reasonably priced, although I needn't worry about the cost because he would take care of everything. He added it had good food for a bar and pretty good drinks as well. *See you tonight.*

* * *

I exited the hotel room forty-five minutes after leaving the convention center for the day. Just as I made it to the lobby, the phone in my purse chimed. I rifled through the bag and pulled it out to find a message from Quincy. He wanted to know where I was. I had advised him midday that I would be making a quick stop by my room to drop off some items from work and freshen up.

Omw. Are you there already?

Nah. Got caught up at work. Running a little late.

I sat in one of the lounge chairs situated around a large fountain in the lobby. *Maybe tomorrow? I'm in the city until Thursday.*

I'm leaving in the morning.

Oh . . . was all I could think to respond with.

How about you drop by the office while I finish up and then we walk over to the bar together?

I tapped back, *I don't know about that.*

Why not?

I reiterated that I didn't know him from a can of paint.

I'm not going to hurt you. He again said he just wanted to put a face to the virtual conversation. He then gave me the name and address of where he worked, adding that there was at least one officer on duty 24/7 in the lobby and plenty of security cameras in and around the building. *If you decide to drop by, cool. If not, I understand. We can just meet at the bar a bit later. It's on you.*

Let me think about it.

No pressure, he said, ending the conversation with, *If you come by the job, I'm on the sixteenth floor, third office on the right when you get off the elevator. I'll leave a keycard at the security desk.*

Okay.

* * *

I entered the office building and just as Quincy had said earlier, there were two guards seated in the center of the large entryway behind an upraised security desk. It was equipped with several monitors and a couple two-way radios attached to a charging station. As I approached, the guard closest to me spoke.

"Evening, ma'am. Can I help you?"

"I'm meeting a friend on the sixteenth floor. I believe he left—"

He interrupted, "Are you Katrina?"

"Yes, I am."

He nodded, stood, and reached across the desk to hand me a silver keycard.

"Thank you."

I continued to the elevators. Once inside, I pressed the button corresponding to the sixteenth floor and swiped the card. The doors closed and the elevator sprang upward. I exhaled deeply and adjusted the purse on my shoulder. I wondered if I'd made the right decision to meet Quincy at his job after hours. Outside of the two security guards, I hadn't crossed paths with anyone entering or exiting the building. Had this been a part of Quincy's plan all along?

I pulled out my phone and dialed Tara's number as the elevator dinged and the doors parted. Reluctantly I stepped out into a dimly lit space littered with thirty cubicles about four feet tall. To the right were three offices and a conference room. Light emanated from the slightly ajar third door. I hung up the phone when Tara's voicemail message kicked on and began walking through the maze of cubes towards the office.

"Quincy?" I called before peeking through the cracked door.

"Come in," a deep voice said from inside.

I pushed the door aside and stepped into the sparsely

furnished office. A single cherrywood desk sat toward the back of the room with a black leather chair behind it. Two armless chairs faced the desk. There was a door on the back wall to the left and on the right, there he was: a shirtless man seated on the floor against a four-drawer vertical filing cabinet with his hands zip-tied to one of the drawers above his head. A black bandanna covered his eyes.

"Oh my God!" Had my body caught up to my racing mind, I would have run screaming like the building was on fire.

The door behind the desk suddenly opened, startling me even further. Demarco emerged.

"Glad you finally decided to join us."

I fell back into the wall, my gaze shifting between Demarco and the blindfolded, bound man who I assumed was Quincy even though he hadn't spoken since he beckoned me into the room. "I don't understand. What in the hell is going on?"

Demarco walked toward me but I threw a hand up to halt his advances. He smiled. I wasn't amused. "Babe, let me explain."

"Please do," I said. "You said you had a meeting this afternoon but yet you're here."

"I was really going to be at the airport. If we'd been on the phone, you would have suspected . . ."

"I would have never suspected this." I gestured with my hands for extra emphasis, completely puzzled, and looked beyond him to the silent man on the floor. "How do you two know each other?"

Demarco explained that the man was indeed Quincy. They'd met through an ad he posted online a few weeks back. The two had been conversing for about a week, hashing out the details of when and where the three of us would meet. When I asked him what he meant, he didn't answer but continued telling his story.

"Stop. Right now."

"What?"

"You still haven't said what we're doing here and why he's tied up and blindfolded."

"I know you've been wanting to add a third for some time," Demarco said, "and I've kind of brushed off the idea, but here he is. A submissive boy toy for your pleasure. Happy birthday."

"Happy birthday?" I stopped to think for a moment. "My birthday isn't until Thursday."

"I know," he said. "If I had done any of this then, you would have definitely known I was up to something so I decided to set this little surprise up a couple days early. Did it work?"

I turned my attention to Quincy without responding to Demarco. "So you've been playing with me all day? You already knew about me the whole time?"

"Yeah," he said. "It was all part of the plan."

"And what if I decided against seeing you?"

"Your dude said your curiosity would get the best of you." Demarco shrugged with a slight smile. "Was I wrong?"

"This is absurd."

"I thought you'd like something like this," Demarco said.

"Where are we?" For the first time, I let my mind wander to the many fantasies I'd had of a potential third party joining us for some freaky fun. "What if someone . . ."

Quincy chimed in, "My staff won't get here until after nine. We got plenty of time."

He informed them that he owned a cleaning company and the architecture firm that rented out the space was a long-time client of his. They usually cleared out the floor around five and didn't return until eight in the morning. He added that he had contracts with several other companies that occupied the high rise but their employees' shifts varied, unlike that of the architecture firm's staff, so we were safe to play uninterrupted.

"You down?" Demarco asked.

I shushed him before I closed the door. I strode to the desk, set my purse down, and dragged one of the chairs across the floor toward the corner where a potted plant rested. "Sit and face the wall."

"Babe . . ."

"You didn't think this little stunt of yours would go unpunished, did you?" I pointed to the chair. "Sit. With your mouth closed."

"Come on . . . please . . ."

"Now." I snapped my fingers. "If you're obedient, I may let you watch later."

Demarco lowered himself into the chair, facing the corner as instructed. I spun around and moved to where Quincy rested on the floor with his legs outstretched in front of him. I knelt beside him and reached for his nipple ring, pulling it lightly at first and then a little harder. He winced.

"Like pain with your pleasure?"

"Yeah."

I twisted the ring between my thumb and index finger until he groaned. "Want me to stop?"

"Nah," he said through gritted teeth.

"Good. I wasn't." I leaned in and kissed his lips. He kissed me back, his tongue sliding into my mouth. My free hand shot up to his throat, forcing his head back into the file cabinet with a thud. "He must not have told you. Ask for permission and then you may receive. Got it?"

"Yeah."

I released his nipple and stood to unbutton my blouse. Tossing it on the desk atop my purse, I glanced over my shoulder to see Demarco with his head pressed into the corner like a naughty child.

"Think you've learned your lesson?"

"Yes," he said in a low voice. "Can I turn around now?"

"No," I barked. "Not yet."

I returned to Quincy and leaned down so his head rested between my breasts. I could feel his warm exhales, the deep inhales as he took in the perfume I'd sprayed on before leaving the hotel.

"You like these titties in your face?"

"Yeah."

I ran a hand over his work pants, feeling a throbbing erection hidden beneath the fabric. "I see."

"You want to suck them?"

"Yeah."

I pressed them into his face. "Beg."

"Please . . ."

Rubbing my hand over his clean-shaven head, I asked, "Please what?"

"Let me taste one. Please, Trina . . ."

I liked the need in his voice, the desire, the way he said my name. I told him to say it again. He did, a second and then a third time.

"You like the way my name feels on your tongue?"

He nodded, my breasts pressed against both of his cheeks.

I shot over my shoulder, "Get up and move your chair over here."

Demarco eagerly sprang from his seat and dragged it across the floor to the spot I pointed to.

"Take everything off but your boxers and sit. I want you to watch another man enjoying me as you have."

He quickly removed his shoes and socks. His pants, button-down, and tank top followed.

"Interlock your fingers behind your back," I instructed.

"Don't want you tempted to touch yourself until I grant you permission."

I turned my attention back to Quincy, straddling him. "Open your mouth."

Quincy obliged, his tongue slithering out as it had done before. I popped one of my breasts from the blue bra that contained them and brought it to his lips. He latched on, his tongue circling my nipple. The metal drawer restraining his wrists rattled above us. I knew he wanted to grab them, me. I wanted to feel his hands gripping my waist, have him palm my ass, but liked him under my complete control even more.

I reached between us and unzipped his pants, finding he had no underwear on. I brushed my hand over the woolly mound of pubic hair and ran my fingernails along his massive erection, feeling him twitch from the sensation. My fingertip grazed the tip where pre-come oozed out. I pulled my hand from between us and tasted his sweetness.

"Like that?"

"Um hmm."

I began gyrating on top of him as he continued sucking on my breast.

"What's on your mind behind that blindfold?"

He released me from his mouth. "How good that ass will feel on this dick."

"I bet you'd really like that," I said. "Me sliding up and down on that wood, you stretching me out like no other man has before."

I peered over my shoulder to see Demarco's reaction. He remained seated with both hands behind his back, his erection standing tall through the slit in his boxers. He licked his lips as he watched.

"Are you enjoying the show?"

"I am," he said before hesitantly asking, "Can I . . . ?"

"You may. Do it nice and slow. No spit."

He brought his left arm from behind his back and began to slowly stroke himself.

I turned my attention back to Quincy, who was tonguing my nipple. "Did he tell you about me?"

"Yeah."

"So you're into girls . . . like me?"

He nodded.

"Tell me how much."

"I can show you better than I can tell you."

I pulled away from his lapping tongue and stood. "Is that right?"

"Yeah."

I unzipped my pants, pulling them and my panties to my knees. "Stick out your tongue again."

He did, his tongue meeting the tip of my dick. He leaned forward and kissed it.

"Put it in your mouth."

He hesitated, kissed the tip again.

"Don't act like you haven't sucked dick before. I know how you freaky trade boys are."

"It's been a minute," he admitted.

"The time is now." I jerked my hips forward, my dick sliding between his lips.

He opened his mouth fully and took me into him, hungrily bobbing his head back and forth. I moaned while gripping the edges of the file cabinet. I closed my eyes as one of Quincy's restrained hands found my exposed breast. He gripped it and kept sucking me, taking me deeper and deeper into his mouth until his nose pressed against my shaved pubic area.

"Come over here and play with his dick."

Demarco got down on all fours and crawled across the floor between my legs. With one hand, he reached into Quincy's pants, pulled out his dick, and began sucking it just as aggressively as Quincy was with mine.

"I meant jack him off but okay."

I palmed the top of Quincy's head to guide him back and forth and closed my eyes again, feeling myself getting closer. My eyes snapped open when I heard Quincy gagging. I looked down to see Demarco stroking Quincy's slobbery dick as foam shot up and out onto his pants and the hardwood floor around us.

"Where do you want it? On your chest? Face? 'Cause I'm about to come."

Quincy kept on sucking. I pulled away from his eager mouth and erupted in his face. I grabbed myself and kept jerking as I continued to spurt nut onto the bandanna, his cheeks, and his open mouth. He licked the liquid on his lips before rubbing them together.

"Put it back in."

I stuck my dick back into his awaiting mouth as he licked around it with his tongue. Demarco crawled up beside Quincy and began stroking his dick at a feverish pace until he exploded onto his stomach and chest. I backed away from the pair, slumped against the file cabinet together and panting.

"Kiss each other."

Demarco gazed up at me, his fist still clenching his erection. I could tell he wasn't interested in being intimate with Quincy in such a way.

"Do it."

He leaned over and kissed Quincy on the mouth. Quincy didn't flinch or shy away but also didn't respond the same as when we had kissed.

"Do you like how I taste on him?"

Demarco quietly sat back beside Quincy.

"You'll be okay." I smiled.

"Trina?" Quincy called out.

"Yes?" I stuffed my breast back into the bra and reached for my blouse.

"Can I see what you look like before you go?"

"No," I said. "That's your punishment for toying around with me all day."

"Damn, you cold."

"I get the impression you kinda like it."

He wiped the corner of his mouth on his shoulder with a smirk.

"Thought so." I pulled up my panties and slacks.

"If you're ever in Bmore, hit me up. Maybe we can play again," he said. "You got my number."

"Maybe . . ." I grabbed the strap of my purse and put it on my shoulder. I looked down at Demarco as he wiped sweat with the back of his hand. "Release him and clean yourself up. I'll be waiting for you downstairs."

CHEF'S SPECIAL

Emma Chaton

You've had a frustrating day in and out of the kitchen. Two cooks out with the flu. A shitty server with an even shittier attitude. Milk that had been left out too long. Mold on one of the cases of strawberries that came in, so all of them had to be tossed. And then getting slammed with dinner guests who had nothing better to do than to carefully rearrange the dishes which you had put so much thought into, because after all, it shouldn't be any problem for the chef to switch out the risotto for quinoa, right?

You're angry, and anyone who's around you knows it. And anyone who knows you well knows to stay the hell away from you when you're like this. Slamming mixing bowls and pots in frustration against the prep table didn't help. Most everybody had gone for the night, but you were still there, pulling out a bunch of apples and peeling them for something (you hadn't even decided what to make yet), to replace the strawberries for whatever it was you hadn't even decided to make with those yet either. Only one of your sous chefs was around, quietly avoiding you as he picked up what was left of tonight's kitchen.

One apple. Two apples. Four. You're exhausted. You're sitting on that one uncomfortable wooden stool mindlessly carving away with your paring knife, one after another, not even sure what you're cutting them for. You've long stopped concentrating on what you were doing, gazing off in the distance. It's well after 2:00 a.m., and you can feel the knots in your neck throb and tense up. It's affecting your shoulders, your lower back, even the backs of your legs are aching. It's been a long year building your restaurant's reputation, and your body is showing the signs of wear. You can't even remember the last time you went out, as you wipe the tiredness from your eyes. When you allow yourself to think about it between slices, you realize it's even been quite some time since you've been with someone. You sigh, thinking that maybe the tension wasn't just in the shoulders.

Your sous chef had been dancing around you for a little bit, trying to dodge your attention and your knife as he made last-minute swipes of the counter. "Sorry, but I've got to get up to that spot right there," he announces, pointing in front of you.

Whatever else he is, you *think* he's a decent sous chef, but in the blur of the day you can't be sure at this hour. A little stocky, clean-shaven across the face and head. Green eyes. And ridiculous ears that won't stay put on the side of his head. Still, he's worked hard for you over the last few months, and largely kept to himself. James? Connor? Alfred? *No, that's the ears*, you think. *Why's he even working this late?* you wonder. Another eager sous chef wanting to move up the line, you imagine. At least he's competent. And here. As he moves in front of you, you lose track of what you were doing, and cut your left index finger.

"Ouch, shit," you hiss, and hold on to your finger for dear

life. It isn't deep, but you hate cutting yourself. You're a chef, after all; aren't you supposed to be above such amateurish things? You rush to the faucet and start cleaning it out, when he appears next to you with a first aid kit, without a word. He starts prepping and cleaning with peroxide and gauze, making a nice little bandage to fit snugly on your finger. You take a deep relaxed breath at his kind mending.

"Thanks." You smile wearily, suddenly realizing you still don't remember his name.

He smiles back at you, nodding. "You seem a little tense."

For a guy who barely says five words all day not related to cooking, he'd managed to pick five words that were a bit obvious. You roll your eyes and shrug.

"You get like this a lot, I've noticed." Your sous chef pauses, taking a deep breath. "I can help."

You're taken aback at this, especially since this may very well have been the most in-depth conversation you've had in eight months. But his words seem loaded. *I can help.* Help how, exactly? Help how exactly, alone in a kitchen after closing time? But you shake off your suspicion, knowing full well lots of sharp things are within your grasp. With a deep breath of your own, you finally ask, "How so?"

Your sous chef takes your unbandaged hand and leads you back to the prep table. "You need to let go. Give up a little control at the end of the day. It'll help."

"What? A fucking breathing exercise?" you snap. Then, embarrassed, realizing how rude you came across, "I'm sorry, I didn't—"

"It's fine." He smiles again, kindly. "Can you give me about five minutes of trust to help you relax?" he asks, patiently sighing, sounding like he's stepped off a commune, and taking yet another deep breath that fills his barrel chest.

Why not? you ask yourself. *What harm can it do?* Besides, you were kind of sharp with him. "Go ahead."

He turns you toward the table and places your hands flat out a good foot apart from each other. He grabs one of the aprons at the end of the table, and with the paring knife, slices through the cloth. Taking the slice he pulled off and folding it twice, he then approaches you from behind. Your sous chef leans in and whispers, "Close your eyes."

Reluctantly, you do as he asks, knowing what he is going to do and not entirely comfortable with it. He ties the blindfold around your eyes, then moves away. You hear him cut away some more of the apron, and you start to breathe quickly as the sound of ripping cloth is amplified. You feel him return. Brushing his lips against your ear, he whispers again, "Do you trust me?"

I sure as hell do not! You weren't sure where this was going exactly when this started, but you now have a pretty damned good idea. But you're exhausted. You're wound up, tired of making decision after decision. And you need something different to break up what you're doing or else you'll end up leaving it all behind, probably after tearing your hair out. With a leap of faith, you whisper back, lying to him, "Yes, I do."

He grabs your hands and ties them behind the small of your back. He is no longer being gentle about it. You feel his hot breath on your neck as he exhales quickly, and begin to notice your own speeding up. You can hear your heart throb in your ears as your pulse quickens. He pushes your shoulders forward and down, holding you against the table. Your hands come to rest right above your ass. Your sous chef is no longer being a gentleman. He reaches in front of your houndstooth pants, pushing hard against you, releases the button, and pulls down your zipper. He's not even pretending this is anything but primal. He pulls your pants and panties around your knees and positions your ass a little lower than the edge of the table.

You're breathing rather heavily, practically panting, and that's when you notice *Jesus, I'm fucking soaking.* You're shivering nervously against the steel of the table, not sure how this will feel, but wanting it more and more. He's still moving behind you. You listen to him unfasten his chef jacket, hear the rustle of his pants dropping around his ankles. The heat coming off his body radiates against your thighs and your ass, and you bite your lip, hoping for what's coming. The head of his cock swipes against your ass cheek, and your heart jumps. For lack of a better word, just that momentary touch feels substantial. You sigh, bite the lower right corner of your lip, and part your legs a little more.

Then you feel it. You hadn't seen his cock at all, but good Christ you can feel it. And feel it. You gasp, your mouth gaping. *He's stretching me! Oh my God!* You groan loudly as he pushes further and further inside you. Your eyes bulge underneath the blindfold, your back arching against your tied hands. Finally, you feel it all, the full length of his cock deep inside you. It's comfortable and uncomfortable, that fantastic pulsing cock. Familiar and foreign all at once. Under your restraints, you squirm on that cock, trying desperately to fuck him, but he's holding you down so that you can't move, pinning you, impaling you. Whatever cares you had, they no longer matter. You're being filled to the core, and want it again and again inside you.

"Oh God . . . just fuck me . . . please," you gasp.

The sous chef obliges, pulling his cock out to the tip, but leaving it inside you. This time when he enters, he thrusts with full force, so hard his balls smack against you. So hard it pushes the table a couple of inches forward. You take a deep breath, gasping for air as over and over, he fucks you deep and hard.

Each time he fills you up, he stays there a moment, lingering, gripping on to your shoulder tightly. You try to break your hands free to brace yourself, but your tensing up seems to make him fuck you even harder. The sensation is overwhelming, and your pussy begins to ache and tighten, trembling around his thick erection.

Pounding you, he whispers, "Whose pussy is this?"

In answer, you unexpectedly find yourself crying out, "Yours!" You're so breathless you can't even get a full sentence out. Finally, you give in. "Oh God, I'm gonna come," you get out, and you feel your body push back against him, trying desperately to keep him inside you, your muscles clamping down and pulsing around that thick cock.

He keeps fucking you, harder, deeper, as you throw your head back and scream out in ecstasy. As if on cue, he takes his hands off your shoulders and reaches for your hands, pulling them back, lifting your body up. There's a tug in your shoulders, and as your body leans upward above the prep table, his cock somehow reaches further inside you. Such an odd sensation, hovering above something that could support such a forceful fucking, and yet the only support you have is his physical restraint on your arms and wrists. His grunts, his thrusts, his scent and yours as he fucks you senseless—all of this is about him taking what he wants from your body. With every deep, hard, Earth-shattering penetration, you lose more and more control.

But that's the point, isn't it? You trust him to take control. To seize control. To surrender to him. As he pushes his thumb in your ass and pulls your hair back, you realize how much you love what he's doing to you—*with* you. How your needs and his are in perfect alignment, an erotic push/pull you can't get enough of. He's fucking you savagely like an animal and nothing else matters outside of this primal fucking, outside of him so deep inside you.

As you finally give up control, you just can't take it anymore, and come again all over his thrusting cock, crying out, shivering on him, feeling your tits bounce hard underneath your chef jacket. You can tell he's getting closer too.

He pulls you off his cock and pushes your shoulders down. Blindfolded, hands tied and on your knees, pants around your ankles, juices dripping down your thighs, you open your lips, waiting for what seems like an eternity for his cock to slip against your tongue. That soft head opens your mouth wider, and you tickle underneath it with your tongue as it pushes in. You taste the sweat and moisture along the length of his shaft, and you moan around this man's thick cock as it makes its way in and out of your mouth. As he fucks you, he groans louder and louder, his fingers running through your hair and getting a firm grip.

Then you taste it. Mixed with your own, you could taste the salt beginning to drip from the head, until he finally comes so hard and so much you can't keep it all in your mouth. And God help you, you really try to swallow him whole, eagerly, hungrily, wanting to savor every last taste of you and him together.

You feel him withdraw, and you sense he is certainly satisfied.

But so are you. You're breathless. Drenched in sweat and come. Unable to move or act without him. But you are calm. Relaxed.

He helps pull you up, removes your blindfold, and sits you on the stool. As he cuts your bonds, he hands you a towel. You look up at him, his shirt open, and that magnificent cock still dangling between his legs.

He asks, head to the side, genuine, and sincere, "Do you need anything?"

Your eyes lift up from his delicious length up to his gaze. Wordlessly, you shake your head. With a smile, the sous chef gathers his things and within a few minutes leaves for the night.

With some regret, you suddenly realize that you still don't remember his name.

FRIEND WITH BENEFITS

Charlie Powell

Up until now, Cami has always tried to be the *chill* part of Netflix and chill. Lately however, that approach hasn't been working so well.

She's been trying not to message Rob. She's not sure he'll get it—is worried in fact that not only will he not get it, he'll completely misunderstand her reason for telling him. And yet, as with everything important in her life, she *wants* to tell him, wants him to be the one to tell her it'll all be okay.

Autumn isn't supposed to be like this. It's always been her favorite time of year, ever since she was a kid. There's something about the change in season that gives her a sense of renewal, even if the trees are shedding their leaves. It makes her think of the things she used to covet as a teenager: new schoolbags, freshly sharpened pencils, never-used markers.

If only those were the things she was craving now. But they're not. The thing she's craving now is a baby.

Except that *crave* is perhaps the wrong word. At fifteen, she adored babies. At fifteen, it would have been fair to say she craved motherhood, and that craving persisted for another ten, maybe even another twelve years. But now she is thirty-five and she feels as if her biology has backed her into a corner. She still wants to be a mother, she's pretty sure of that, but right now all she wants is another five to ten years to keep doing all the things she loves—late night bars, travel, *men*.

There's Rob, of course. But even if she does decide that now is the right time to embark on motherhood, it won't be Rob that she embarks on it with. She adores him, sure, and he adores her, but he already has a primary partner. If she had a kid, how would they continue to make it work? Diary management is difficult already. Often, what with work and friends and jobs, they have to plan weeks in advance when they want to see each other.

There's no reason why today would be any different, why he wouldn't already have plans. But she calls him nonetheless.

He answers, and suddenly she's lost for words. It's 10:00 a.m. on a Sunday when she has no other plans and she knows as soon as she hears his voice—his voice that has so often been able to soothe and comfort her—that this time it won't be enough. She needs to see him in person.

"You're horny?"

"I don't know"

"Sad?"

"I . . . no, not exactly."

"Would it help if I came over?"

She wasn't expecting this, but she's grateful. So *fucking* grateful.

"Yes."

"Okay, I can do that. I have a few hours free this afternoon. And Cami?"

"Yes?"

"When I fuck you, how do you want it?"

They've spoken to each other like this for as long as she can remember. To outsiders, she knows it might sound abrupt— cold, even. But she loves it, the way he forces her to put her desires into words, the way the back and forth between them acts as a kind of foreplay, the way every exchange shimmers with anticipation.

Usually, she'd say something like "I've been thinking all week about sitting on your cock—sinking onto it slowly so I can feel every thick inch" or "I'm desperate to have your dick in my mouth," but right now, none of that is true. She hasn't thought about him much at all until today—she's been too wrapped up in worrying about the future.

She takes a deep breath. She doesn't want the words to come out wrong. "I'm not sure I want you to fuck me?"

They couldn't have come out more wrong if they'd tried.

This time, it's him who's momentarily silent. "I . . . okay. Okay, I'll be over in a bit."

It's the first time she's not been sure sex will solve the problem. In the past when her mental health has tanked, which it does, regularly, all she's wanted is physical contact. But today, she feels that if she doesn't talk about this it'll only continue to eat her up inside once he's gone, no matter how many orgasms she's had.

"Are you breaking up with me?" he asks when she opens the door to see him standing there looking like something from an advert for autumn, all ruffled hair, flushed cheeks, and plaid shirt. She hasn't been outside all day, hadn't realized how cold the weather has turned.

"What? No!"

He looks confused. "You wanted to see me, it sounded urgent, but you don't want to fuck. You *always* want to fuck. What am I missing here?"

"I want to talk."

"About us?"

"No. About some shit I'm having a hard time with."

"Then we'll talk. Tea?" He heads for the kitchen. He's always been right at home in her place, and she loves that. It makes him feel like a solid part of her life, rather than someone who's just passing through.

They sit next to each other on the sofa with their drinks, but she still can't relax. Her leg jiggles uncontrollably and tea sloshes over the edge of her mug, soaking the jersey wrap dress she's wearing. She heads for the kitchen to fetch some paper towels. While she's dabbing herself down, she gazes blankly out of the window, watching the leaves drift slowly from the trees and smoke rise from a bonfire next door.

"Rob?" she calls.

"Yeah?"

"Can we go for a walk?"

"A walk?"

"I need to get out of here for a bit. Clear my head."

"You'll need to wrap up. It's freezing out there."

"What about you?"

"I've got some stuff in the car."

They head for the woods and Cami starts to feel better almost immediately as she kicks through piles of dried leaves. She's wearing her warmest scarf and a bobble hat, and she's holding the hand of one of the best men she knows. Rationally, she knows her life is good. If only her anxious brain would calm the hell down and realize that too.

"Go on, then," Rob says, when they've walked about a mile. "You said you wanted to talk, and I'm all ears. Spit it out."

She turns to face him, grinning. "Honey, you know I *never* spit it out."

"Hey, don't you get smart with me, or I'll make you pay for it later."

"You won't understand."

"Try me."

"Fine, fine. I want to have a baby."

She waits for the look of horror to appear on his face, waits for him to tell her that that's completely out of the question for them, but he does neither of those things.

He says, "Keep going."

Once she starts explaining, she feels as if she might never stop. She tells him everything: her fears about choosing a donor, her concern that it's not fair to deprive a kid of a relationship with their father, her worries that the IVF will be painful, or worse, that it won't work. She confesses she's scared that one day she'll regret not having tried harder to find a traditional relationship, that she's not sure she can afford to do this alone, that she hates the idea of having to rely on her parents for childcare. And yet, she wants this. She's always wanted it. It's just . . . it's just it feels so unfair to have to know for certain when the time is right, to have such a small window, and to not be able to know for sure whether she'll enjoy being a mother, or whether it can never actually live up to the fantasy of motherhood that she carries around in her head.

While she's saying all this, he just listens; he doesn't say anything when she starts to cry, either. He finds a clean tissue in his pocket and passes it to her, but then he just holds her and lets her sob for a bit.

"I'm sorry," she says eventually. "I'm just being ridiculous."

"You're not," he says. "In fact, saying you're being ridiculous is the first ridiculous thing to come out of your mouth. Of course thinking about this is going to be stressful, and you're right, it's totally unfair that women have to make this decision in their thirties, and it's completely normal to not feel ready and to want more time."

It's like a huge weight has been lifted from her shoulders. Even in her wildest dreams, she'd never have hoped that someone would acknowledge her fears in this way. And she certainly wouldn't have imagined that having her fears acknowledged would make her feel so damn horny.

"You know what I said about wanting to fuck?" she asks.

"About *not* wanting to fuck," he corrects, gently.

"I think I've changed my mind."

He does that face—the one between a grin and a smirk—that always infuriates her because it makes him seem so damn smug, but also makes her want to suck his cock immediately.

"You do surprise me," he says.

"Is that weird?" she asks. "You know, because I was crying and stuff?"

He takes her hand and moves it to his dick, which is already swelling under her palm. "It's not weird."

"It turns you on?"

"No! God, it's just not weird, is all. *You* turn me on."

"I could go down on you right here," she says. "There's no one around."

There's something about the idea of kneeling in a crunchy pile of leaves and taking his cock as deep into her mouth as she can that really appeals to her.

"You could. I might have a better idea, though."

"Oh?"

"I'll show you back at yours."

* * *

When they arrive home, she takes off her boots and moves to unwrap her scarf, but he stops her. He gestures that she should go upstairs just as she is, and he follows behind her. He's also still wearing his outdoor stuff.

"Give me your scarf," he says, and she does.

"Lay down on the bed."

She can see what's going to happen now, but that doesn't make it any less exciting. She toyed around with some plastic handcuffs once, but no one has ever tied her up like this before.

She begins to unbutton her coat, but once again, he stops her. "Leave it. Just lay on the bed."

One at a time, he takes her arms and binds them—over her coat—to the headboard, the first arm with his scarf, the second with hers. Next, he pulls down her thick, black winter tights and her underwear and uses her tights to tie her left leg.

In her underwear drawer, he finds a second pair of tights, and then her right leg is tied, too. She's surprised at how little she's able to move, given his improvised kit, but she's not complaining.

And then she's completely at his mercy.

It's odd, how much more exposed it makes her feel, the fact that she's not naked, especially when he takes off all his clothes and circles the bed like an animal considering its prey. She can't take her eyes off his thick cock, jutting proudly from his body. She can't wait to feel it inside her.

But Rob has other ideas.

He pushes her coat and her dress up around her waist, and then he kneels on the bed beside her, his gaze leveled directly on her cunt.

"It seems to me," he says, "that it would be fair to say you've been thinking about things that scare you lately. Is that right?"

Cami nods.

"And that you're trying to find the courage to confront those fears?"

Another nod.

"So how do you feel about trying something else that used to scare you?"

"Nervous."

"Nervous as in you don't want me to do it?"

She thinks for a moment. In a way, the thing she knows he's referring to—him going down on her—and the fact of having a baby, are not so dissimilar. They both rely on her trusting that her body will do what it's supposed to. She's never been good at that. Until now.

"No. I'd like to try."

"Good girl," he says, and she feels both her mouth and her cunt get wet.

"One extra challenge," he says. "No nervous jiggling. Pleasure is one thing, but if you're trembling with anxiety, I'm going to stop, okay? I can't promise you'll get any cock later, either, unless you do what I say."

"You bastard."

"You love it."

The problem is, she kind of does.

For the first thirty seconds or so that his mouth is on her, she thinks she's made a terrible mistake. All she can focus on is what she might taste like, and the fact that he could be hating every minute because she's not shaved bare. And then suddenly, her body overrides her brain and she couldn't care less what happens, or what he's thinking, as long as he doesn't stop until she comes.

Her anxious thoughts have vanished, every single one of them, as if her mind were a disc that had been wiped. He has two fingers inside her, thrusting, and his tongue is flicking rhythmically against her clit. She is only vaguely aware that she is screaming his name—her own voice sounds strange to her, as if it were somebody else making all the noise.

His strong hands hold her thighs wide apart, his tousled head the only thing she can focus on. Her eyes are screwed shut with the sheer intense pleasure of it all and then the pleasure crests and breaks, leaving her exhausted and panting beneath him.

When she looks like she's begun to recover, he asks, "How was that?"

"Amazing," she says. "I loved it."

He moves up the bed to snuggle beside her. "All that time you were so sure you'd hate it . . ." he murmurs.

She flinches. Is he suggesting that she's letting doubts get in the way of having a baby, too?

"I need time to get my head around stuff," she says. "It's just who I am."

He smiles. "I know," he says. "It's just who you are, and who you are is also wonderful."

He's silent for a moment, and she wonders if he's fallen asleep. And then, from where his face is nuzzled in her shoulder, she hears him whisper, "And if you decide it's right for you, I know you'd be a wonderful mother, too."

THE WEIGHT OF COMMAND

Anne Stagg

Captain Salgado of the GCS Epona. *Mission Log: 257913.12. Received distress signal from civilian-transport Boudicca at ship's time 0300, stating they were under attack from a Vespertine warship. We proceeded to coordinates. Pause recording.*

What a shit-show, Beatriz thought as she sipped her tea. The fragrant ginger and honey brew had cooled since her yeoman had shoved it into her hand an hour ago. The film of cloying sweetness coating her tongue made her grimace.

Everything had gone tits up the minute the *Epona* dropped out of the light-stream and into regular space. If tactical hadn't started firing right away, she wouldn't be alive to worry about cold tea.

Scrubbing at her face with both hands, she stifled a groan. The weight of captaincy left her breathless, crushing the reason out of her until she was gasping for air.

Stop feeling sorry for yourself.

The communication light on her console blinked, followed by a staccato series of buzzing sounds that made her teeth ache.

When she punched the comm button, a jolt of pain shot up the length of her arm.

"Fucking hell." She shook her hand out. "Salgado, here."

"Go easy on the comm button, Captain." Commander McKissick, her first officer, sounded worn as the heel on a pair of old boots.

"The last time I checked, you had a null psychic rating. Have you planted some surveillance cams in here?"

"Call it an educated guess. We've been on this mission, what, eighteen months? You've had that thing replaced three times."

"That's fair. What do you have for me?"

"Doctor Rejick sent a final casualty list."

"Go ahead," she said, voice steady, though the skin at the nape of her neck prickled with anxiety. The skirmish had lasted longer than she'd wanted.

I didn't want it at all.

"The *Boudicca* reported twenty wounded, mostly plasma burns from close-range weapons fire when the Vespertine tried to board her," McKissick said. "Four are critical. One dead— their captain. We've got seven wounded, two are critical, but the Doc says they'll pull through."

The first glimmer of relief broke through the wall of exhaustion. One loss hurt, but compared to Beatriz's expectations, it was a miracle.

"And Kimura? How's he doing?"

Ezume Kimura, a xenobiologist, was McKissick's husband. He'd been one of those injured when the *Epona* took a nasty hit to her port side.

"His leg's broken, and he got a hell of a knock to the head, but he'll be fine. Thanks for asking. Speaking of—"

"Wait, let me guess," she said, a smile tugged at the corner of her mouth. "I'm expected in Medical without delay."

Her wife, Dr. Velodona Rejick, was Chief of Medical Services. She would want to lay eyes on Beatriz after the battle. Reassure herself that she was safe. They both needed the affirmation after violent encounters.

McKissick chuckled. "Now who's spying?"

"Point taken."

Simmering arousal low in the cradle of her hips warmed her, yet she shivered like cold fingers were caressing her spine. Accepting help was hard for her. So was letting go of the personal discipline cultivated during her time as captain. Submitting to her lover's will was a surefire way to set duty aside. But it didn't stop her from bucking beneath another's yolk.

It was no surprise Velodona knew Beatriz required a break from the overwhelming burden of command. They had been together for a decade, and the Doc's people, the Ax'Il, were both empathic and telepathic. The abilities made her an excellent doctor and an incomparable lover. There were times when she understood Beatriz better than Beatriz understood herself.

"I expect I'll be out of pocket for about two hours while she checks me over." Pausing, she reconsidered with her next breath. *You're not a kid anymore; you can wait to see her while he checks on Kimura.* "I'm glad Ezume is all right. You sure you don't want me to tell Doc R. to cool her jets so you can visit him?" she added.

"You go. He's zonked on pain meds. He wouldn't even know I'm there. Gamma shift is coming on in thirty minutes, anyway. All we've got scheduled is cleanup and repairs until we hit Ordillis Station."

"Thanks, Commander. Salgado out," she said, wincing when she pressed the comm button.

The hush of the medical bay always struck Beatriz like the silence most people attributed to the ocean's depths—a fiction invented to mask the violence hidden in the stillness. The sea had currents swift enough to snatch a person away in seconds. Pressure on the ocean floor was so intense it could crush a human skull.

Med Bay is like that, Beatriz thought as the doors whisked open. *Calm and pristine until your eye catches a glimpse of the suffering.*

"If you can't get that maudlin shit under control, I'm going to confine you to quarters," Velodona said.

Beatriz jumped. She hadn't noticed her wife stepping out of the last exam room in the row.

The doctor continued, "We can't have you moping about the ship like some hell-bound sailor."

You're a pain in the ass, Beatriz thought to her partner.

"At least I'm not polluting the corridors with gloom." Despite the joke, the doctor's voice was tender. The Vespertine's brutal attack on the *Boudicca* shook everyone on board. The teasing was her way of telling Beatriz she was unharmed.

"It might surprise you, but some of the crew find comfort in their captain displaying an appropriate level of gravitas," Beatriz said.

"They don't share a bed with you. I do."

Velodona laid a warm, broad palm on her shoulder. She lowered her voice before continuing, "I sensed your need the moment the danger passed. Come with me. I'll take care of you."

The command went straight to her spine and Beatriz mustered the strength to remain on her feet. The tickle of Velodona's breath against her ear reminded her of the night before. They'd fucked like their bodies had been immersed in honey. Each movement was deliberate, each breath meant to be shared. Velodona had wrapped Beatriz in her limbs and whispered filthy thoughts as she'd thrust inside her until they were both senseless.

Differences in their bodies never hindered their lovemaking. The Ax'Il's features resembled humans from the waist up, but the similarities ended at the hips. Water covered their planet. Instead of legs, the Ax'Il had evolved with eight tentacles. Beyond their ability to swim at incredible speeds, they had also adapted to other terrain in the years since they had ventured into space. Their skin was dark as obsidian, their eyes a hypnotic violet. Strong emotions enriched their hue. Velodona's eyes were currently the same shade as ripe blackberries.

Beatriz leveled her shoulders and pointed to the row of glass-walled exam rooms. "Where do you want me?"

"Follow," Velodona said, choosing the room closest to where they stood.

Beatriz nodded. She knew that the walls became opaque and soundproof at Velodona's command. No one would see or hear what happened inside. But the power Velodona wielded, the ability to expose Beatriz's submission, was thrilling.

Her mind stilled as lust coalesced in her core. She would be wet before they began, her body craving the freedom Velodona's dominance created.

"Full privacy on, exam one," Velodona said after they were both inside. The glass on the walls became frosted, then darkened to an opaque gray.

The room was utilitarian, sterile, with just a gurney, a chair, and a med-supply cart. Everything else the staff needed could be made by the matter-configuration unit on the wall.

Velodona shed the tunic covering her upper body and laid it over the back of the chair. A plum flush radiated outward from the six nipples on her smooth chest. When they'd first become lovers, Beatriz had lost herself, suckling each bud and tugging on the titanium hoops piercing each nub.

"Strip," Velodona commanded once she'd settled in the

chair. Her tentacles waved in a serpentine motion. The movement belied the anticipation beneath her unruffled demeanor.

Beatriz didn't need a psychic rating to know she was wanted. Body alight, she yearned for the glide of her lover's skin against hers.

"You're fucking beautiful," Beatriz said, peeling off her captain's jacket. Shedding the visible trappings of her command lightened her mind and heart.

"Thank you. But I don't recall asking for your opinion, did I?" Velodona's voice lacked the teasing cadence from earlier.

"No, you didn't." She blushed, embarrassed by the way squirming excitement accompanied any correction.

"Well spotted. When do you speak?"

"When you ask a question."

"Good. Now tell me what you say if you need me to slow down or stop."

A surge of arousal swelled within her, and she felt the wetness on her outer lips. The ritual preceding their play was the same each time. Beatriz associated repeating her safewords with deliverance and fulfillment.

"*Suas* to keep going. *Lenta* to slow down. *Pare* to stop." She shuffled out of her trousers, quick to shake them off her feet. The combination of desire and haste caught her off balance, and she tumbled to the floor. Her hip smarted from its collision with the deck plating.

The doctor's brows knit with concern. "Please tell me you didn't break anything."

"I'm okay." Beatriz shook her head, giggling. "So, that happened."

"It did." The doctor's laugh was resonant, joyous. It reminded Beatriz of the trilling guitars she'd heard when she visited the New Azores colony on Carentina Major.

Her mother's family had sprouted from the archipelago of volcanic islands off the coast of Portugal back on Earth. But that was five hundred years ago before the oceans had risen, drowning the Azores and their crag-mouthed calderas. Beatriz imagined it was the spirit of people who had drawn sustenance from rocky soil and tumultuous seas that propelled her into the blackness of space.

Velodona rose, her movements as graceful as an open flame. She offered Beatriz a hand. "Up you get. It's fascinating," she said, flicking Beatriz's nose. "You're a master strategist. A fierce warrior. And yet you can't get your pants off without catastrophe."

Beatriz bit her lip, holding her retort back. She hadn't been given permission to speak.

"There's my beautiful, obedient pet," Velodona crooned, brushing Beatriz's curls behind her ear. "Now be still."

A tentacle slid up the back of Beatriz's thigh, stopping to brush circles over her buttocks. It dipped into the crease, tickling the puckered furl, before slipping lower, parting the folds of her vulva.

Groaning, Beatriz ground down on the soft point of flesh stroking her, heedless of the growl rumbling in her lover's throat.

Velodona's hand shot out, and a stinging warmth flared in Beatriz's cheek.

"Greedy thing," Velodona said. "Look at you, taking something from me without bothering to ask first."

Beatriz was left cold when the pressure disappeared. She was bereft, naked, and ashamed of the transgression, but schooled enough to stay quiet till she was told to speak. Velodona lifted her chin, bringing them eye to eye.

"Pet, tell me what you did wrong."

"I was selfish. I took pleasure without asking." She tried to not fidget, wanting to cover herself, lick the wetness of her cunt from the tips of her lover's tentacles, be forgiven. The snarled threads of guilt and passion were pulled too taut to untangle.

"And who does that pleasure belong to?"

"You," Beatriz said, contrite. Remaining still was a struggle. She wanted to revel in the slickness of Velodona's kisses, feel the thrust of a tentacle in her pussy, her mouth, her ass.

Disassemble me, piece by piece, and fill me. I want to be nothing but a creature of sensation. A thing made from your touch, Beatriz thought.

The yearning for absolution was ferocious and all-encompassing, gathering in Beatriz like a hurricane over the open sea. It weighed on her conscience, regardless of the justification.

"On the bed," Velodona ordered, tone stern. "On your back."

Compassion and care would come later.

Beatriz scrambled onto the bed, crisp sheets rasping against her overheated skin. She curled her hands over the edges of the mattress. Velodona smirked. It was a sharp expression, pleased, but the black of her skin was shot through with threads of icy silver denoting a thread of unabashed cruelty in her demeanor.

Beatriz bit her lip to keep herself from begging to be used.

"We're going with restraints today. I'd wanted to be soft with you, love you with gentle touches, but you need a harder hand. Tell me what you are?"

"I'm a greedy thing." The words burned in Beatriz's throat, and her eyes stung with tears, yet the well of her sex fluttered, desperate to be filled.

The restraints on the bed were padded with a material designed to not chafe. Her wrists and ankles were tethered to the edges of the bed, spreading Beatriz open. A final restraint looped over her stomach, binding her to the bed, and prevented her from arching into her lover's touch.

Climbing onto the bed, Velodona wrapped four of her tentacles around Beatriz's legs and arms, adding another layer of restraint. Immobility was a profound relief, Beatriz keened.

She peered down the length of Velodona's body, gazing at the center of her body where her tentacles met and a fleshy beak jutted out. It was erect, like a stiff cock, but not as rigid. The shaft was more akin to a tentacle with an aperture at the tip that opened and closed like a small mouth.

Velodona reached down and took herself in hand. "You want this, don't you?"

Beatriz moaned. The small cups on the underside of Velodona's tentacles gripped her, rippling across the length of her arms and legs.

"I do. Please," Beatriz cried out, her body fighting against the bonds. The touch wasn't enough. The words *more, more, more* beat at the backs of her teeth. "Please, I need to be full. I'm sorry I was selfish."

"Settle, pet," Velodona said, tightening her grip on Beatriz's limbs. "Check in with me. Do you want me to keep going?"

"*Suas.* Yes." Just saying it aloud calmed the anxiety in her blood.

"Say '*You'll give me what I need.*'"

"You'll give me what I need."

"Again," Velodona said, voice trembling.

"You'll give me what I need." Beatriz licked her lips, before throwing all of her want into one final plea. "Please, I'll be so good for you."

"You will, won't you?" Velodona lowered her body, the tip of the cock-like tentacle at her center caressing Beatriz's clit. The tiny lips at its tip suckled while the shaft quivered against her opening.

Velodona's natural lubrication added to Beatriz's own wetness. Their combined slickness dripped down the crease of her ass.

Quaking, a torrent of heat swept through Beatriz as the walls of her pussy tensed. All other thoughts disappeared, her vision narrowing to Velodona's face.

The rest of the universe disappeared. Even Beatriz's sense of self fell in the face of Velodona's mastery. Gone was the fear of her ruthlessness and her willingness to do anything in defense of her ship and those who served with her.

There was nothing else.

Velodona thrust inside her, and she howled at the sudden fullness. Ravaging Beatriz's mouth with her own, Velodona swallowed her cries while her body writhed above her.

The tip of a tentacle swept through the pool of slick beneath them. It slid between the cheeks of Beatriz's ass. Pulsing against the furled muscle, it dipped inside, slow and insistent until the flesh yielded to her.

Pulling back, Velodona panted, "Open for me, love. I want all of you. Will you give me everything?"

"*Suas.* I'm yours." The words were spoken without hesitation. "Take it. It's for you. I would give you anything. *Tudo.*" *Everything.*

"There you are, my pet," Velodona murmured. "I want your orgasm. Give it to me. Come." She thrust two fingers into Beatriz's mouth and reached down to grind against her clit with her other hand.

Beatriz sucked hard, cheeks hollowing. Every inch of her was possessed. *Owned.* The inner walls of her cunt spasmed.

"Did you hear me? Come."

A final slap against her pussy robbed Beatriz of breath, and she seized, her existence reduced to that single moment. She felt nothing but pleasure, and then even that faded, and she was weightless, free.

A CONSTRUCTED THREESOME

Dr. J.

In the distance, I heard a truck engine. After a door slammed shut, stomping feet through the front door followed.

"Hey, Lucas, where are you?"

"Keep walking toward the back, Justin."

I pounded the last nail into the board on the platform and grinned to myself as I prepared for my thirtieth-anniversary celebration. Two of them. The beginning of my marriage coincided with the opening of my construction business. Walking around my creation that sat in the middle of the partially hung drywall, I grabbed a corner and rocked it, checking for stability. Even for simple projects like this, my inner craftsman showed through.

When Justin reached the large family room, he stared at the wood and metal structure in the center. He turned and busted out a smile.

"Damn, I'm getting hard just thinking about how this will go down."

He rubbed his crotch and walked closer.

"Well, you're here to help me get the focus right." I gave his dick a quick squeeze. His hands landed on my shoulders, and his playful fingers dug into my muscles. Ava's ringtone coming from my pocket broke us apart. When I hit answer, her sobbing floored me.

"Ava, baby, what's going on?"

As she blubbered, it was difficult to catch her words. "Slow down. Breathe. Tell me what you're talking about."

"We have to cancel tomorrow night. I had the perfect gift set up for us, and it's all falling apart."

For three decades, Ava had been the rock and the driving, sexual force of our relationship. You don't stay together with someone this long without love, trust, and sexual adventure. I wanted to start our next thirty years by showing her I was fully committed to taking on a leading role in our sex life.

"I've got us covered, babe."

She sniffled. "Really?"

"It's *the big* 3-0. I want to do my part."

"Are you sure, Luc?"

"Afterwards, you can tell me how I did, okay?"

"Okay. I'll go anniversary shopping to do my part."

"That's my love."

When I ended the call, I shoved my cell back in my pocket and turned to Justin.

"Are we in trouble, Lucas?"

I winked at Justin. "Nah, the first part of the plan fell into place."

My arrangements would take precedence for tomorrow night. Ava had planned for a troupe of folks to dance naked for us. I intercepted a call from the company verifying the date, and she had no clue I'd canceled them.

Justin ambled around my stage, looked up to the adjustable bar with attached metal rings and knobs, and patted the side table. "This is something else, Lucas. You are a master at your craft. Not just your specific surprise, but this house. Ava will freak out. You have pulled off the impossible."

"Thanks for the kind words, J, and I'm happy you agreed to it all."

Dodging Ava's immediate disaster, I may have pulled off the impossible feat of an anniversary surprise, but she's the reason Justin is here.

Two years back, Ava announced she wanted to explore a threesome. I reluctantly agreed when she wanted it to be with a man. We had met many people interested in being with us, but when we met Justin, we knew we had located our sexual unicorn. Never had I thought I'd be in a polyamorous relationship, much less with a man, but Justin added the perfect flavor. Open-mindedness may be the secret to our thirty years.

Justin's renowned photography drew Ava to him. Maybe we all connected in the creative world. I loved watching him fuck Ava, and when she asked to see us together, I threw myself into it for her. Tonight's celebration would be incomplete without Justin.

"Did you get my email, J?"

"Yeah, hang on." Justin looked at his phone. "You had pretty detailed things you wanted going on. I have to ask; do we get to improvise?" He waggled his eyebrows, and I shook my head laughing.

"You know how we roll, man. Consider it a sexual menu from which to choose. The bigger job is the element of surprise."

Justin continued reading.

"Yeah, that's a huge element. So, I'm riding with Ava in the limo to meet you here?"

"Yes, you get to blindfold her."

"Our witchy woman will not like that."

We both laughed. Ava's representation of the world was visual. She liked to survey her landscape, and everything must look just so. But tomorrow tonight, I wanted her in a feeling place: this was all about sensation.

"Do you think my presence will give away the surprise?"

Would it?

"I don't believe so, but you could throw her off with an anniversary present."

"What are you thinking, Luc?"

"How about a Shibari arm binding demo on the drive over? That'll get her into sensations. She's wanted you to do that, to experience the feel of the knots before we bind her for a sexual experience."

"Great idea. Ava loves decoration and showing her boldness in public." He stared at me for a second. "Colored rope, too. I'll find out what she's wearing then plan to decorate both arms."

"Good luck with that."

"I have my ways, Lucas." He rubbed his chin as I saw him putting a plan in motion.

"Okay, but make sure you leave a loop at the wrist ends so I can attach her hands on the bar." I pointed to the sound system. "Do you think this will fool her?"

I grabbed the remote from atop the metal box and hit the on button. Justin strained to listen as I turned up the volume.

"It sounds like a club."

"Yeah, it is. I recorded it the night we were at Embers. I'm setting the stage, pun intended. She'll think we're in a crowd."

"I can see her shaking now, Lucas."

"Okay, so remember to put the noise-canceling headphones on her before you get out of the limo."

Ava's probably expecting our tried-and-true fancy dinner celebration with her last-minute debacle, but not this anniversary.

"I think we'll have fun, Luc. It looks like you have everything under control. Call me if you need anything, and I'll see you tomorrow night."

"Thanks, Justin. Same to you." I clapped his back. "And I'm looking forward to everything."

I had arrived at the construction site when my phone rang with the expected call.

"Lucas, Ava is throwing a fit about the blindfold. She has threatened the driver if he drives off."

"Give her the phone, Justin." In the background, my spitfire spewed her favorite rant words.

"Lucas Mark Johnson, I am not parading around in public with my eyes covered."

Yes, my witchy woman had arrived, right on time.

"Darling, when have I ever paraded you around in public?"

"I know you are taking me to Antoine's with last-minute planning and all. I refuse to be led into that restaurant wearing this mask."

I chuckled under my breath.

"Do you think for this big anniversary, I'd pick Antoine's?"

"What? That's not where we're going?"

"No, it's not. Let Justin put the blindfold on you." I closed my eyes and imagined the look Ava was giving Justin. He'd be earning sainthood tonight. "Ava, darling, I want you to get with my program."

All the sounds from the limo stilled, and then she whispered, "You have a program?"

"You'll find out after you're blindfolded."

"Lucas, tell me."

Ava's "do it my way," seductive voice called to my cock, and it wanted to respond. My call to her body, mind, and soul had to be bigger. "If I wanted to tell you, there wouldn't be a blindfold. You are mine tonight, Ava, to pleasure as I see fit. I'm honoring our first thirty years and ushering in the next. Now let Justin do his work, so we'll have a night to remember."

I knew her so well. It would be at least thirty seconds before she agreed.

"All right, Lucas, but if you parade me around Antoine's, there will be hell to pay."

"Not Antoine's. Put Justin on the phone."

"Yeah, Lucas?"

"Just a heads-up, the headphones will be as bad, but I think you can handle it. See you shortly."

Right on schedule, the limo pulled up, and I was at the front door to aid Justin with Ava. When he helped her out of the car, and she righted herself, I witnessed a vision. The black cocktail dress, the intricate design of purple rope on each arm created by Justin brought out her sensuality. She gripped Justin's arm as he reached the steps. I motioned for him to stop. Standing in front of Ava in the night air was intoxicating. I lifted the headphone off one ear.

"Hey, beautiful."

She turned her head to my voice. "Hey, Luc." She twisted her body around trying to catch the sounds.

"I see you decided to join my party."

"Did I have a choice?" An edge of frustration in her voice landed on my heart.

"You always have a choice, even if you don't like it when I'm in charge." She jutted her jaw out as she straightened her stance. "Thank you for having J do the rope. I feel kinky, and I can't wait to see it." She paused. "Ah, I don't hear traffic, so we're not at Antoine's. Are those tree frogs croaking? Where the hell are we?"

"You are so hot when you're riled up. Get ready for this adventure like it was thirty years ago." I grasped her hand and squeezed. We had eloped, at her insistence, taking our best friends with us to Vegas.

She chuckled and sighed. "I was the insistent one then, but if you're with me, I'm good." Her trusting voice, the one I remembered from our wedding night, touched me. "I will always be with you. Let's get this party rolling."

I covered her ear and motioned for Justin to go in ahead of us, so he could activate the sound system. I waited a few moments, nuzzling Ava's neck, admiring her as I traced the rope knots. I was turned on and wondered how long I could make this event last. When I felt the bass notes rumble, I guided Ava up the steps and opened the door.

Ava clutched my arm as we walked, much like during our short wedding processional. As we approached my surprise, with the music blaring, I removed her headphones.

Ava shouted at me, "Where are we?"

I ignored her question and spoke in her ear. "Would you like a drink?" She nodded.

Justin handed me her favorite one, and I held it under her nose.

"The bubbles tickle, Luc." She gasped. "A St. Germain martini. You remembered." We had discovered it on our tenth anniversary. It had turned her into a sex maniac.

"Take a sip." I lifted it to her lips, relishing the ease with which she tasted. When Ava stopped sipping, she nodded her head to the beat of the music.

"Luc, I need a gulp since you brought me visually impaired to a club."

That's my wife, bolstering her courage. This time she threw her head back a little further and opened her mouth wider. All I could think about was how many times those gorgeous lips had been wrapped around my cock.

"Ava, I hope you enjoyed the appetizers in the limo because dinner is a long way off. Come this way. There's a special place for us."

"As long as you have martinis for me, I'm good."

I walked her to my platform. "Two steps up, love."

Justin came to her opposite side and grasped her arm as I had.

"Oh, my God. Justin, you're still here? What is going on, Luc? Talk."

"Not yet."

When she reached the top of the platform, we positioned her under the bar. As the music boomed, I stroked her cheek and kissed those luscious lips.

"I'm giving you what you wanted. Lift your arms."

"I don't understand. What's happening?" she asked, her tone laced with irritation and interest.

"Ava, you trust me, I know." I stroked her arm and then kissed her again. "If you want to find out, lift."

When Ava lifted her arms, I affixed the rope loops to a clip on the metal ring. I traced my fingers down her arms, feeling her softness, and she shivered. The sexy dress Ava wore tonight would be a causality of the event, but so worth it. I could only imagine what she was thinking.

Justin had positioned his camera with the remote trigger and had been snapping pictures all along. He signaled me when he was satisfied with his shots and moved toward the sound system. After we undressed and prepared our surprise, he turned off the club sounds. I watched Ava fidget, a real bonus of my surprise.

Sex with Ava was unprecedented and always hot when agitation was present.

"We're not in a club? You have me bound. What is that smell?"

"No, Ava, no club, but if you can name the scents, the blindfold comes off."

She wiggled like a worm on a fishing hook. Her breasts jiggled, and when Justin eyed me, I thought my dick might explode. She twisted her head in different directions and sniffed.

"It's musty and a little wet. Hmmm. Concrete dust. I swear I smell, pressure-treated wood. Lucas, are we at a construction site?"

The eagerness in her voice pushed me forward, and I lifted off the mask.

Her reaction was priceless. She stared at my bare chest with her mouth hanging open before scanning down to my tool belt riding my naked hips, my semi-hard cock, bare legs, and my work boots. After she gazed around the open, high beam ceiling and the stacked drywall against the partially installed wall, she saw Justin decked out the same way, and a tear slipped down her cheek.

"Happy anniversary," I said, as I wiped the drop.

"I get a threesome at your construction site?"

"I have it on good authority it was what you wanted."

"Wait until I get a hold of Jody."

"Is that to hug or kill her?"

Two months back, Ava's best friend Jody tattled that while on girls' night, playing Truth or Dare, Ava picked truth. She wanted to be bound up at a construction site for a threesome. My brain detonated because that was something I could make happen, but there's no way she could know about the rest.

Ava grinned. "I guess that depends on how well you execute this fantasy."

"Always trying to run the show." I held out my hand. "Justin, the electric scissors, please."

Her eyes, the size of saucers, missed nothing. With the scissors in my grasp, I dragged them across her lips. She shuddered, and I smelled her arousal like an uncorked bottle of vintage wine. I flipped the switch, and they whirred to life.

"My dress?"

"Your dress."

With the ease of a master, I started at the hem and sheared the dress up the middle. When the shredded clothes landed on the floor, Ava watched me intently.

"Holy hell."

As she hung there grinning, I looked at Justin.

"Why should Ava have all the fun, Luc? I wanted you to have a present, too."

Around Ava's breasts were intricately knotted thin ropes, which met in the space between her breasts and ran down her abdomen. The ropes diverged past her belly button and created two circles around her legs like panty lines. With this and the cord on her arms, she was a stunner.

"Do you like it, Luc?" asked Ava, moisture seeping out the corner of her eyes.

"Oh, yes. Thank you both." My chest pounded and I rubbed my cock on her thigh.

"You feel good," she said.

"I'm guessing this is better than Antoine's?"

"So much better."

Stark naked and dangling from my bar in her purple rope art, Ava was a siren made to worship. Justin must have felt it too because his camera clicking exploded.

"I'm your subject tonight, J?"

"You and the rope work." Ava dropped her head back to view her hands.

"Spectacular J, thank you."

"Justin, hand me the compressor hose, please."

When it was tight in my hand, I hit the button, and a stream of air burst forth.

Ava tried to reposition her legs, but I stopped her movement with my hand.

"This is my arena, Ava. I wield my tools how and where I want them." She pouted before I blew the air through her hair. She accepted it like it was a massage. When bursts teased her sensitive nipples, her body convulsed.

"Needy?" I turned toward Justin. "You want to help Ava out?"

As I alternated the direct air to each nipple, Justin kneaded her breasts and sucked her nubs. Ava's body moved like a wave, rising and falling with the action.

"Spread your legs now, Ava." I dropped to my knees to see her wetness; I smelled her arousal, earthy and robust. I intended to drive her insane with the air on her clit. If she thought the hot tub jets were sensational, this application would change her mind. I had a front-row seat to her response.

"Luc, this is so, so naughty."

"And you love it," I said, as I whipped the first blast of air on her clit. She jumped back with surprise.

"It's phenomenal."

"Justin, we can't have her moving around like this."

"My cue to improvise, Luc?"

I chuckled. "Go for it, buddy."

Justin dropped to his knees with her ass in his face. I fired up the compressor again on her clit, and she backed into him.

"Oh. My God." said Ava. Her staccato words suggested surprise.

"What's Justin doing, love?"

"He's squeezing my ass and licking—"

"Something you like my dear? Is his hot, fat tongue wiggling down your crack and pressing right into your backdoor? I love watching him drive you crazy."

The metal clanked as Ava tried to position herself. She writhed and gasped as Justin worked his magic tongue. The lust on her face confirmed my plans.

"Justin, let me know when you've had your fill of rimming my wife's ass." He stood, nodded at me, and repositioned himself.

"Oh, Justin. I love the tool belt grinding into my ass. You sandwiched your cock in my crack."

"I did." He reached in his tool belt and pulled out a tube. "Let's see if this lube helps it ride your cheeks before it finds heaven." He dripped the lube down her crack. I shot more air on her bundle of nerves and watched her dance back into him. It turned me on when she bucked her pelvis to feel his hard cock.

"Do a little dance for me, baby." She was at my mercy with the whims of my hand blasting the air. She and Justin rocked and moaned. I shoved my fingers between her legs into her wet lips. Her moisture covered me in an instant. My woman was a sex machine. I blasted her clit while I finger-fucked her hard. Justin held her tight as the first orgasm flew through her.

"Tell me, Luc. How are we doing this?"

"Baby, we'll fuck you until you see fireworks."

"Together?"

Justin applied more lube.

"Isn't that what you wanted?" I asked.

She nodded her head with sharp, quick bobs.

As Justin rocked his cock up her crack, it pushed her pelvis closer, teasing me. I unfastened my tool belt, letting it fall to the floor along with the compressor nozzle. I inhaled the most intoxicating arousal, like my favorite wine, aged to perfection, and I had to taste. Every time Justin pushed her body forward, my tongue dipped into her vulva. We'd created a pendulum effect.

"Is this how you envisioned it, Ava?"

Between her gasping, garbled words emerged: "No, it's better."

I latched my hands onto her thighs, fingering the rope, and let Justin's movements drive her pussy into my face. I ate her out like I never had and her screams of pleasure soaring through the air made me scrabble.

"Justin, get the table, slide it here." When it was set under the bar, I hopped on, and Justin adjusted Ava so she could sit on my erection. "Tilt the bar forward, so Ava's body bends toward me for your access."

Her thighs shook as Ava hovered over me. I grabbed her hips and centered her over my cock. "Ease on down, baby."

"Forget easing, I want to gobble you up, Luc." Her tight pussy sucked me in and clamped down. As her decorated breasts hung toward me with her hard nipples, flushed skin, and glazed-over eyes, I was a goner.

"You ready, Ava?" She nodded her head. "Justin, lube and go as you please."

Ava mouthed, "I love you."

I heard the camera clicks. Would there ever be better anniversary sex than this? My wife hung by her bound hands from my constructed platform, sexier than I have ever seen her, ready to be drilled in the ass by our guy, with my dick hard as steel inside her. As Justin's hands crept over her shoulders, I pinched Ava's nipples as she moved on me. I felt the pressure of Justin's cock against mine as he fully seated in her ass, and then the three of us ground together.

Could I have envisioned this for us thirty years ago?

Nope.

But I'm glad we got here. Ava carried the lead baton for our sexual pleasure in the first thirty years, and now it was my turn. Her love-filled gaze, throaty moans, and pelvic thrusts suggested I was off to a good start.

"Ava, how is the sex in our new house?"

She gripped the rope loops in her hands. Her face morphed into confusion or near orgasm.

"Our house?" she panted.

"I'm building it for the three of us," I grunted.

"Our place?" Ava's eyes sparkled. "J, you committed to us?"

I sat up flush against Ava's body and reached my arms around to Justin. He wrapped his arms around Ava and me. Ava beamed.

"It's official," said Justin.

"We thought you'd like a ceremony," I said.

"This is better than my wildest dreams. Fireworks for all. Hold me tighter, guys."

The orgasms crashed through all three of us and the camera shuttering signaled we'd have proof of all our creations.

As for me, I couldn't wait to hear if I executed the fantasy to Ava's liking.

PLUG IN THE MODEL

Céline

It was the last day.

It was the last day and Sofie couldn't help but feel sad and dejected. It had lasted a week and a half, spent posing for hours at a time, sometimes in silence, observing Karo, and sometimes in conversation, during breaks between two sessions, talking about the world of art they both were a part of.

Three more hours and it would be over. After this, the painting would take on a life of its own, and she and Karo would go their separate ways. Because Karo was the artist, the genius, and Sofie was just a model. A good one, but that was it. She knew Karo didn't see past her body, that was the reason she had been chosen for the series. Karo wanted to represent age and pain, and after more than fifteen years away from the painting studios, Sofie had decided she could pose once more, because for the first time since her surgery, she had felt somebody wanted to see her scars.

They had met, a contract had been signed, information had

been exchanged, and Sofie had found her way to Karo's private studio, directly under the roof, full of easels, canvas, paint, and winter light. Sofie had undressed, let Karo tie her hands together with a white cotton rope and help her climb on a pile of wooden boards stacked together. Sofie then had to slide the rope onto a hook and the session would begin. Depending on the tension Karo wanted to see in her body, they would take away one or several boards from the pile, stretching Sofie's body as much as they deemed it necessary.

Today, Sofie climbed on the pile, felt the cold of the iron hook against her skin and let the shiver waft over her skin, enjoying it even, because it was the last time she would feel it. She knew the pose by heart now, she could find it herself, and didn't need Karo's guidance anymore. Nevertheless, they stayed close, ready to catch her if she fell. Today, she understood the knot was extra tight; her hands didn't have as much space between them.

Karo moved toward her, stopping in front of her stomach and raised their beautiful black eyes toward her face.

"Do you need an extra board?" they asked, their voice running across her belly, making her tremble. She tightened her grip on the rope and ground her teeth before answering.

"I'm fine."

It was by that time that Karo would usually step away, walk to the easel, mix paints, and start working. But not today.

Today, for some reason, they stayed in front of her, looking at her with hooded eyes.

"I need to look at your tattoo," they explained after a while, during which their gaze didn't leave her.

"Of course," Sofie replied in a whisper, already fascinated by the face that kept coming closer and closer to her tensed stomach, elongated by the position.

She loved her tattoo, an artistic embroidery of flowers and

insects along her chest, hiding the scars of her surgery. It had taken weeks to get ready; she had wanted the insects to look like jewels on her white skin, and the work on the colors by the tattoo artist had proven more difficult than initially thought. But after five years, the details still looked as vivid as during the first weeks.

"May I touch?" Karo asked, already rubbing their hands together to warm them up.

"Yes," Sofie whispered, closing her eyes.

For a few seconds, nothing happened, then the touch came, and Sofie exhaled. The finger was still cold, raised goose bumps in its trail, along her arms, back, and legs. Despite the tension in her position, she moved her thighs, closing the gap to contain the throbbing in her lower belly. When she looked down, Karo seemed as undisturbed as ever.

"Do you mind?" they asked without looking up, reaching to their back pocket and drawing out a thin brush.

"What do you want to do?" she wondered.

"This."

They raised the brush and started tracing the lines of her tattoo. It was lighter than the finger, startling her. Sofie moved back, her arched feet leaving the pile of boards, and she suddenly found herself hanging from the ceiling. Without so much as a bat of an eye, Karo grabbed her waist and helped her find her footing again. This time, Sofie couldn't hold back the whimper in her throat.

"Will I have to hold you so that you don't move?"

"I don't know. Maybe."

"What a model you make."

The sarcasm was palpable but Sofie was too flushed to get offended, she could feel her chest rising faster and faster as Karo traced the infinite loop of plants and flowers, again and again.

Drops of sweat were gliding down her spine; she could follow the trail to her ass, and the sensation just added to the one Karo created.

"Okay, I think I'm done," they suddenly said, stepping back. "Do you need a break or can we start?"

"I'm fine," Sofie answered.

She didn't want to step down the pile, she didn't want to move around, because movement would dissipate all the sensations, and she just wanted to enjoy them, bask in them. It had been such a long time since someone, anyone, had touched her there, so long that she had thought that, after the surgery, she would lose all sensations. But not today.

Karo went behind the easel, looked at their paint and started mixing, quick and professional. Sofie suddenly felt inadequate. Here she was, flustered and uncomfortable, whereas Karo was set on their goal, never wavering, master of their emotions. In that moment, Sofie realized, again, that she wasn't anything else besides a model. Not a full being, and certainly not a creature with desire. She was a means to an end, and she should have felt grateful for having been chosen by Karo Paz, a genius artist whose pieces she had admired for years, whose philosophy and thoughts on art echoed her own. At this minute, however, Sofie felt unseen and rejected, the wave of the sarcasm finally hitting her full force.

A grunt snapped her out of her spiral of self-pity. Karo was moving the easel closer. They squinted at her chest for a few seconds before repeating the maneuver, then settled down four feet away.

"There's so many colors, I want to get them right," they explained.

"Okay."

"You don't talk much today," they noted, finally starting painting.

Sofie could hear the whisper of the brush on the canvas, and it made her shiver. She wished it was running on her skin again instead of the painting.

"What would you like to talk about?" she finally asked, her whole body tingling.

"Why are you so nervous?"

"It's the last day. I want to enjoy it," she tried to say.

Behind the easel, Karo looked at her with an arched eyebrow.

"You're so tense, you could snap like a bowstring," they countered. "What's going on? Usually, you're fluid, like a reed."

Sofie closed her eyes and bit her lips, gulping down the answer that came up in her throat. Instead, she said, "I'm sorry. I think I'm just sad."

Karo made a low growl, a noise Sofie had learned meant "suit yourself," and kept on painting. The next half hour was silent, until Sofie asked for a break. Karo went out to get some coffee and Sofie made a few yoga movements on the carpet to try and unravel the knots in her stomach and shoulders. Karo came back and offered her the cup, saying it was black tea instead of coffee.

"I don't need you more stressed than you already are."

"I'm sorry," Sofie said, taking the beverage.

It was chai tea, honeyed and creamy, and it made her feel better. Because it meant that Karo was seeing a little more than she thought. Chai tea was what she was drinking the first time she came to the studio; she had explained she found it reassuring when nervous. The fact that Karo remembered filled her with joy.

"Thank you," she said with a smile, and Karo smiled back, a rare feat.

"Here you are. Ready to go back up?"

Sofie nodded and soon, she was on the hook again, her hands

grabbing the rope to keep her balance. But when Karo didn't move away, instead staying close and looking at her tattoo again, the knots came back, the tension rising in her muscles as all the beneficial effects of the tea disappeared.

"What's wrong?" Karo asked again when they saw her stomach tense up.

"It's just . . . you're so close . . ." Sofie said before thinking better of it.

"Does it disturb you?"

"Yes . . . I don't know."

"You don't know?"

Karo looked up and Sofie looked down. They stared at each other for a moment, then Karo climbed on the pile of boards and Sofie found herself flushed against their body, her breath caught in her chest. Karo's face was so close, she could have counted the wrinkles around their eyes, but all she could do was to stare at their mouth, red and wet, as tempting as a glass of wine. Their hand moved on her neck, their fingers threading through her hair.

"May I?" Karo asked against her lips.

"Please."

The kiss wasn't what she had expected. It was not soft and coaxing, it was powerful and intrusive, a demand rather than a question. Sofie surrendered as desire came. Her nether lips were taking more and more space between her legs, her lower belly aroused by the heat that seemed to pour from Karo's body into hers.

When Karo moved away, they had a satisfied smile, unlike anything Sofie had seen before, not even in official pictures and portraits.

"So that's what's going on? Why didn't you say so?"

They jumped down and looked at her.

"I didn't think you'd care," Sofie whispered, having trouble finding her wits after the rush.

"My models are always people I find beautiful. I thought that was obvious."

"It's not the same."

"You've been naked in front of me for the past week, you think it does nothing?"

"I don't know . . . you always look so absorbed, so focused."

"You don't know what I do each time you leave."

Sofie stretched her neck to better look at them. Their satisfied smile was still in place. They took a step closer and when they spoke, their breath ran on her skin.

"I take my toys and I pleasure myself, thinking of you, imagining you in different positions until I come, screaming your name. What do you say to that?"

"Help me come down," Sofie begged.

"What for?"

"So that I can kiss you back."

"I don't think so."

Sofie opened her eyes wide, fear running down her spine. Karo climbed up again and took her face in their hands, suddenly softer that what she could have anticipated.

"If you want to climb down, I'll let you, but this is how I want you. What do you say?" they repeated.

"What will we do?"

"We'll play, of course. Instead of my model, you'll be my canvas and I'll get rid of that tension you can't let go. Now, doesn't that sound fun?"

"Yes," Sofie said, licking her lips.

"So what do you say?"

"Yes," she repeated with more power in her voice.

"Good girl," Karo said before kissing her again. This time,

the tongues were involved, dancing with each other until Sofie was breathless. It was clear from this point forward that Karo was in charge, and she was along for the ride.

"Now, let me see," Karo exclaimed while jumping down. They put one hand on her waist, the other moving on her stomach and belly. No foreplay, it seemed, since the fingers were heading down to her lips, already parting them, exploring the region with fierce enthusiasm. Sofie moaned and arched her back. Karo chuckled against her skin.

"No problem there, it seems. What about your ass?"

The finger that was probing her vagina suddenly left and went further, poking around the entrance to her hole, and Sofie answered the call, pulled on the rope to come down further to meet it, to let it enter. But the finger retreated and Karo stepped back, crouched down and withdrew one board from the pile, stretching her entire body. She let out a breathless cry, her toes shifting along the wood, and Karo's smile broadened.

"Let me taste you," they demanded.

They placed their hands on each side of her waist and pulled Sofie toward them. She barely had time to register the tongue slithering out of their mouth before contact and then she forgot everything, because it was so invasive and taunting, barely there and then sucking with full force, as if to draw out the color from a marble. Sofie was utterly defenseless. Stretched and barely able to find her footing, she could feel the orgasm rising, but the tension in her legs to try and keep upright prevented it from going past the point of no return. Pleasure became torture, especially when she tried to raise her legs to knot them around Karo's shoulders, but they pushed her away, talking into her fold with a laugh.

"Not yet. I say when."

"Please, please," begged Sofie, the excitation coming closer and closer to the line that would turn into pure frustration.

"I say when," they repeated.

One last lick, long and hard between her lips, one last sucking action on her clit. Sofie thought she would scream but Karo moved away, finally, wiping their mouth with the back of their paint-stroke hand.

"I love this." They smiled at her. "Look at you."

"I can't," Sofie breathed.

"True. Give me a minute."

Karo disappeared into one of the rooms opened to the studio and Sofie was left rubbing her legs together to try and soothe the throbs of her sex. Karo came back carrying a tall mirror they put against the easel, affording her a full view of her taut body. She was flushed, her inner thighs wet with a mix of her juices and Karo's saliva. On her chest, her tattoo was on full display, shiny with perspiration.

After a full minute of observation, Karo stepped in front of the mirror and took a wand vibrator out of their back pocket.

"This is where we're going to play," they explained while taking a small glass jar and pouring red paint into it. "I'll hold the wand in one hand, the brush with the other, and we'll see what kind of painting your pleasure can draw."

Sofie whimpered, a mix of fear and anticipation bubbling up. She didn't know this Karo, with reddened cheeks and a sparkle in their eyes that had nothing to do with the joy they could have when painting. This was a game, a give-and-take, a race for sensual pleasure.

Karo came back in front of her and turned on the device. The soft hum filled the air, covered her shallow breaths. Karo dipped the brush in the paint and positioned it in her navel. The wand was then gliding along her leg, going up and up until she could feel the vibrations in her sex and her spine, with Karo tracing a tight spiral on her stomach all the while. At first, Sofie thought she could keep still, but the vibrations were treacherous, one moment in her leg and the next on her clit. She slithered under the brush, caught by the rope on which she stretched and stretched, looking for an escape when there was none to be had.

"Please, stop!" she cried, tears in her eyes, unable to handle more.

The wand was turned off, Karo put down the brush, grabbed her by the waist again and buried their face between her legs, licking and sucking until Sofie came, abruptly and quickly, with no time to ride it properly.

Silence fell. Sofie felt Karo's breath against her pubic hair, a gentle breeze that was soothing after all that heat. Karo grabbed the wooden boards they had taken away before and placed them on the pile, allowing Sofie to stand on the four corners of her feet. Her arms grew heavy against the rope, but the cotton was so soft it wasn't painful, just a nice bite on her flesh. She knew once this session was over, she would have marks for hours afterward.

"Admire yourself," Karo ordered, stepping away. "I'll be back."

After they left the room, Sofie could hear them foraging somewhere in the bedroom. Sofie did as asked, looking at the lines the brush had painted on her belly. As anticipated, the spiral started from her navel, moving outward. If at first the line was nice and smooth, it didn't stay so long. Sofie could see the vibrations of the wand reverberate in the line, which became wobblier and wobblier, fainter and fainter on her skin as the color ran out. A blotch of paint was visible where she had given up, had begged Karo for release, near her hipbone.

When Karo came back, they had an anal plug and a bottle of lube in their hands. Sofie recoiled, an instinctive reaction that they noticed. They kneeled in front of her and caressed her calves with both hands, a gentle gesture she didn't expect.

"Have you done it before?" they asked.

"A long time ago," Sofie said, her voice hoarse.

"Then you know it can be good."

"Even like this?" she asked, her eyes moving upward to the cotton rope.

"Especially like this."

"You promise to be nice?" she asked again.

"How about sweet?"

"That'll do."

Karo smiled and rose, climbed on the pile of boards and they started kissing again. Karo ground against her and Sofie raised her legs, crossing them on their back to prolong the contact, and in doing so, allowing them access to her rear. A finger came, gentle and shy, coating her with her juices, flattering her hole into opening. Sofie arched against Karo when their finger entered her, poking around, stroking her inner tissues engorged with desire. Karo kept on kissing, her jaw, her throat, her collarbones, then marked a pause before daring to kiss the first scar of her surgery, tracing it with their tongue. Using some lube, another finger entered. Sofie relished the sensation, feeling exposed and vulnerable, and above all, seen. The fingers came in and out, caressing her inside with a delicious thrust impossible to resist.

"You're ready," Karo breathed against her chest.

Sofie let go of their waist, found the wood of the board and regained some composure, while Karo climbed down again and grabbed the plug. They lubed it up and down, coating it with the liquid while Sofie looked at the ballet of the fingers, liking the process to finger painting. They took a position in front of her, asked her to put at least one leg on their shoulder. She obeyed, opening her ass again. She saw Karo's hands disappearing between her legs, the cold sensation of the lubed plug against her hole and the pressure, resolved and unnerving, that kept on opening her, stretching her. And then the sensation, expected but still surprising, of her muscles closing on the base of the plug, settling it in its place inside her.

She heaved, unable to speak, filled to the brink.

"Good girl," Karo smiled in her hair before rising. They turned around, grabbed the brush and the wand and came back to her. Before starting, they withdrew three boards. Sofie was now on the tips of her toes, always looking for balance. She could feel the plug pulling her down, pulling on her arms and sides, asking her to let go. The wand was turned on and the brush placed at the top of her back between her two shoulder blades. While the wand was again climbing up her leg, the brush came down her spine, tracing the path her sweat had before, all the way down to the opening of her hole, tickling and making her squirm under it. Soon, the wand was against her pubic bone and the vibrations were coursing through her stomach, the plug trembling in her ass, shaking her from the core. Her limbs, restrained by the rope and gravity, were still trying to break free, her body trying to escape from too much sensation and yet, she couldn't.

The orgasm rose again, from deep inside, flew in her veins, pleasure taking over every nerve, every cell in her chest, until it again became too much to bear and she asked Karo to stop. The contact of the brush against her skin disappeared, the wand between her legs was withdrawn but not turned off. When Karo came in front of her, she could see they had tucked the instrument in their jeans. Before she could imagine what would follow, Karo climbed up to meet her and started kissing her again, the wand vibrating between their two bellies.

Sofie moaned in their mouth, bit their lower lips in protest. Karo moved away and grabbed her by the ass, pressing into her, this time their mouth busy with licking and biting the highlights of her tattoo. She raised her legs and anchored herself to them, tugged on the rope in a desperate effort to touch them, to run her fingers through their hair and feel the flush of their skin. Again, she begged, but Karo refused with a throaty laugh and kept on nibbling at her chest.

The wand was still on, pressing against her clit, sending its vibrations into her stomach, past her chest and shoulders, along her arms and all the way up to the tip of her fingers, as if a thousand brushes were being traced against her skin. The plug was still weighing her down, echoing the vibrations deep inside, and making her pulse against Karo's body. She had the feeling she would soon crack open.

For the third time, the orgasm came; this time she accompanied it by grinding into Karo, imposing her own rhythm. They rose up and plastered their face unto her. Both growled into each other's mouth, looking after the other, waiting and counting until they could come together. Sofie bit Karo's mouth with all her might, didn't feel Karo's fingers digging deep into the flesh of her ass, her whole body rippling around the plug.

Moments later, they were both on the ground, smiling and panting. Karo's lip was bleeding lightly, they wiped the blood on their skin, mirroring the stroke of a brush. Sofie didn't try to contain her smug expression.

"Come on," Karo said after a while. "I have to finish your tattoo."

The opening exhibit happened a month later.

Sofie had been invited, of course, and went without expecting much. She was surprised, and proud, and humbled, and flushed when she understood her portrait stood at the center of the event, a core piece around which the rest of the paintings were displayed. At first, she had thought the background, on which her taut body was exposed, showing off the bright colors of her tattoo, was a dark brown, but upon closer inspection, she noticed the patterns. On the lower half was the wobbly spiral Karo had drawn on her belly, and in the upper half were the five lines they had traced on her back.

The folds of the cotton rope looked like molten silver in the light. Her cheeks were flushed and her expression was one she knew she hadn't displayed during the sessions. It was one of pure ecstasy, one Karo could only have seen on the last day.

"I'm not selling it," Sofie heard behind her. "This one is mine."

ABOUT THE AUTHORS

REBECCA E. BLANTON (aka Auntie Vice) is a blogger and podcaster. Their current work focuses on the intersection of BDSM, identities, and feminism. Their work also includes two nonfiction books about BDSM and submission. Their podcast, Fat Chicks on Top, contains discussions about how bodies mediate our experience in the world.

JACQUELINE BROCKER (jacquelinebrocker.net) writes erotica and has had several short stories and novellas published. She is an Australian who lives in the UK with her husband and their cat. When not writing, she crochets, teaches Scottish Country Dancing, and gazes longingly at pretty Bullet Journal spreads on Instagram.

CÉLINE is a Europe-based French writer. This is her first contribution to an erotica anthology and she is working on changing that fact.

PAGE CHASE (pagechase.blog) is the alter ego of a mild-mannered librarian who wants to put her creative writing degree back to work.

ROSALIND CHASE (rosalindchase.com) is a LAMBDA Award finalist and winner of the Bisexual Book Awards highest honor, Bi Writer of the Year, for her debut novella, *Lot's Wife: An Erotic Retelling*.

When not reading, writing, or teaching, **EMMA CHATON** is a terrible oil painter and an even worse baker. She greatly enjoys entertaining thoughts that she's not supposed to have, or allowed to have.

POSY CHURCHGATE (posychurchgate.com) started writing erotica in 2016. She writes fiction and non-fiction, embracing kink curiosity. Happily married and heterosexual, she includes personal experiences in every scenario she creates. Her catchphrase: "Libido is like a muscle. Use it or lose it!" When not reading or writing, UK-based Posy spends time with her family and dogs.

Born in Brooklyn and raised in the New South, **ALEXA J. DAY** (alexajday.com) loves stories with just a touch of the inappropriate and heroines who are anything but innocent. Her literary mission is to stimulate the intellect and libido of her readers. She lives in Upstate South Carolina.

SONJA E. DEWITT is an author and narrative designer with a passion for romance, classic video games, and professional wrestling. She has an MFA in Game Design that she uses to write interactive romance novels. When she's not writing or watching wrestling, she draws comics and raids the occasional dungeon. For more of Sonja's work follow her @SonjaRedDeWitt on Twitter.

D. FOSTALOVE has been published in numerous anthologies, including *Brief Encounters, Baby Got Back*, and *The Big Book of Submission, Volume 2*. He is the author of *Unraveled: Sealed Lips, Clenched Fists* and *When I Miss You*.

Often quirky, always queer, **ELNA HOLST** is an unapologetic genre-bender who produces anything from stories of sapphic lust and love to the odd existentialist horror piece, reads Tolstoy, and plays contract bridge. Find her on Instagram (@elnaholstwrites) or Goodreads.

DR. J. (drjauthor.com), a retired sex therapist, writes erotica while enjoying island life on the Atlantic coast of Florida. After providing authorly presentations, she gallivants across the countryside tasting wine and spreading sex-positive cheer.

TRYSTAN KENT is the nom de plume of a perverted renaissance punk rocket scientist and dedicated voyeur with a penchant for pantyhose, stockings, and all things nylon. Trystan has penned nine novels and dozens of quickie reads on everything from shoe spanking to cupcake sex to voyeuristic orgies. trystan@sexwithotherpeople.com

EVAN MORA is a kinky queer writer whose tales of love, lust, and other demons have appeared in more than thirty anthologies. She lives in Toronto with her partner and menagerie of two- and four-legged kids. When not writing, she loves food, wine, and all manner of earthly delights.

CHARLIE POWELL (sexblogofsorts.com) has been an avid reader and writer of erotica since her teens and has a particular interest in disabled and flawed characters, unusual safewords, and shame. She lives in the UK and has been published in a number of anthologies including the Best Women's Erotica series.

SIENNA SAINT-CYR's fiction has appeared in the Love Slave and Sexual Expression series, anthologies like *Silence is Golden* and *Best Women's Erotica of the Year, Volume 4* and nonfiction in *Kintsugi: Powerful Stories of Healing Trauma*. They own a publishing company with a focus on shifting toxic culture.

ANNE STAGG (annestaggwrites.com) is an author and poet. They are an active advocate for the creation of healthy, affirming sexual spaces for women, the LGBTQIA+ community, and the BDSM/kink community.

VERONIQUE VERITAS (veroniqueveritas.home.blog) writes fiction and poetry. She has been interested in writing all her life and is excited to continue creative writing in different genres. Through writing erotica, she hopes to be part of a more sex positive future and help readers embrace their authentic desires.

Unbeknownst to her dissertation committee, **T.R. VERTEN** has long been a spy in the house of academia, creating an aesthetic manifesto in disguise. You can find her writing in the reissued novella *Confessions of Rentboy* as well as anthologies from Cleis Press, the New Smut Project, Republica, Burning Book, and Ravenous Romance. Intermittently on Twitter @trepverten.

ABOUT THE EDITOR

RACHEL KRAMER BUSSEL (rachelkramerbussel.com) is a New Jersey–based author, editor, blogger, and writing instructor. She has edited over sixty books of erotica, including *Best Bondage Erotica of the Year, Volumes 1* and *2; Dirty Dates: Erotic Fantasies for Couples; Cheeky Spanking Stories; Bottoms Up; Spanked: Red-Cheeked Erotica; Please, Sir; Please, Ma'am; He's on Top; She's on Top; Come Again: Sex Toy Erotica; The Big Book of Orgasms; The Big Book of Submission, Volumes 1* and *2; Lust in Latex; Anything for You; Baby Got Back: Anal Erotica; Suite Encounters; Gotta Have It; Women in Lust; Surrender; Orgasmic; Fast Girls; Going Down; Tasting Him; Tasting Her; Crossdressing;* and *Best Women's Erotica of the Year, Volumes 1–6.* Her anthologies have won eight IPPY (Independent Publisher) Awards, and *The Big Book of Submission, Volume 2, Dirty Dates,* and *Surrender* won the National Leather Association Samois Anthology Award.

Rachel has written for *AVN, Bust, Cosmopolitan, Curve,*

The Daily Beast, Elle.com, Fortune.com, *Glamour*, The Goods, Gothamist, *Harper's Bazaar*, Huffington Post, *Inked, InStyle, Marie Claire, MEL, Men's Health, Newsday, New York Post, New York Observer, The New York Times, O: The Oprah Magazine, Penthouse, The Philadelphia Inquirer*, Refinery29, *Rolling Stone*, The Root, Salon, *San Francisco Chronicle, Self*, Slate, Time.com, *Time Out New York*, and *Zink*, among others. She has appeared on *The Gayle King Show, The Martha Stewart Show, The Berman and Berman Show*, NY1, and Showtime's *Family Business*. She hosted the popular In the Flesh Erotic Reading Series, featuring readers from Susie Bright to Zane, speaks at conferences, and does readings and teaches erotic writing workshops around the world and online. She blogs at lustylady.blogspot.com and consults about erotica and sex-related nonfiction at eroticawriting101.com. Follow her @raquelita on Twitter.